PRAISE FOR TESSA

"No one writes hot, dirty-talking alpha heroes like Tessa Bailey!"
—*NYT* bestselling author Laura Kaye

"There are not many authors whose books completely, utterly, and totally wreck me. Tessa is at the top of that list, and I thank the stars for the day she started writing. As soon as I get a book from her, *nothing* else gets done until I finish it. My world is a better place because Tessa's books are in it."
—*NYT* bestselling author Sophie Jordan

"Sexy, witty, and completely irresistible, Tessa Bailey's writing is addictive. I can't get enough! Her dirty-talking heroes keep me up all night and always bring me back for more."
—*NYT* bestselling author Kelsie Leverich

"Tessa Bailey is one of my favorite authors. You know when you pick up one of her books, you're in for one hell of a sexy good time that will pull on your heartstrings even as it heats you up. I cannot recommend her highly enough."
—*NYT* bestselling author Katee Robert

"Forget 'melt-your-panties' heroes. Bailey writes 'rip-your-panties-off' alphas with a capital A!"
—*USA TODAY* bestselling author Samanthe Beck

"Nobody writes hot guys, feisty girls, and fan-yourself sex like Tessa Bailey. Her books are addicting, and you'll continue to root for her characters long after you turn the last page!"
—Megan Erickson, author of *Changing His Game*

UP IN

SMOKE

UP IN

A CROSSING THE LINE NOVEL

SMOKE

TESSA BAILEY

Entangled Publishing, LLC
2614 South Timberline Road
Suite 109
Fort Collins, CO 80525

Visit our website at www.entangledpublishing.com.

Edited by Heather Howland
Cover design by Heather Howland
Interior design by Jeremy Howland
Photography from Shutterstock

Paperback ISBN 978-1-63375-013-5
Ebook ISBN 978-1-63375-014-2

Manufactured in the United States of America

First Edition June 2015

10 9 8 7 6 5 4 3 2 1

For the girls who don't fit in.

CHAPTER ONE

You can take the man out of the SEALs...

Connor Bannon stared across the empty conference room at the clock, watching the second hand tick past 3:00 p.m. Impatience prickled the back of his neck. He hated being late. Hated *other* people being late. If the navy had taught him one thing, it was how to show up on time. Even now, when his military career wasn't even visible in the rearview mirror and the consequences weren't nearly as severe, his ass showed up when it was supposed to. He couldn't be late if he tried.

Apparently he'd been banished into the midst of an undercover squad that didn't share the same quality.

Connor tapped his fist against his knee, breathing through the need to look at the clock again. The blank whiteboard and the room's six empty chairs mocked him. He didn't like going into meetings blind. It went against his nature to be unprepared, but he'd been given no choice. All he knew was Bowen Driscol and Seraphina Newsom were on the squad, sent from New York City to Chicago in exchange for favors, same as him. For the first time since his short-lived stint with the SEALs, he was going to be on the right side of the law.

Or the wrong side, depending on who was doing the asking.

He'd be working with cons, criminals who wanted to stay out of prison. That was where his knowledge started and ended, truly pissing him off. If they'd been given the same options as him, they'd decided helping the Chicago Police Department catch criminals such as themselves was the lesser of two evils.

Another valuable lesson he'd learned from the SEALs? If it doesn't look like a bomb, it's probably a bomb.

The door of the conference room flew open, crashing against the opposite wall. Connor's hand flew toward the small of his back, searching futilely for his gun—a gun the uniforms had taken away from him upon arrival, *dammit*. He shot to his feet instead, focusing on the...threat?

"Relax, trigger. I like to make an entrance."

A girl sauntered into the conference room, her combat boots jingling with each step, as if there were bells attached. She wore a shirt that said *Bitch Don't Kill My Vibe* over a pair of ripped jean shorts that ended just below her ass. An ass that he'd noticed even before he registered her bright pink hair. *Who the fuck?*

She tossed a frayed canvas bag onto the table and sprawled into the seat across from his currently empty one, head tilting slightly as she regarded him. Amusement transformed her features from merely beautiful to interesting *and* beautiful. From distracting to *the* distraction he didn't need. Like she fucking needed the extra push.

Since when did he get mad at girls for being good-looking?

Very slowly, she looked him over. Connor felt her gaze slide over his crotch and bit back the urge to adjust himself, to hide the wood he'd sprung in honor of a girl who'd been in his presence for thirty seconds. He didn't like this. Didn't like feeling out of control of the situation. He let people see only what he allowed, but somehow this girl had walked into the room, said eight words, and thrown him off his game.

"Well." She sat back in her chair and winked at him. "I guess the nickname 'trigger' is appropriate in more ways than one."

Connor sat back down and dug his fingers into his knee, forcing himself to show no outward reaction. He hated the nickname she'd just christened him with, but he'd be damned before he let her know. "Your name, please."

Her lips twitched. "So formal, aren't you, baby?" A flicker of calculation entered her eyes before disappearing, but it told him to expect her next move. She dragged her full lower lip between her teeth and propped both feet up on the table, giving him a view of her thighs that clogged the breath in his throat. She crossed her feet at the ankles, but not before he glimpsed where those legs led. The tiny patch of denim covering her pussy. "Call me whatever you want. Just don't expect me to answer."

Jesus Christ. If she made him any harder, he'd have to excuse himself. "I wouldn't say your name unless I had a good reason."

She swayed her feet back and forth. "Give me your best one."

The urge to shift in his seat was strong. "You've already looked right at it."

Her feet stilled. He caught a flash of surprise and uncertainty, confusing the hell out of him. Had he read her signals wrong? One minute she was challenging him, and the next, she looked frozen in the headlights. Or maybe he'd just called her bluff? His ability to read people had been his saving grace more than once since being dishonorably discharged from the SEALs two years ago. Working as a street enforcer in Brooklyn for his cousin's underground crime ring, the skills he'd honed in the navy had been utilized on a daily basis. Often in ways he didn't like to recall, but forced himself to, anyway. To remember what he'd been reduced to.

But reading this girl was difficult, even for him. She'd flashed her thighs at him as if wanting a reaction, but when he'd given it to her, she'd clammed up. Whatever the reason, he refused to show another ounce of interest. He *wasn't* interested. This girl couldn't scream trouble any louder. He was through with trouble. Done.

"*So.*" She finally recovered her entertained expression. "What kind of piece were you reaching for when I walked in?"

He simply narrowed his eyes at her.

"Hey, you're preaching to the choir. They took my favorite Ruger." She pouted. "Has my initials painted in Wite-Out on the side and everything."

Oh, I get it now. She's crazy. "Why are you here?"

His abrupt question didn't faze her. "Three o'clock meeting, same as you. Some people just don't value punctuality."

The way she smirked when she said it made him think she'd read his mind upon walking into the room. But that was impossible. Who the fuck *was* this girl? A tempting weapons enthusiast who also happened to be perceptive? He needed to know more. Just enough to solve the formula she presented, so he could pack up his curiosity and store it away. "I wasn't asking why you're in this room. What landed you on this squad?"

She inspected her fingernails. "Ah. The old *what are you in for* conversation. I don't want to play." Her boots abruptly hit the ground. "Just kidding, I'm in. But you have to go first."

"Nope."

"Impasse," she whispered, walking her fingers across the table. "I could guess why you're here, but you'd dislike that more than simply telling me."

Connor said nothing. He *would* dislike that. Guesswork had

always been a source of irritation for him. He dealt only in facts. Again, he got the feeling this girl saw more than most people. The air of mayhem she wore like a second skin probably made people underestimate her. He wouldn't be one of them.

"You have a military background. But you're not there now, are you?" She leaned across the table and he caught a whiff of smoke. Not cigarette smoke. Like the strike of a match, or the lingering scent of incense. "It isn't difficult math, soldier."

"Don't call me that."

"You don't like trigger, baby, or soldier." Her tongue lingered against her top lip. "If you don't like any of my nicknames, better tell me your real one."

Connor almost laughed. Almost. The nicknames had been her roundabout way of getting him to spill his name first. He'd nearly walked right into it. Why were they waging a battle over something so minor? When this meeting started, they would find out each other's names anyway.

It was time to let this girl know he didn't play games. At least not the kind that took place while fully clothed. As he leaned across the table, he watched her blue eyes widen and knew she had to be a blonde underneath that pink hair. Her eyelashes and eyebrows were light, her coloring fair. *She'd look goddamn perfect against my black sheets...arms stretched over her head, unable to free herself. Not really wanting to get free at all.*

"I never said I didn't like you calling me baby."

Dammit. Had he said that out loud? He'd decided not to show her any more interest. Once he made a decision, he stuck to it. Every time. He resented her for being the one to make him deviate. If she weren't leaning so close, her small tits pressing against the front of her shirt, maybe he'd have kept his resolve. He'd always liked women with bouncy little tits, and he'd lay ten to one odds she wasn't wearing a bra. "Maybe I just want to hear you call me that under different circumstances."

When her confidence visibly wavered, Connor wanted to curse. These contradicting sides to her were only increasing his need to know more, and he did *not* want to get involved. Couldn't afford to. Her chin went up a notch, and that show of fire amidst the uncertainty turned him on. "What circumstances would those be?"

Too soon. Too insane. He'd just met this girl. They'd be working together. He couldn't sit here in the light of day and detail the many activities he'd like to perform with her. Even if he wanted to, just to see her reaction. To see if she wanted him, too. But what would he do if she did? Drag her onto the conference room table, tug her shirt up to her neck, and get a look at those tits? He'd have to get her back to his apartment if he did that, damn the meeting.

Change the subject. "Why do you smell like smoke?"

Her eyelashes shielded her eyes a second before they flashed wide, hitting him square in the chest with the force of their impact. "I set things on fire."

Any other time, the expression on the hot, bearded ex-soldier's face would have made Erin O'Dea dissolve into a fit of laughter. It wasn't the usual response men gave her when she played the crazy card. Not at all. Maybe that was why she wasn't laughing. This guy wasn't typical. Didn't fit her profile of what men should be like. They all wanted to get inside her until she performed her fun little reveal. *Surprise, sweetheart. I'm a convicted arsonist. You might be next.*

Cue haunted house cackle.

They never asked why she'd done it or questioned the circumstances, simply vanishing into a puff of smoke. Exactly as planned. This guy wasn't vanishing, however. He hadn't flinched, not once, and the trickle of relief in her chest pissed her off. The words "proceed with caution" flashed across her consciousness, sparking and flaming around the edges. This man *would* ask why and question the circumstances. Having only met him mere minutes ago, she shouldn't be so certain of that fact, but it would be reckless to put him in the same category as other men who scared easily. His steady green eyes were so intent on her, she worried her mask might slip underneath the weight of them. She didn't want him to be the first person to ask her why. She didn't want *anyone* to ask her why. Her secrets were all she had. After you'd lived behind bars among hundreds of women with your privacy stripped clean away, you held on to what you could. You didn't let it go for a pair of muscular biceps.

This one just needed a few more nudges and he'd lose interest. It was possible he already had and could hide his emotions better than most. She knew all about that. Although some people, her stepfather mainly, *wanted* her to be certifiably crazy, it was probably only half true. Yeah, she was a little off. For good reason. The man sitting across from her would recognize it soon enough and stop looking at her like he wanted to devour her, bite by bite.

His gaze became too much to bear and Erin focused on the window. Only one pane of glass between her and the outside. She could survive anything, face anything, as long as that was the case. Which was why she was here. You could only dodge so many bullets before one caught you in the back. This place, this job, was her bullet between the shoulder blades. *Woman down.*

Working for cops. Hell must have been having a fucking snowstorm. She hadn't spit on the sidewalk on the way in for no reason. Cops were the enemy. The men and women who took away her freedom. Laughed as they stripped away her dignity. They thought handcuffs and a gun made them smart, but it only made them complacent. At age twenty-five, she'd already proven that. Twice.

The ex-soldier's raised eyebrow told her she was smiling. After what she'd just said to him, he probably thought that smile meant she was a lunatic. Mission accomplished. For the first time since she'd sworn off men, she regretted sending one running. But it was entirely necessary. This man—this big, rough-hewn *male*—was an enforcer. More than that, he had a brain working behind all that stoicism. Even if she were inclined to call him baby in certain *circumstances*, it would be disastrous. It didn't take a rocket scientist to figure out he would be dominant in bed. The way he was clenching his fists as if fighting for control, even with her a full two feet away, told her that. He'd be the type to hold a woman down while he pounded out his lust.

That image might have turned her on at one time. Now it terrified her.

Still. She allowed her gaze to drop to his lips. Who knew she could find a beard so appealing? It wasn't rugged, but close-cut. Well-maintained. He looked like a man who could survive on his own in the wilderness with nothing but string and a Windbreaker. Capable. Made of steel. What would that beard feel like against her cheeks, her chin? If she leaned a little closer across the table, he might let her find out. If he hadn't already decided she belonged in a straitjacket. *Take a number, pal.*

"You'd better decide now if this meeting is important to you," he growled. "Because if you keep looking at me like you want to kiss me, neither one of us is going to be here for it."

Hooo boy. Something she'd thought long gone shimmied in her belly. "That's pretty confident."

"Realistic."

Erin drummed her fingers on the table before reaching one hand out, intending to tug his beard. "I'm just curious about what this feels like. In places."

He caught her wrist in midair before it made contact. "You touch me, you'll find out."

Ice formed beneath her skin, so freezing cold that it burned like blue fire. Her muscles tightened to the point of pain. She focused on her breathing. *In and out. In and out.* Just a little tug and her hand would be free. Nothing could contain her. She'd made sure of that. He might harness a lot of power in that muscular frame, but she didn't sense that he would use it on her. Unless she asked. Which she sure as hell would *not.*

Her brain commanded her to pull out of his grip, but her body wouldn't obey. She focused back on the window, zeroed in on the patch of gray sky visible through the glass. "Please let go," she whispered, furious when her voice shook.

He dropped her hand like it was on fire. She didn't like the way he was looking at her. Eyes seeing too much. Discarding theories, thinking of new ones. Like he knew a damn thing about what was wrong with her. Half the time, *she* didn't know.

"My name is Connor."

Erin went still. Inside and out. She felt warm all of a sudden, like someone had draped a fleece blanket over her shoulders. If she thought she'd had him at least partially pegged, she'd been wrong. He didn't have to give in to their silly name war. He'd done it because she'd shown a chink in her armor and he wanted to give her a victory.

Connor.

"What about a tiny little kiss?" *Shit.* Where had that come from? "No tongue."

"This isn't summer camp." Those hands clenched. Unclenched.

"If you want to kiss me, you'll get everything. I'm not going to hold back."

His gruff tone made her shiver. That voice held promises she couldn't begin to interpret. It had been so long since she'd let a man touch her, but she knew instinctively that Connor would be a whole new experience. One she definitely wasn't ready for and never would be. Still. She felt...gravitated to him. She'd originally leaned across this conference table to unnerve him. It worked with most people. Invade their personal space until they back off for good. Now that she was this close to him, though, she found herself wanting to stay there. It didn't hurt that he'd released her hand without hesitation. Maybe it was premature or bad judgment on her part, but his action had made her feel safe. She didn't feel safe very often, if ever.

Deciding to trust the instinct that rarely failed her, she climbed onto the table and crawled on her hands and knees the remaining distance. Connor's facade slipped just a little, lips parting on a gravelly exhale, broad chest shuddering as he watched her. "That wasn't a challenge," he grated.

"Everything we've said so far has been a challenge." Erin knew he liked what he saw as his gaze ran the length of her back, snagging on her ass. She gave it a quick shake. He groaned low in his throat, and she was shocked to find herself excited by it. "Kiss me. Just...don't touch me, okay?"

"*Jesus.*" He dragged both hands down his face. "You've got the wrong guy for that, sweetheart."

Of course, that made her want the kiss even more. She was drawn to fire. Connor had enough inside him to burn down a major city. The fact that he kept such a tight leash on it only made her want to watch it crackle and race. "I didn't say *I* couldn't touch." She gripped the collar of his shirt and dragged him forward, bringing their mouths an inch apart. "Just you."

A muscle ticked in his jaw. "I'll make you beg for my goddamn hands on you."

Ah, Connor. You have no idea what you're up against. "You're welcome to try."

As if he wanted to reassure her, but the need to do so pissed him off, he seized the table's edge with such obvious strength, the wood groaned beneath her. After a blistering perusal of her body, he brushed their mouths together once, before running his tongue along the seam of her lips. The room blurred around them. *Oh. Oh wow.*

Out of the corner of her eye, a figure loomed in the doorway. "Well I guess the 'getting to know each other' phase is under way."

CHAPTER TWO

Connor shot forward to block the girl from the newcomer's view. She'd gotten up on that table for him, and no one else got to enjoy the scenery. No one but him. His hands reached out of their own volition to drag her off the table and set her behind him.

They grasped at thin air.

Panic flared for two reasons. One, he didn't like taking his eyes off the man framed in the doorway when his identity hadn't been established. He'd been told to expect a roomful of convicts, after all. He needed to know who posed a threat and he wanted to know *immediately*. Especially now, when the threat could be directed at the girl. Two, not being able to touch her made him anxious. Ridiculous, really, since he'd only held her wrist and she'd nearly had a full-blown breakdown. It had only made him want to touch her more. Smooth out the fear with his hands. Gentle her. Tame her.

Connor whipped his head around, needing to get eyes on her. She gave him a pinkie wave from her chair. How had she moved so fast? And dammit, how could she look so serene when the barest hint of contact with her mouth had shot electricity down his spine?

He split his attention between her and the new guy. Although "guy" seemed an informal moniker for someone who held himself as if expecting to own the room's attention. Not a con, then. Captain Derek Tyler? He'd been told back in New York to expect a man who brooked no bullshit, and the description fit. Most importantly, he wasn't a threat to *her*.

Connor lowered himself back into his seat. He thrived on control. Always had. What she had inspired in him since entering the room didn't compare to anything in his thirty years of experience. He'd watched the girl vacillate among terrified, curious, and confident so many times his head was still spinning. So many things seeming to war for precedence in her head… and he'd found himself wanting to battle them all. What would it be like to harness all that vitality?

Initially, she'd wanted him to back off. Her admission that she liked to "set things on fire" was meant to scare him away. Instead, his mental response had been, *it's a good thing I know how to put them out.* He'd been doing it for the last two years. Cleaning up after his volatile cousin, who'd preferred to solve matters through violence. Guns, intimidation, fists. You name it. Connor's life had been filled with violence. Images imprinted on his brain since childhood, then the navy. He'd fit seamlessly into the Brooklyn operation without a hiccup and he'd resented that. Resented that a place had been carved for him there all along, waiting for him to screw up and go the hell back where he belonged.

Resented how easy doling out pain had become. Feeling too easy, too…good. A numbing distraction from the direction his life had taken.

He'd found a way to get free of it, though. Finally. For that very reason, this pink-haired pyromaniac should not appeal to him. Chicago was supposed to represent a new start for him. For his ailing mother. The word "complicated" didn't even begin to describe "she who still had not been named." He had issues of his own to solve. He sure as hell didn't have time for this. For her.

For Chrissake, she didn't like to be *touched*. His hands were everything to him. Whether they were being used as weapons or to give a woman pleasure, they were always at the ready. Being on the receiving end of her come-ons without being able to touch would be pure torture. She tested his restraint while simultaneously demanding he exercise more than ever. No, he needed to set aside his fascination with her and focus on the job. This one would drive him straight out of his mind. It wouldn't be the first time he didn't get what he wanted. He'd survived every time. He'd survive without having the girl beneath him. Probably.

But God help anyone *else* who tried to get her there.

Connor gripped the edge of the chair and reeled back the irritation produced by that thought. His attention landed on the presumed captain who'd interrupted them before he could get a satisfying taste of the girl. The man looked slightly perturbed, but the faint frown lines between his eyes gave Connor the impression he looked like that most of the time. He was splitting his attention between Connor and Fire Girl, looking more than a little fascinated.

"See something interesting, Captain?"

The other man took his time answering, opening up a manila folder and thumbing through some paperwork, although he looked suitably impressed by Connor's deduction. "That's how you talk to your new boss?"

"I do when he's late."

"I have a city to run." He threw an irritated glance toward

the door. "Not sure what everyone else's excuse is, but I intend to find out."

"Maybe they were delayed by your goons at the front desk." The girl spun her chair around in a circle. "And I don't have bosses. Merely oppressors."

Derek didn't blink. "You're free to leave at any time, Ms. O'Dea."

O'Dea. Connor tried not to show a reaction to that piece of information. Across the table, she tossed her pink hair and laughed. "If I wanted to leave, I'd be halfway back to Florida by now."

"Yes, I'm aware of your specialized skill. It's why you're here."

She spun around again. "I love when my reputation precedes me."

Florida. Specialized skill. Connor didn't have time to ponder what exactly Derek meant by that before another girl walked into the room. Marched, actually. She tucked her short jet-black hair behind her ears again and again, curious brown eyes landing on all three of them in the space of a heartbeat. "They took my laptop at the front desk. I want it back."

"Have a seat, Ms. Banks."

"Polly. Polly Banks." she corrected, taking a seat beside O'Dea. "Since we were all blackmailed to be here, we should dispense with formality."

"I like her." O'Dea reached over and released Polly's hair from behind her ear. "Can we keep her, Daddy?"

For someone who didn't like to be touched, she sure liked to be on the other end, didn't she? If they hadn't been interrupted, would she have touched him? Where? Connor was distracted by his leading thoughts when a man hobbled into the room. He wore an oversize sweater, fisherman's weave. A wide-brimmed hat was pulled down low on his forehead, and he tipped it at the two girls. When he reached the chair beside Connor, he practically fell into it with a groan.

Connor sent Derek a questioning look, but the man just stared back levelly, a hint of a smile on his mouth. "Meet Austin Shaw. He'll be joining you on the squad."

Polly hummed. "At least the Chicago PD aren't ageists, in addition to being thieves."

"What she said," O'Dea chimed in. "Cool hat, Grandpa."

"Thank you, dear." Austin's voice wavered with age. "I've had it years. It was an anniversary gift from my wife, Martha. You likely weren't even born the first time I wore it."

O'Dea's hands fluttered in a series of claps. "We're keeping him, too." She smirked at Connor. "You're the only one I'm not sure about yet."

"Fooled me," he growled.

Derek cleared his throat and the room went silent, a fact that annoyed Connor even more. This guy might be a captain with the Chicago PD, but that didn't mean shit where he came from. He was just another man ruled by the almighty system. Connor knew all too well how the system could hang you out to dry if you didn't play ball its way. "You have no choice in who you keep. Let's get one thing straight right away. This is my squad." Derek encompassed them with a look. "I picked the six of you out of hundreds for a reason. As soon as the final two get here, we'll talk about what it is."

Huh. *That's strange.*

Erin looked down at her chest, wondering if the warm fuzzy she'd just encountered in her midsection was visible to the naked eye. She might hate the idea of being strong-armed into being here, of having her past held over her head and used as a bargaining chip to gain her obedience. But unless you counted the thousand-woman team whose uniforms consisted of orange jumpsuits, she'd never been part of a *group* before. Yeah, they had a jerk-wad leader who had already felt the need to assert his male superiority over them, but everyone at this table had their rear ends to the fire. They were in this rowboat headed down shit creek together and something about that felt vaguely comforting. As comfortable as a convict could reasonably get knowing her second-class citizen status made her dispensable, and therefore she would be placed in dangerous situations.

But hey—at least it was for the good of a team. With an adorable old man mascot.

She sneaked a glance at Connor. He was still looking at her. She wished like hell he'd stop. Also, if he could keep going that would be great, too. It felt like being touched without all the anxiety that came along with it. His mouth had felt so good—

"Nice of you to show up," Derek said, giving the two latest arrivals the stink eye. "Now sit down. We've got work to do."

Erin stared in fascination at the new couple standing in the doorway. And despite their obvious differences, there was absolutely *zero* doubt that they were a couple. They were tethered in some invisible way she'd never witnessed before. The man was a fighter. Every taut line of his body made that unquestionable. Not only did he look ready to take on any threat to the girl standing beside him, he was *dying* for someone to try so they could lose. Where Connor was sturdy and unmovable, this dark blond in his worn leather jacket never stopped moving. His fingers flexed, his eyes scanned, his energy sparked. A complete contrast to the girl who'd taken hold of his hand as if to reassure him.

Erin realized she was openly gawking at the girl, but didn't care. Two years ago, she'd spent Christmas Eve locked up in Dade Correctional. Bored and restless, she'd found her way to a makeshift church service, an event she'd normally avoid like the plague, but they'd been giving out fruit punch. Sitting in the back row, she'd listened to the story of Mary and Joseph traveling toward Bethlehem, where Mary would eventually squeeze out Jesus. This girl standing in the doorway, casting an air of calm over the room, was how she'd pictured Mary. Still, serene…eyes brimming with warmth.

"Oh captain, my captain." The fighter slapped a hand over his heart, punctuating the heavy Brooklyn accent he spoke with. "Try not to endear yourself to me too quickly. We just got here."

Derek trained cool eyes on him. "You're on my time, Driscol. Don't make me regret it."

Driscol kept his smile in place, but it had lost any trace of humor. The Virgin Mother holding his hand whispered something in his ear and after a second, he nodded. Giving them all a suspicious once-over, he led her to the remaining open seats. He guided his girlfriend into one of them gently and stood behind her with arms crossed over his chest. When he jerked his chin at Connor and received a grunt in return, Erin realized they knew each other. Two strong personalities like that didn't form truces right off the bat. There might be an air of tension there, but there was also familiarity.

"You were *all* given a choice," Derek boomed. "Prison time or my time. One or the other. If you thought I was the lesser of two evils, you were wrong. You each have a skill that landed you in this room and I intend to use those skills to make Chicago safer." He twisted the gold wedding band on his finger. "There will be a high level of risk involved. If at any point prison sounds safer to you, I won't stop you from leaving. But if you're here, you show up on time and work hard. No fucking around."

Mean Daddy. Erin raised her hand, but didn't wait to be called on. "When do we get our guns back? I feel naked."

"No guns. No *weapons*, period, unless it's cleared by me." Derek waited for the protests to die down. "We meet every morning whether we're actively working a case or not. If you fail to show, don't bother coming back. I've made myself accountable for the six of you and I don't take the responsibility lightly." Each of them received a meaningful look. "I'm sure some of you share the opinion that police officers aren't perfect."

"Amen," she muttered.

"Understatement," Polly purred.

The captain paced in front of the table. "It might surprise you that I agree. I don't think we catch every angle because we're trained to think a certain way." He rapped a knuckle on the table. "You were born to think another. I'm going to use that."

Everyone remained silent a moment, absorbing that. Erin felt a reluctant twinkle of respect for the captain for admitting his department was flawed, but immediately squelched it, like two damp fingers subduing a candle flame. *Dick.*

"Let's hear everyone's skill," Connor rumbled, sending goose bumps racing up her arms.

"Seconded." Driscol rocked back on his heels. "Need to know who we're working with."

Alarm crackled in Erin's veins. She should have anticipated this. Her particular skill set could potentially give away her weakness and she didn't like that. Didn't like anyone having a means with which to defeat her. Feeling Connor's gaze on her, she turned away and focused on the window.

She heard Derek flip his folder back open. "I think it's important, too. Knowing one another's strengths will force you to utilize one another. In addition to being talented criminals, you each have a tendency to be a lone wolf. That ends now, or this will never work."

Polly's chair squeaked beside her. "Don't keep us in suspense, Hitchcock."

"Yes, it's almost time for my heart medication," Austin said, before dissolving into a coughing fit.

"Fair enough." Derek sighed. "Even though each of you has signed a confidentiality statement, rest assured I'm only going to define your role, not enlighten the group as to how it earned you a ticket to prison."

Erin relaxed enough to face the group again. Connor was still looking at her, so she sent him a tongue-lolling grin. He rolled his eyes.

"We'll start with Polly," Derek continued. "She's a hacker, but we'll be kind and refer to her as a tech specialist."

Polly nodded briskly. "Hacker will do. No need to soften it."

Derek gestured to the Virgin Mother. "I misspoke earlier when I said you were all given the choice between my time and prison time. Seraphina is a trained undercover officer. She's the only one in this room with experience in the field, so you'd be wise to listen to her."

Erin sagged with disappointment. Now she had to hate the Virgin Mary.

"Bowen Driscol—"

"I'm here for *her*," Bowen broke in, cutting Derek off. He leaned over Seraphina and planted a fist on the table. "I protect her first. The cases come second. Take it or leave it."

Derek and Bowen squared off across the table. Even Erin stayed completely still, intoxicated by all the testosterone floating in the air. Finally, Derek moved on, but Erin noted that he hadn't given in. The captain liked to pick his battles. A lesson to remember.

"Connor Bannon. Former Navy SEAL." Derek tapped the folder against the table. "That pretty much makes him capable of anything. Infiltration, hostage removal, explosives." Erin's heart started to pound at the mention of explosives, red plumes of smoke streaking across her vision. *So pretty.* She tucked the image away for later and focused. If Connor had been good at his job, why didn't he have it anymore? Her already-considerable interest in him grew. "Connor is good under pressure. He'll be in charge whenever I'm not present."

If she hadn't been watching his face closely, she would have missed the jolt that went through him. He hadn't been expecting that announcement. It had caught him off guard, but he still managed to retain his *ask me if I give a fuck* expression. It made her want to bake him a fancy cake overloaded with rekindling candles. Or get that kiss. Kiss, fire, kiss, fire. Definitely the kiss. After all, the kiss might be fire in itself.

"Erin O'Dea," Derek said.

"Present."

She managed to drag her attention away from Connor to focus on Derek, but not before she saw the big ex-SEAL mouth her first name. *Erin.* Her nerves were playing a game of ping-pong inside her throat at the impending reveal of her special talent. So far her instincts hadn't blipped on anyone in the room, but it was too soon to tell what kind of people they were under the surface. If they were the kind of people who would test her boundaries. Her claim to infamy tended to provoke and challenge. See if they could prove the rumor wrong.

Derek's voice forced her to tune back in. "Her nickname is Erin 'she's getting away' O'Dea. That should tell you everything you need to know. She gives new meaning to the words 'escape artist.' There isn't a set of handcuffs or a concrete cell that has been able to hold her for long."

Not entirely true, she thought, but refrained from saying out loud. All eyes were on her. She could feel them roving over her skin, making her itch. Being the center of attention only worked for her when it was on her terms. Not someone else's.

Erin traced the shape of a half-moon onto the table with her finger. "The police are so adorable with their jangly set of keys and iron padlocks." She scrunched her shoulders. "I just want to pinch their little cheeks."

She caught Seraphina stifling a laugh and decided she only needed to half hate her. Derek, to his credit, didn't take issue with her characterization of cops, only moving on with a weary headshake. "Not that I don't love the pink hair, Erin, but it makes you too recognizable. Deal with that by tomorrow."

Dammit. She'd known they'd nix the do. Never one to agree to anything outright, she propped her boots on the table, allowing the bells to jingle. Bells that only made a noise when she gave them permission. It was how she'd trained herself to make the quietest exits possible. "I'mma think about it, Captain. Proceed with the introductions."

Derek's jaw ticked as he eyed Erin's boots, but he didn't comment. "Last but not least, we have Austin Shaw. Simply put, Austin is a con. He can weave himself into any situation and immediately belong there. He speaks several languages fluently and the ones he does not, he can pull off an authentic accent for. He's everything and nothing. A lifeguard, a bartender, a millionaire. He's exactly what he needs others to see."

The five of them exchanged baffled looks, but only Bowen spoke up. "You're talking in the past tense, right?" He scrutinized the hunched-over old man. "No offense, Pops, but unless we're working a missing dentures case at a retirement home, I don't see you going undercover."

Austin took off his hat and tossed it on the table. At the same time, he straightened, his spine shedding all signs of age within a split second. He shrugged off the coat and ran a hand through his tousled brown hair. Erin's mouth fell open. Austin wasn't an old man by any stretch. He was a young man…a *gorgeous* one at that. She caught Connor's dark frown and shrugged.

Looking like he'd just stepped off the pages of *GQ* magazine, Austin stacked his hands behind his head, sending Polly a wink as he did so. "Now, ladies and gents," he said with a faint British lilt. "Any questions?"

CHAPTER THREE

Connor tossed his oversized duffel bag onto the hardwood floor and looked around his new apartment. The police department had rented two units on the top floor of a building in Logan Square where they would live rent-free as long as they were cooperating with the undercover squad. Apparently since Bowen and Sera had already set up home base independently, Derek had anticipated Polly and Erin sharing one remaining apartment, while he and Austin shared the other. The girls had seemed indifferent about the arrangement, quickly gathering their things and heading home to check out the new digs.

He and Austin had been a different story altogether. Neither one of them had cottoned to the idea of sharing space with a virtual stranger they knew next to nothing about, protesting rather loudly when Derek dropped the news. After his little stunt, Austin had turned out to be outspoken as hell, so Connor had just sat back and waited. Derek, needed at another meeting, had basically told them both to fuck off and live in a Dumpster for all he cared. Austin claimed he already had a place to crash, so Connor had taken the apartment for himself.

Not bad. Back in Brooklyn, he'd split time between a run-down one bedroom and his mother's dilapidated house in the Bronx when she felt too sick to be alone. He'd never lived in this much sunlight. It streamed in from several windows, even a skylight located just above the eat-in kitchen. The furniture they'd provided was functional, which was all he needed. Nothing flashy, just four white walls and a place to lay his head. Each bedroom was about the same size, so he took the one with a view of the street. That way, he could see anyone coming or going.

On cue, he saw Erin and Polly walking up the sidewalk. The giant cup of coffee in Polly's hand explained how he'd beaten them to the building. Erin stooped down and picked up a short fallen tree branch and lit the end on fire with a lighter produced from her pocket, holding it up like an Olympic torch and jogging in a circle. Without flinching, Polly reached over and doused the flame with coffee.

Connor shook his head. Jesus, how had he forgotten in the space of an hour the effect that Erin had on him? She was a hundred yards away and yet his body reacted like she was naked and straddling him.

Fuck. He shouldn't have thought of that.

Five stories down, Erin caught sight of him standing in the window and blew him a kiss.

Jesus. She'd be living right across the hall from him. Maybe he should have taken a page from Austin's book and looked for other accommodations. How would he concentrate with her so close? He'd made only the barest contact with her body and still he knew what she'd feel like. All flexible angles and smooth, supple skin. He'd seen right where he wanted to be that afternoon. Just beneath that patch of denim. He wanted to shove her legs open and bite her there. Make her sorry she ever flashed her sweet spot at him. Make her grateful she had.

Everything in between.

Connor stepped away from the window, wishing he weren't the kind of man who hated the idea of two women carrying their own suitcases up the stairs. If he weren't, he'd step into the shower and jerk his cock to the fantasy he'd been harboring since leaving the station. Erin on her hands and knees on the conference room table once again. Only this time, she'd be facing the other direction as he fucked her silly from behind. He'd never heard her speak in anything but that throaty purr, but her satisfied screams somehow already rang in his head.

Did it make him sick? He'd never been ashamed of his preference for rough sex before, but Erin had already shown signs of fear from a simple touch. He couldn't even imagine her reaction if she could see the images his mind refused to stop projecting. Why had she inspired this restless urgency in him? The need had always been there, but never so demanding. So necessary.

With a curse, he stomped out of the apartment and down the stairs to help Erin and Polly with their luggage. They sat in the tiny foyer outfitted with mailboxes, perched on their suitcases and drinking coffee. They weren't talking, Polly looking deep in thought while Erin tried to pick a mailbox lock with her fingernail.

She brightened when she saw him. "Baby, what took you so long?" Her elbow found Polly's ribs, unseating her. "Told you he'd come down."

"Yes, our fearless number two in command." Polly smiled politely. "I've heard good things, but nothing directly from you. I don't think you spoke once during the meeting."

Connor picked up a suitcase in each hand. "Had nothing to add."

"No?" She followed behind him. "You didn't even feel

the need to point out he's turned us into a parody of the Mod Squad? I certainly did."

Actually, he *had* noticed. "As long as we're not required to wear bell bottoms."

Polly laughed, but it was such a girlish sound compared to her no-nonsense demeanor, he looked back in surprise. Polly didn't seem to notice anything amiss, but behind her Erin had a hand smacked over her mouth to hold in her own laughter.

"What about Derek?" Polly asked. "He's wearing a wedding ring and I'll admit he's quite attractive, but I can't imagine him with a wife. Seems like he's already married to his job."

Connor had zero desire to gossip about the captain's marital status, so he breathed a sigh of relief when Erin piped up. "We should invite her over for empanadas and find out."

"That's a very specific plan," Polly commented. "But unnecessary. I'd rather hack into her financial records."

The bells on Erin's boots tinkled. "More empanadas for me."

He turned on the landing and went up the final flight of stairs, setting both suitcases down in front of their door. "Check the locks when you go inside and make sure they're working. Windows and doors. If they're broken, let me know."

Erin pulled a bobby pin out of her pocket and inserted it into the lock. Two twists and one jiggle later and the door swung open. "This one is decent."

Polly dangled a key. "Next time, we could use this."

Connor decided he better go in and check the locks himself. Erin might be an escape artist, but hopefully not *everyone* would be able to open their door quite as easily. Otherwise he'd be sleeping on their couch until the locks were fixed to his satisfaction. Being that close to Erin would be the ultimate torture if he couldn't push her up against a wall every time they were in the same room. As if she could read every last one of his thoughts, she sashayed past him through the doorway, trailing a hand over his abs as she went, sending heat spiraling to his groin. Polly pursed her lips and followed.

Their apartment had the same general layout as his, only it was located at the back of the building, giving them less sunlight. Erin walked into one bedroom and immediately came out looking pale. She stood in the living room a moment fidgeting, before entering the second bedroom. Connor waited for her to come out, barely noticing when Polly rolled her luggage into the first bedroom Erin had rejected. Still no Erin.

Feeling impatient with himself for wanting to follow her into the bedroom even though it was an epically stupid idea, Connor busied himself by checking every window lock and testing the front door from the inside, finding them secure. On his way to double-check the bathroom window, he saw Erin standing in the center of the bedroom, completely still. Facing the small, rectangular window, her shoulders were bunched tight. A coiled spring ready to launch.

"Hey," Connor said. "You all right?"

Erin spun around. "I'm fine. It's going to be fine."

Her eyes were unfocused. He didn't like it. Which was ludicrous since she'd been like this off and on since he met her. "Everything is secure."

She smiled, but it looked sad. A little forced. "Not from me."

"No, not from you." *Go back to your apartment. You don't know how to comfort anyone. Or why she even needs it in the first place.* He cleared his throat, looked away. "I'm right across the hall."

"I'm aware of that. I'll probably think about it all the time."

Her honesty brought his head up. "Why is that?"

She blinked. "Because we kissed. It was all very sexual,

wasn't it?"

"Yes." He shook his head, torn between painful arousal and the need to laugh. Where the hell had this girl come from? "You could say that."

"I just did." She plopped down onto the floor, pulling her legs up to her chest. "Go back to your apartment, baby. I'm acclimating."

Connor stayed put a moment, reluctant to leave her alone when she looked so lost. Shit, he just wanted to keep looking at her, period. But when she closed her eyes and started to hum, he felt like an intruder. With a final glance in her direction, he went home to unpack.

It was the *sound* that sent her over the edge. Every time.

When she was thirteen, the sound had started getting louder. It hadn't been her first time being locked in the closet, but it was the longest. Her stepfather had left her a packet of ramen noodles and a bottle of Evian. By then, she'd learned to ration and she'd learned the hard way. This time, though, she heard no noises on the other side of the door. No chairs scraping across the floor or water running. By the time she realized her stepfather wouldn't be coming back, she'd been too weak to do anything about it.

Maybe it was a side effect of dehydration or simply her brain craving some kind of activity. The sound had started quietly, like moth's wings beating against a screen door. Over the course of time, the volume of it had swelled until it sounded like a biblical swarm of locusts was trying to break the closet door down. She'd made the mistake of trying to drown it out with screams, but it had only grown louder. More intense.

Needing to move, needing to escape the sound, she'd started to kick at the wooden back panel of the closet. Kicking and kicking until the soles of her feet ached. Just as she was about to give up, her foot had broken through into a crawlspace she hadn't known existed. As she'd sobbed and slipped her way to freedom, the noise had muted. She'd sworn to herself that no one would ever lock her up again. If they tried, she would get free every goddamn time, no matter what it took.

Night had fallen hours ago, but she still sat in the middle of her new bedroom floor. If she looked closely, she could still see Connor's outline in the doorway, and she wished she hadn't told him to leave. Safety. He made her think of safety, and she desperately needed to feel it right now. She didn't do well in new places. Without any knowledge of the various means of egress, hollow spots in the wall, or who lived around her, she felt limited. If her window led to a viable escape route, she wouldn't be in this state. But it didn't. Neither bedroom had one, thanks to them being in the back of the building. She'd looked down into an alley surrounded by cinderblock walls and she'd seen a trap. A death trap.

It had shut her down cold, forcing her to tunnel into herself. But she had to get up and move at some point. Sitting here wouldn't ease the thrashing of locust wings paralyzing her mind. Only finding a safe place would. Move. *Move*. Where would she go?

Erin rose unsteadily to her feet, stumbling against the bed frame when she found both of her legs asleep. Several minutes later when she could move without falling, she left the bedroom. She paused at the front door, once again attempting to examine this certainty that being around Connor might dull the harsher edges of the sound, the fear, but she couldn't hear her thoughts over the roar. Tears burned behind her eyelids, but she told herself to grow a fucking pair and blinked them back. If she made any noise, she might wake up Polly, and no way could she explain herself. Especially to her new roommate, who so obviously had her shit together.

Only one option.

In a move of desperation, she opened the door and closed it quietly behind her. It only took her a few seconds to let herself into Connor's apartment. As soon as she crept inside, the noise started to recede. She told herself it was the fire escape attached to the living room window and the view beyond that calmed her. The identical fire escape she'd seen extending from his bedroom window, as well. Not his cool, smooth scent that dotted the air. Like freshly sanded wood rubbed with pine needles. She told herself it was the view, the promise of freedom, but she inhaled through her nose like a resurfaced diver as she padded toward the window. She would just curl up here and be gone before Connor woke up in the morning. Easy peasy. The sound died down a little more.

"What are you doing, Erin?"

Roaring. Battering. Her hands flew to her ears to muffle the noise, but it didn't work. She couldn't draw a full breath. Connor stood in the dark, shirtless above black sweatpants, talking to her. None of his words broke through. She lurched toward the window and looked out onto the avenue running in front of the building, trying to breathe, but the guarantee of escape didn't help this time. Connor's heat at her back should have alarmed her. When the noise got this loud, the fear this great, it took her a long time to come back from it. Miraculously, though, his heat was absorbing it. Taking the weight off of her. Her body sagged back against his in relief, but she batted his arms away when they tried to close around her. *Too much. Too soon.*

"What do you need?"

His voice bathed her ear with a feeling so delicious, she felt it down to her toes, alleviating anxiety as it went. *More...*she needed *more* of him. In her own way. Even as Erin turned to face him, she had no idea what would happen until she saw his concerned face, his masculine lips hovering above hers. "You're fighting it off," she whispered. "I thought it was the window."

"I don't understand, sweetheart." He looked frustrated, but not with her. More because he wanted to comprehend. His fingers touched the glass. "Don't you have a window in your room, too?"

She shook her head. "It's a mirage. There's a trap set for me."

Motherfucker. Why couldn't she say what needed to be said? The words weren't coming out right. He was going to think she was crazy. Just like everyone else.

Connor was silent a beat. "Tell me what you need."

Erin leaped, no idea where she would land. "Take. I need to take." Yearning struck her in the belly, thick and undeniable, but it teamed with regret. "But I can't *give* anything. I—"

He cut her off with another step. Closer. So close. But not touching. Light spilled in through the window and highlighted his strong jaw, clenched so tight. His chest and arms, carved with muscle, should have been forbidding, but the smell of freshly rubbed wood and pine, combined with his quiet strength, made him a haven. He stood without moving and let her look him over, not trying to rush her into a decision or make her mind up for her. It made her need him even more. Her flesh pulsed between her legs, nipples tingling behind the material of her shirt. It had been so long since she felt desire of any kind, and it crashed through her now, obliterating the fear. She had no choice but to cling to it. To him.

Erin slid her fingers around his biceps, sucking in a breath when they flexed hard under her touch. She reversed their positions, bringing his back up against the wall. Frustration was evident in every line of his body. Leashed restraint. *She* was the one leashing it, along with her own fears. This wasn't the type of man who let a woman handle him. The power in that settled over her like a thick cloak. She pressed his hands, palms down, against the wall and implored him with a look. *No touching.* His only acknowledgment was a tightening of his muscles. Bracing himself.

She didn't, *couldn't*, waste another second. The craving to touch, to release, was growing and she needed to appease it before it took her over. Connor watched through fevered eyes as she unsnapped the button of her jean shorts and let them fall to her feet. She could see the outline of his substantial arousal through the sweatpants and moaned into the silence. That was for her. He was aroused for *her*. Wearing only her panties and T-shirt, she grabbed on to his broad shoulders and hiked her legs up around his waist.

"Fuck." The back of his head hit the wall. "*Fuck*."

"Oh, *God*."

Her hips circled once and she whimpered, wanting to get closer and unable to. She needed pressure *right there*. It ached so badly. Connor seemed to comprehend her predicament or share it with her because he braced the breadth of his shoulders against the wall and pushed his hips out, tilting them at the perfect angle. "You won't let me touch you, Erin? You sure as hell better ride me rough for the both of us." He gave an upward thrust of his hips. "My cock is big and angry because you made it that way. That makes it your responsibility. *Move*."

Erin dug her fingernails into the muscles of his shoulders and started bucking her hips. The fact that he could support her weight and the frantic movements of her body made her ist. Intense hunger radiated from him, scorching her to move faster. Her writhing motions, the back her hips, caused a groove to form along the seam p panties, widening with her every movement to cradle Connor's erection. If the thin material of her panties and his sweats were to vanish, he would have been inside her in a heartbeat. They were that close to being joined.

"Look at you. Grinding that little pussy on me." His voice sounded raw, heated. "I'd fill you with every goddamn inch so quickly, you'd scream for me to take it back out. Maybe it's better this way, giving just your clit a ride. But know that I'd like to be pounding you full of me, Erin. *Full.*"

His words should have made her nervous, but reassurance shone in his eyes, swirling through the heat. No matter what came out of his mouth, he wouldn't break his silent promise. Thank God for that, because Erin's thighs were starting to shake violently, the beginnings of exhilaration firing in her belly, lower. Oh yes, lower. Her panties had grown so wet, the cotton had taken on a different texture and it dragged perfectly over her clit. She gripped his hips with her thighs and bucked faster, *faster*. A new sound filled her head, sending the other one running with its simplicity. *I need him and he's giving me what I need and I need him and he's giving…*

A sob burst past her lips as her orgasm loomed closer. "Please, Connor. Connor, please."

"*What are you begging for?*" The question cracked like a whip. "You're the hottest goddamn thing I've ever seen, thighs spread wide open as you dry-fuck me to insanity…and I can't even *touch* you. I should be the one begging." He groaned as she picked up speed, angling his hips more, giving her everything. "I've never begged a fucking day in my life, but you're going to make me, aren't you?"

Her muscles clenched. The flesh between her legs seized. Yes. *Yes*. "I can't. I don't…"

"You *will*," he gritted out. "Jesus Christ, look at you. You'll be worth my pride."

Erin got lost in a flash of blinding light. The climax sped through her with a force that her body almost couldn't withstand. A scream launched from somewhere deep inside her chest, but ended in a violent shake. She couldn't plant her feet because they were dangling off the ground, couldn't run from the intensity. It was ceaseless; the tightening at her core wouldn't stop. Before she registered her own actions, she'd fastened her mouth to Connor's and just as quickly, she found her way out of the blinding light into a soft, gentle glow. There were jagged edges here, but she knew how to navigate them. She heard his fists connecting with the wall as she pushed her tongue deep and tempted his to meet hers. To bring her down from the heights to which he'd sent her. The second his mouth opened to hers with a deep growl, her body went boneless, sliding down his rock-hard frame.

Connor's rigid length dug into her belly and she could feel the pain coming off him in waves. She lifted the hem of her shirt so she could feel it against her stomach, and smooth flesh greeted her. The head of his erection was visible over the top of his sweat pants, round and damp. Her hands itched with the need to touch him there, but she hesitated. Could she please a man like him? She'd learned how to intimidate men by being overtly sexual, but she hadn't called her own bluff in so long. No, she would *try* for him. After what he'd done…

Above her, his breathing grew stunted and shallow, as if it were being ripped over razor blades. "I can only take so much, Erin." He skirted past her and strode away, toward the bathroom. The door shut behind him and silence fell in the apartment. Not complete silence. Her pulse still pounded loud enough to echo in her ears. But his presence leaving the room had the effect of a mute button being hit. She closed her eyes and listened, finally hearing Connor in the bathroom. Heavy breathing, the occasional groan. Something anxious twisted inside her at the realization that he was touching himself. A multitude of emotions had her drifting toward the bathroom. Curiosity, lust…affront that he'd taken the privilege away from her.

She opened the door and stopped in her tracks.

CHAPTER FOUR

Connor felt Erin behind him in the bathroom. He'd left the door unlocked for a reason, but when he made eye contact with her in the mirror, that reason seemed unworthy of the moment. Out in the living room, she'd made him feel useless and exultant at the same time. The latter made no sense, so he'd focused on what she *hadn't* let him do. She hadn't let him touch her, taste her. He'd stood there like a rodeo bull and let her use his body to get off. So yeah, when he'd walked into the bathroom, raging with lust so thick he couldn't breathe, he'd thought, *fuck it, let her see. I'm not ashamed of a damn thing.*

He'd mistaken the fact that she'd humbled him for taking away his pride.

She stood behind him now with her lips parted and cheeks flushed, watching him stroke himself off like a hormonal teenager. It shouldn't have made him *hotter*, not when he didn't fully understand the problems she obviously had knocking around inside her beautiful head. He should stop now and make her explain, tell her she couldn't touch him anymore until he knew what she was going through. But there wasn't any turning back. Not right now, not with his cock heavy in his

.and, ready to erupt.

In the mirror, he could see her fingers smoothing against each other, as if she were imagining what it would feel like to replace his hand with her own.

Jesus. He liked having her watch. If her expression had been any different, it might have been another story. The look of wonder, the renewal of arousal that transformed her as she came slowly closer, had him clenching his teeth to prolong the moment. *Fuck*, though, it *hurt*. The front of her panties were wet from riding him until she came. Her flat stomach peeked out under the edge of her shirt, reminding him once again how crazy he was to yank it up and see what she hid underneath. At the same time, she looked like an innocent who'd stumbled upon something very, very bad happening and *God,* it made him want to corrupt her even more. *Sick. I'm sick.* His balls drew up tight…the tingling began at the base of his spine…

"You should leave," Connor grated, squeezing his eyes closed. Christ, any minute now…he couldn't wait any longer. Looking at her, knowing he couldn't touch her, was *killing* him. At the same time, his mind was projecting images in a desperate attempt to send him over the edge and find relief. Erin straddling his face, hands cuffed behind her back. Erin's eyes going blind, ankles around her ears, as he drove into her like a madman. "*Go*, Erin."

He didn't hear her move. One second she was standing at the door, the next she was standing on the rim of his bathtub, just beside his left shoulder. Closer. Her tits were eye level and it took every ounce of self-control inside him not to suck them into his mouth, right through her T-shirt. A tiny moan dropped from her lips as she leaned close, watching his hand work his stiff cock. She placed her open lips on his neck and dragged them higher, where she licked at his ear.

"What are you doing?" he demanded. *Do it again.*

"What feels right," she whispered, stroking her fingers over his chest. "Tell me what you're thinking about. Is it me?"

"*Of course*," he shouted. "You don't want to know any more than that."

"Yes, I do." She lightly scraped her fingernails down his back, and he growled. "I want to know what I'm missing out on. Tell me."

Against his better judgment, he let his lips come within a breath of her straining nipples, shifting beneath her shirt with every breath. Torture. This was *torture.*

"You said you want to fill every inch of me. Is that what you're thinking about?"

"*Yes, goddammit.*"

Her eyes turned glazed, unfocused. In his entire life, he'd never seen anything like her, vulnerable yet regal at the same time. She lifted her right hand and sucked two fingers into her mouth, before sliding them down the front of her panties. Her mouth parted on a gasp as she sank them into her pussy. "We can play pretend, can't we?"

Connor's body lurched with the force of his brutal climax. His vision dimmed under the weight of it, but he fought to keep his eyes trained on her hand, moving subtly inside her panties. His wild groans bounced off the walls of the bathroom as he stroked out the last of his come, aware that it was landing on her bare legs and unable to feel an ounce of regret over that fact. Right at the end, when the tremors were beginning to die down, she removed her fingers from her panties and dragged them across his lips, ripping an aftershock out of him, coating his palm with the effect.

"Dammit, Erin. *Dammit.*"

She slipped both hands into his hair and massaged his scalp, gently pulling on the strands. Until he swore it was the only thing holding him upright. "Gorgeous man," she murmured. "Amazing man."

"No. I'm not." How could he stand this close and not bury his face against her chest? Her stomach? It felt like a ritual he was neglecting to complete. "Don't mistake me for something I'm not."

"I make a lot of mistakes, but coming over here wasn't one." He heard her heavy swallow. "I'm sorry I made you hurt. I'm sorry I can't…"

The need to reassure her cut through everything. Her toes curled into the edge of his bathtub, chipped black nail polish on her toes. Without the bravado she'd worn like a second skin since he met her, she looked exhausted. Her eyelids drooped, making the heavy circles under her eyes look more pronounced. Now that his need had been momentarily slaked, shame plowed into his stomach like a battering ram. He shouldn't have let the situation get away from him. Whatever she was harboring on the inside was more important than his attraction to her, mind-numbing though it might be.

He rearranged himself back into his sweatpants and took a deep breath. "Why *did* you come over here, Erin?"

"The window in my room might as well be painted on. It doesn't go anywhere."

"Explain."

She glanced toward the mirror, flinching at her reflection, before hopping off the tub and leaving the bathroom. He grabbed a towel off the rack and followed her. When he entered the living room, he felt a flare of panic at not seeing her, but breathed a sigh of relief when she stepped into the light coming in through the window.

Evidence of his release was still visible on her legs and he put a stranglehold on the surge of pleasure it gave him, seeing it on her skin. He handed her the towel, wishing he could be the one to clean her off. She stared at the towel for a beat before comprehending why he'd brought it. As she wiped her legs clean, there wasn't a hint of embarrassment in her expression, only methodical concentration. When she'd finished, she held on to the towel and looked out the window.

"See, from here, there are twenty-two steps to the street." Her words sounded subdued, but concise. "One step onto the fire escape, five down the first set of stairs, five down the second. One when I hop down onto the asphalt. From there, if I run at a sprint, I can be in front of the building in ten steps. There's a security light that goes on if it senses movement, but the bulb has been taken out. It's the first thing I did when I got to the building this afternoon."

Connor's chest felt like someone had lobbed a sandbag onto his chest. Dots were starting to connect, though. Escape artist. Needs to be near windows. He wasn't ready to ponder the reason she'd developed the skill, but he had to know. It felt like his responsibility. "Your window doesn't have a fire escape?"

Erin scoffed. "I could get out without one. No problem." She rapped on the windowpane with her knuckles. "There's a closed-in area below my window, only accessible through a basement door. Fifteen-foot-high cinder-block walls. I could potentially get over them, but it would kill my timing. And I wouldn't have any visibility on the other side. It's a trap."

It was unbelievable, really. The way she appeared so self-possessed while calmly discussing escape routes. So unlike the unusual behavior he'd already come to associate with her. It made something inside him hurt. "Does someone want to trap you, Erin?"

"Yes," she whispered, then shook herself. "Don't ask me

that again."

It took Connor several moments to calm the rage. Was her need to have a way out associated with her aversion to being touched? He'd known there had to be a reason she didn't like hands on her, but now that he drew closer to an explanation, he was afraid to know the whole story. Afraid to have his depravity confirmed. God, what he'd just done in front of this girl couldn't be excused. Nor could the desire to do it again. To do whatever she'd allow him to do.

"I'm going to sleep here tonight." She sat down on the floor, just beneath the window. "I'll figure out something tomorrow… a different place to stay. This won't work."

No. He almost shouted the word. Maybe he'd known her less than a full day, but no way was he letting her stay somewhere he couldn't watch her. Where he couldn't keep her protected. Especially now that she'd admitted someone wanted to trap her. "Stand up, Erin," he said more sharply than intended. "You sleep in my room tonight and I'll take the spare. We'll switch apartments in the morning."

She came to her feet slowly. "You would do that?"

"Of course I would."

Her smile turned him inside out. She pushed up on her toes and laid a soft kiss on his lips. "Good night, baby."

She walked away, leaving him holding his breath and unable to stop himself from watching her through his bedroom doorway as she nestled like a kitten into his sheets. After some consideration, he dropped down onto the couch—just in case she decided to go for another midnight ramble—wondering what the hell he'd gotten himself into. Because he knew with irrevocable certainty that he would give Erin whatever she needed, whenever she needed it. He'd help her battle her demons any way he could.

God help them both if his own demons came out to play.

CHAPTER FIVE

Erin lit a match and let it fall to the ground, crushing it with the toe of her boot. The bells attached to her shoelaces jingled, mingling with the passing traffic. She was late for the squad meeting. Risky, yeah. Derek hadn't been playing around yesterday when he'd threatened to kick them to the curb if they didn't fly straight. Not to mention, the reason for her hesitation to go inside was so *stupid*, she wanted to give herself a dead arm, if such a thing were possible.

Her hair. She'd dyed it back to blond this morning, having sneaked out of Connor's apartment early to make a drugstore run. Gone were the hot-pink tresses that had acted as a warning to all who approached her that they weren't in for a normal conversation. She'd stared at herself for too long in the mirror, torn between hating how normal she looked now and wondering if wearing her natural color for the first time in ages would *force* her into normalcy.

Nothing could. She knew that. Maybe that was the real issue. This job, this new hair color, it signaled a step away from how she'd been living her life since age sixteen, when she'd finally taken off on her own. Leaving the past behind in a dancing whirlwind of flames. It had followed her, that whirlwind, heaving its smoky breath down her neck, watching and waiting for her to falter. Waiting for its chance to devour her. She wasn't scared of the flames, only the too-familiar face that stood behind them.

Now that this job had given her a function, now that she'd caved and gotten a more professional look, her barriers were gone. Her excuses. She couldn't say *fuck the man* anymore and leave them eating her dust. She'd signed on for this squad because the face behind the whirlwind was closing in. Her twenty-fifth birthday had finally come to pass and she had something it wanted. Money. Money she had never asked for and didn't know what to do with. An unexpected blessing, but an even bigger curse. Her plan had been to hunker down and prepare for the storm, but now that she was here, it felt permanent. Like a cellblock or her bedroom. She'd traded one prison for another. Even more confusing, she knew that once she got inside and saw Connor it would be okay.

She lit another match and tossed it toward the gutter. A mixture of gutter water and God-only-knew-what put it out with a sizzle. Connor. Had she conjured him out of some secret place in her mind? It wouldn't be the first time she'd done something like that, but it would be the first time it felt so *good*. On the way out of his apartment this morning, she'd stopped to watch him sleeping on the couch. His big body hung partly over the side, one hand resting on the floor, far too large for the piece of furniture he'd slept on. For her. So she could have a bed near a window. Accepting favors from others sat squarely at the top of her no-no list. Being beholden to anyone made her nervous.

She didn't feel that way with Connor. It only made her want to reciprocate. Do something to help him, make him happy, too. Yet she had no way of doing that.

He likely thought she'd been abused. She had. But not in

the way he might imagine. When she'd tried to explain her fear of being touched to the prison shrink, he'd kept digging, kept pushing for the *real* reason. It hadn't been enough for him that, to her, touch came before being restrained. There hadn't been many instances in her childhood, maybe *none*, where touch had led to anything else. Hugs, pats on the back, encouragement. No. Touch had been a means of putting her somewhere. Keeping her there. Locking her in her bedroom so adults could argue in peace, dragging her into the closet, cuffing her and shoving her into the back of a parked car.

Then came the closeness. Air compressing in on her, like thousands of sticky hands. Cutting off her oxygen, bathing her skin in clammy sweat. Before she'd learned how to get free, the space confining her had become a representation of touch. It closed in on her and held her still, made her scared to move, paralyzed her. Her first time in prison had been torture. The guards, the other inmates, had learned her weakness early and exploited it. Touching, pulling, pinching.

Erin gasped when the lit match she held in her hand burned her fingers. It jolted her into action. No more stalling. No more thinking about the past. She wouldn't explore this odd assurance that once she laid eyes on Connor, the emotional teeter-totter tilting inside her would stabilize. For now, she would go with it. And make sure she always had a path leading out.

She breezed into the closed-down community center with a loose-hipped gait, a small smile playing around her mouth at the sound of her boots' bells tinkling. They couldn't silence her completely.

This morning, she'd woken up with a text message from Derek on her phone explaining that there had been a last-minute change of plans as to where they would be meeting. Yeah, sure. Like that guy didn't have everything planned down to the tiniest detail. This recently abandoned building would be where they would meet from now on, and it suited her down to the ground. The fewer cops she had to deal with, the better. But when she heard voices coming from the basement, she stopped cold.

God, her Achilles' heel hadn't been tested this frequently in a good, long while. They had to meet in a goddamn *basement*? Erin took a deep breath and eased down the stairs. As long as she kept the staircase to her back, she could get through twenty minutes. If it got to be too much, she would make an excuse to leave.

And if they refused, she'd simply burn the place to the ground.

Although the thought of Connor being trapped in a burning building made her sick. She wouldn't let herself acknowledge the pull of knowing he stood just beyond the door. What was it about this guy that fought off the noise, the flames? She shouldn't be craving his presence so soon.

Erin pushed open the door. Derek broke off in midsentence and everyone turned to look at her. Her eyes unerringly sought Connor where he stood in the back of the room...prying plywood off a window? Sera stood a few feet behind him with a sympathetic hand outstretched, as if she could heal him with her Virgin Mother vibes. *My job.*

Connor held a metal crowbar, but it dropped to his side when he saw her, his gaze running over her as if checking for anything wrong. But she could only stare at the foot-wide space he'd opened up. A window. Obviously the building was on a slope, because through the wood he'd managed to pry free, she could see an empty parking lot, and an avenue lying just beyond. Her body could fit through it easily...from where she stood, there were approximately forty-eight steps between her and freedom. Breath filled her lungs. Had he done this for her

Connor buried the crowbar into the final plank of wood and ripped it off the window. Then he tossed both of them to the ground with a clatter. "Where were you?"

She didn't flinch under his barked question. "I had a hair appointment. You like?"

He gave a sharp shake of his head and threw himself down into a metal folding chair. Bowen gave a slow whistle from across the room as Sera returned to him and sat down. "When a woman asks you that question, the answer is always yes, man."

Erin couldn't take her eyes off Connor. Deep grooves stood out between his eyes; sweat beaded his forehead even though the basement was decidedly cool. He'd been...worried about her? And he'd used the time to make the space bearable for her. Why? Why would he do that for her? She didn't know, but it made her feel wonderful. Like she belonged. Like someone had listened to what came out of her mouth and remembered it.

She searched around the room for the closest available chair and found it beside Austin. Challenging anyone to comment with a dark, sweeping look, she grabbed the chair and dragged it over to Connor, the rusted metal scraping a loud protest the entire way.

Connor watched her through narrowed eyes as she approached, obviously still angry with her for showing up half an hour late, or possibly for sneaking out of his apartment that morning without a word. It didn't matter. She shoved the chair up beside his, close as it would go, and parked her ass right beside him. And just because it felt right, she buried her face in his shoulder.

"Thanks for the window."

...nd his molars together against the adrenaline
...ugh his nervous system. Had it really only been
...he'd worried about his demons coming out to
...Here he was, less than twelve hours later and he felt dizzy
with the need to expend energy. And not in a healthy way. This
wasn't good.

When Erin hadn't walked in at ten o'clock for the meeting,
his skull had started to buzz. It had been bad enough waking up
this morning to realize she'd sneaked right past him, bad enough
that she hadn't answered the other apartment door when he
knocked. She'd confessed to him last night that someone
wanted to "trap" her, and the possibility of that happening on
his watch had conjured up a feeling he knew too well. Helpless
anger. Impotent rage.

If something happened to her...if somebody touched her...

No amount of breathing exercises or happy place
visualization had been able to ease the buildup of rampant
anxiety. He recognized this part of himself. Thought he'd had a
handle on the hereditary violence that had whirred inside him
since adolescence. But he hadn't anticipated Erin blowing in and
rearranging everything. If this didn't send a loud and clear signal
to his brain to stay away from her, nothing would. He required
order or the careful layers he'd pasted together over his damaged
insides would strip away, little by little, and reveal what was
hidden beneath. Too bad she was chaos personified. Disorder on
two albeit sexy legs. She'd rip those layers off so fast, he'd get
whiplash.

Two other times in his life, he'd felt responsible for another
person. One was his mother. She'd been through enough in fifty-
five years and deserved to finally start over. Find some peace.
That peace is why he continually sold his soul. First to the navy,
then to his power-hungry cousin. Now, to the Chicago police.

Anything to make up for what she'd been through at the hands of his father. Anything to atone for the fact that he'd been too small, too weak as a child to help her. To save her.

The second person he'd felt responsible for had been his one-way ticket out of the SEALs. Coming to Chicago was supposed to mean a clean slate, leaving that shit in the past. He could sense impending disaster ahead when it came to the girl beside him. She was a wild card. An unknown variable. He couldn't control her. Couldn't keep her in one place without worrying if she'd vanish. Fuck, he couldn't even *touch* her.

As Derek started talking at the front of the room, Erin smashed her nose against the side of his neck, breathed deeply, and sighed. He tried to ignore her when she pulled back to look at him, but the lure of her gaze was too strong to resist. Christ, she was even more compelling up close. She smelled like hair dye and matches, not exactly the most intoxicating of scents, and yet he couldn't get it into his lungs quickly enough. A deep satisfaction rolled through him when he saw that the bags under her eyes were gone. She'd slept well in his sheets. Her hair spread out on his pillow. Unbelievable. The storm inside him had ceased with her near. It never happened this quickly, usually taking hours to subside.

"What?" he asked, needing a distraction from the kick of lust the image of her sliding around in his sheets had conjured.

"I drank all your orange juice this morning."

"I noticed."

She propped her chin on his shoulder. "Can you get the kind without pulp next time?"

How could he concentrate when their mouths were so close together? "Are you planning on making a habit out of drinking my orange juice?"

A beat passed. "If you stop buying it, I'll know you don't

want me over anymore."

"I'll buy the damn juice."

God, her smile. "I was going to come over anyway."

Derek cleared his throat, drawing both of their attention. "I don't repeat myself, so I'd suggest paying attention. Especially you, Connor. I can't be here twenty-four-seven and it'll be everyone's ass if you don't know what's going on."

Erin bristled. "I drank his juice."

"Are you sure it wasn't Kool-Aid?" Austin drawled from his lean against the wall. "We're all expected to drink that, apparently."

Polly snorted and went back to inspecting her nails.

"Continue," Connor bit out. Not even his time in the navy had made him comfortable with authority. "You were giving us a profile of Maxwell Stark, but hadn't gotten to why."

"That's right. Stark." Derek crossed his arms over his chest. "City treasurer for Chicago. He came up through the ranks quickly and we have a good idea why. He's running for mayor at the end of his term as treasurer. We believe he used city pension funds to finance a private project in exchange for campaign donations."

"A crooked politician," Bowen said from his usual place behind Sera, who was busy taking notes on a legal pad. "The shock might kill me."

"You said he moved up through the ranks quickly," Sera commented. "This must not be the first time he has misused funds."

Derek nodded. "Stark has done it once before. Once that we can *prove*, anyway." He made eye contact with each of them. "Last year, his assistant Tucker May took the fall for him in a similar situation. Stark had accepted a bribe from AllStock Warehouse to support their proposal to open a store in Chicago. They had met a lot of resistance from local small business owners and council members, but they were ultimately approved. There was an internal investigation, and a sizable amount of money exchanged hands before they broke ground."

Polly looked bored. "Doesn't everyone just shop online now?"

"We kept an eye on Tucker May while he served time downstate," Derek continued. "His cell mate turned informant in exchange for a reduced sentence—"

"Snitches get stiches," Erin sang.

Derek hung his head a moment. "What do you think *you* are, O'Dea?"

"Oh yeah." She waved him on. "Keep going."

"Thank you. May confided in his cell mate that Stark knew about the AllStock Warehouse bribe money. Stark orchestrated the whole thing and pinned it on him with a second set of books, claiming he'd never been the wiser."

Austin dropped into a chair beside Polly and winked at her. "Stark sounds like a real peach."

"His father is a career politician at the state capital, so he's been bred for this sort of thing," Derek said. "And he's smart about it."

Sera shook her head. "What good does May's cellblock confession do? He's already been convicted. It's his word against Stark's." Bowen laid a hand on her shoulder and she reached up to cover it. "It's not unusual for a prisoner to proclaim his innocence. They all do."

"That's where it gets interesting." Derek walked to the whiteboard and uncapped a blue marker. "May took the fall *willingly*. Stark promised to oversee his investments while he served his time, in addition to a bag of cash when he came home. But those investments failed under Stark's watch. May wasn't quite so ready to play ball anymore."

"Wasn't?" Bowen shifted on his feet. "Something happen to him?"

Derek nodded once. "May disappeared."

"From prison?"

Erin shrugged. "It's not as hard as it sounds."

"May was cooperating with us." Derek paused to let that sink in. "He had the proof we needed that Stark took the bribe. He's also in possession of evidence that Stark approved a private development in exchange for campaign funds."

"Stark got to him," Connor said, his voice sounding rusty. "Found out he was going to talk."

"That's the assumption," Derek confirmed. "We need to find him."

"What if May is dead?" Erin wanted to know.

"Yeah," Austin chimed in. "Stark doesn't sound like the type to leave that kind of liability hanging around."

Derek tapped the blue marker against his palm. "Each of you will be working a different angle. If we can't find May, we trap Stark a different way."

Erin flinched against him at the word "trap" and Connor quashed the urge to drag her onto his lap. Not for the first time, he wondered if she could handle what came their way. She might present a cavalier attitude to everyone else, but he'd seen what lay just beneath last night.

"This is where you six come in." Derek uncapped the marker with his teeth and made a circle on the whiteboard, writing "Stark Campaign Headquarters" through the middle. "Sera, this is where I want you. Finding out everything you can. Listening, asking the right questions. We've built you a solid résumé and alternate identity that gets you in as a campaign staffer. Working close—"

"Nope." Bowen started shaking his head. "No fucking way."

"—but not *too* close with Stark. The mayoral election isn't for a few months and he's only there a few times a week." Derek gave Bowen a challenging look. "Are you saying she's not capable of handling it?"

Feeling an unwanted spark of sympathy for Bowen—he knew from experience that the guy *lived* for his girlfriend—Connor spoke up. "I think he's saying *he's* not capable of handling it."

"Not my problem," Derek returned.

"Can you get me in there as a"—Bowen snapped his fingers—"whatsitcalled, too?"

"A campaign staffer. And no. Best I can do is put you on surveillance outside headquarters."

Sera murmured something to Bowen and he fell into the chair beside her, looking numbed out. Derek sighed and moved on. "Polly, I need you to set Sera up with a mic that feeds out directly to me...and Bowen. If you can get your hands on Stark's financial records—"

"Cake."

"—then try to track down any and all suspicious activity."

Polly scrolled through her phone. "This barely passes as a challenge."

Derek ignored her. "Erin, getting in and out of prison is your specialty. Find out how May did it. Or Stark did it for him, as the case may be."

Erin shot forward in her seat. "Dude, I thought the point of this little dream team was to keep me *out* of prison."

"This time, you'll be there as a visitor," Derek said drily. "Connor, go with her. Tomorrow morning, I have you scheduled for a visit with May's cell mate. See if you can get anything else useful out of him. Suspicious behavior before May went missing, anything that could point us in the right direction."

"On it."

"What about me?" Austin made a sweeping gesture over his body. "You're going to sideline your most valuable player?"

Connor decided he didn't like Austin. Especially when Erin chuckled under her breath at his mock outrage.

"You'll be utilized when the time comes."

"Is this meeting over?" Bowen asked.

"Yes, but keep your phones on in case I need to be in touch." Derek capped the pen and shoved it into his back pocket. "Let the games begin."

CHAPTER SIX

When Connor walked into his apartment, Erin gave him her best smile. She'd used this particular smile only one other time in her life, and it had ended in her first successful bank robbery, so she felt good about her chances of Connor complying with her request. At nineteen, she'd gotten tired of living in the back of her car and reasoned the bank wasn't really *using* that money. Not actively. She'd used this exact smile to gain entry to the bank after hours, tempted the armed guard into the vault with the promise of a quickie, and subdued him with his own nightstick.

"Hey, roomie," she said from her perch on the windowsill.

Connor stared at her long and hard before striding into the kitchen. She saw what he was holding, though. A plastic bag of groceries, including a gallon jug of orange juice. Her smile widened, which only put a meaner scowl on his chiseled face. "Where did you go after the meeting? I turned around and you were gone. You have to stop *doing* that."

"Getting gone is kind of my thing." She hopped off the sill. "Besides, I had to test the escape route you so thoughtfully made me. My estimation was off by two whole steps in my favor. Good work, baby."

Connor looked up at the ceiling as if he were praying for patience to drop out of the heavens. It gave Erin a chance to look him over. God, he looked good when he was angry. His wide chest seemed even broader, muscles more pronounced beneath his gray T-shirt. Like she could climb his body and he wouldn't even notice. His jaw was rigid with tension. Ticking, ticking like a bomb ready to go off. A bomb that would start a glorious five-alarm fire. The image made her shiver. Again, she marveled over the fact that nothing about him made her nervous. She recalled the fear that had careered through her bloodstream yesterday when he grabbed her wrist. Some nerves couldn't be remedied, but even being around another person this long was a feat for her. Twenty minutes into most acquaintances, she started to get antsy. Afraid the other person would get too close and start feeling comfortable. Comfortable enough to touch her.

Erin took the orange juice out of Connor's hand and set it on the kitchen counter. "Do you want the good news or the bad news?"

His green eyes went on alert. "Bad news?"

Erin nodded and hopped up on the counter. Something hot and shivery raced over her skin when Connor's gaze dipped between her thighs. She became all too aware of how the black material of her shorts molded to her core. Too aware of what he'd do if he got those shorts off her. *I'd like to be pounding you full of me, Erin. Full.* "Yes, bad news," she forced past suddenly dry lips. "Polly won't switch apartments. She can't. The pigs have already hooked up the high-speed cable and started setting up central command. That's what she's calling it, anyway…"

Connor dragged his attention up her body, making her skin feel hypersensitive. "So what's the good news?"

"I make a pretty decent frittata."

He arched an eyebrow. "You want to live here'

Erin nodded slowly. "It won't be forever, ju
start paying us and I can afford somewhere els
room doesn't have a fire escape, but..." She gave her best smile
another whirl. "We could switch bedrooms."

Connor ran a hand down his face. "Erin, you know I want
to help—"

"I know. You're a loner. So am I." She picked up the jug
of orange juice and picked at the label. "I wouldn't ask if I was
brimming with options."

His laughter was dark. "Being a loner has nothing to do
with it."

She shouldn't ask the question, especially since she already
knew the answer. Too bad playing with fire ran in her veins,
a need so thick and heady she couldn't deny it. Asking was
reckless and inconsiderate and inexcusable of her. What else
was new? "What *does* it have to do with?"

Connor took a step into her personal space. Her breath
caught, but she didn't flinch. Not an easy feat on the receiving
end of such intensity. "Don't ask if you don't want to know."

"Tell me," she whispered.

He sucked his upper lip into his mouth. "I haven't been in
the same room as you, Erin, when my cock wasn't rock hard and
ready to fuck. You know it, too. You know I want to plant it deep
inside you. Watch you shift around trying to get used to being
crammed so motherfucking tight." His pupils were dilated,
chest rising and falling unevenly. *Breathtaking man. Burn for
me.* "I'm hard right now just thinking about what you're hiding
under those shorts. I want to lick all of it. I want to bite and fuck
it. If you think I can survive this way all day, all night, you have
overestimated me."

Erin's mind reeled. With excitement. Apprehension. Most

ɔverwhelmingly, pain that she couldn't give him what he needed. She wanted to be the girl who could. *Desperately*. But she couldn't. She'd experimented with touch before. How much she could take, how much she could give out. *Giving* had never been a problem for her. *That*, she could control. The tricky part was finding someone she could trust not to get lost in the moment and forget the ground rules. In the past, she'd sought partners who liked to take a passive role in bed, reasoning they would be less likely to touch, which proved correct. But *she'd* been unsatisfied. One part of her sang at the thought of being consumed, but it was overshadowed by the part of her that was terrified of it.

The second she'd met Connor, she'd sensed what he had churning inside him. He'd just confirmed her theory with his words. If she were capable of giving herself over to him, of exploring their mutual attraction without reservation, she'd be flat on her back immediately. Pinned. Unable to move. A thought struck her. Was she so drawn to him because he was the perfect mixture of what she needed? A man capable of satisfying her physically, but who had enough self-discipline to stop if things got too overwhelming for her?

It was selfish of her to ask to stay. Usually she wouldn't bat an eyelash at her narcissistic behavior. It suited her not to give a shit how her actions affected others. But Connor inspired something…*give-a-shittish* inside her. In the conference room, he'd stopped touching her immediately when she asked. Last night, he'd let her take from him what she needed. This morning, he'd carved out daylight for her in that stifling basement. Much as she hated being in someone's debt, she owed him. She should get her suitcase and find somewhere else to stay. Put them both out of their misery and only deal with this startling gravitational pull at work.

"Say something," he demanded.

"I'll go."

His brows drew together. "Are you testing me?"

Erin hopped off the counter, feeling a kick in her chest when he automatically stepped back to give her space. So they wouldn't touch. Yeah, this was the right thing to do. "No, I'm not testing you. This time. But I wouldn't get used to such generosity."

He paced the kitchen, but came to a halt when she started lacing up her sneakers. "What — you're leaving *now*?"

"Uh, yeah. I only have a few hours before it gets dark. Doesn't give me much time."

"No." Connor gripped the kitchen counter and leaned over it. "No. Just no."

What was wrong with him? He told her he couldn't handle her living in the same apartment, now she was doing the right thing and he looked like she'd informed him a flaming meteor was headed toward Earth. She walked toward her suitcase where she'd left it propped near the window and looped her fingers around the handle. That simple act of finality pierced her armor and she suddenly hated herself for being such a goddamn mess. "Look, I'll meet you at the prison tomor — "

"Put down the suitcase."

Erin spun around with a gasp to find Connor standing two feet away. "Jesus H. Christ. *Warn* a sister."

His gaze was concentrated on her hand. "Why haven't you put down the suitcase?"

"Do you suffer from short-term memory loss? I'm out, baby. Hitting the bricks."

Slowly, his hands came up, palms out. Surrender. He closed the distance between them. One step, two. What the hell was he doing? The concentration etched into his handsome face started a hot burn deep in the pit of her stomach.

She wanted to run.

She couldn't move.

"We kissed last night." His attention focused in on her mouth. "Can we do it again now?"

"I don't know." Her lips burned at the thought of it. Last night, she'd been in the moment, so consumed by her climax, she couldn't remember if it had hurt. She wanted desperately to find out. If for no other reason than to give him *something* that he wanted. "Y-yes."

Connor's gaze went smoky as he leaned in and kissed her. There was an initial smarting of her lips, the way skin feels after a slap, but it blurred and dimmed. He started out simply trading breath with her. Or maybe he just wanted to make sure she wouldn't run Flintstones-style out the door. Only their lips were touching, eyes open to take each other's measure.

He sipped at her bottom lip, then the top. His eyelids drooped, then concealed his darkened green eyes completely. Something inside her twisted up tight, holding her off the ground so high she felt weightless. They had kissed last night, but it hadn't felt like this. She'd been out of her head with pleasure. Right now, she was present. Too present.

Connor's breath went shallow along with hers, but his hands remained in the air where she could see them if she needed to. His taste proved too appetizing, the scrape of his beard too delicious. Erin opened her mouth to the kiss, knowing through some divine intuition that he would anticipate it, which he did, masterfully. He slanted his lips over hers, drawing on them with an anguished groan. When their tongues brushed together, she sensed his hands turning to fists but couldn't open her eyes to confirm. His mouth demanded every ounce of her attention, its needing of hers, its perfect shape and texture. The rich scent of pine and shaved wood curled around her, drugging her, finishing off what his mouth started.

With only their mouths touching, she should⸍
so aroused. Liquid lightning flashed inside her, leav⸍
its path. A squeeze between her legs released a shaky whi⸍
She knew she could ask him for anything in that moment and
he'd give it to her. He'd let her work out her need on top of him,
riding his length as she'd done last night. He'd leash his nature
and let her be broken, let her take from him.

Which was precisely why she didn't ask.

Connor broke away, allowing them both to suck in oxygen.
"Stay. I'm sorry. Stay." He bent his knees to bring them eye to
eye. His spoke of torture, but he was trying to hide it. "Look at
me. I can handle this. I want you here. Don't leave."

"I don't know if *I* can handle it," she whispered.

His heavy breaths ceased. "What do you mean?"

She drew out a lighter from her back pocket and ignited the
flame. It cleared her head a little, allowing her to search for the
right words. Words that wouldn't sound crazy. "I like touching
you. It makes me feel really…good. And there isn't a whole lot
that makes me feel good, you know?" Her throat closed up.
"I wish you could touch me, too. I don't think I can stay here
knowing I'm hurting you by making myself feel good…and I
don't think I can *stop* touching you. It feels like a must."

A flare of panic flashed across his face. "I shouldn't have
said what I did earlier. You just caught me off guard." He
massaged his forehead with four fingers. "Did I scare you? Is
that why you're really leaving?"

"No." She shook her head. "No."

"Okay. Jesus. Okay." He was silent a moment, but gears
were turning behind his eyes. "You need to touch me and I need
you to stay. Let's give each other what we need. All right?"

Why was this so damn *confusing*? She'd only met this man

yesterday and they were already tangled up in her web of fucked-up issues. He should want to be clear of her, shouldn't he? No one else had ever bothered with her this long before. "Why? Why do you need me to stay? I—"

"I won't rest," he growled. "I'll think about you somewhere, scared like you were last night, and I'll go fucking crazy."

Her heart lurched, dislodging her pride. "I've been taking care of myself for a long time. If the only reason you want me here is to play nursemaid to the crazy girl, that's not going to work for me."

"You know there's more to it. You *know*." He visibly centered himself with a deep breath, appearing to debate with himself. "I've got my own skeletons, Erin. They don't rattle so much when you're around. Your touching me…it makes me hot. But it soothes elsewhere."

She knew her expression was pathetically hopeful, but couldn't find a single shit to give. "Yeah?"

"Yeah," he repeated. "I'm not going to lie, Erin. Yes, I want to sleep with you like hell. But only if it's healthy. Would you trust me enough to go slow? A little at a time?"

Her pulse hammered out of control. "*You* touching *me*?"

Connor watched her closely. "When you're ready. Not before. *Never* before."

This is where she should climb down the fire escape and vamoose toward the street. A weight pressed down on her rib cage, making it difficult to draw a breath. It felt like the point of no return. But Connor's eyes grounded her.

Safe. He's safe.

"Okay, baby. Slow."

His body drained of tension. "Thank you." He leaned in and brushed their lips together, gently, reverently. "First, we talk."

CHAPTER SEVEN

Yes, because you're such an accomplished talker. *Asshole.*

Didn't matter. He'd talk a blue fucking streak as long as she didn't leave. Back in the kitchen, he hadn't kept himself in check and she'd picked up her suitcase. Actually picked it up. Ready to leave for God knows where all because he'd felt the stupid need to enlighten her on his permanently aroused state. Until that moment, it hadn't fully registered exactly how badly he needed her close. None of it made a bit of sense, either. Not the edginess he felt when she wasn't in his sight line. Not the decision to sacrifice his sanity just to keep her safe. Keeping her with him was all that mattered. *Keep, keep, keep.*

He hadn't planned on asking her to trust him. To allow him to help her overcome her fears, at least where he was concerned. But he'd had to be honest with himself. His appetite wouldn't allow him to remain in purgatory indefinitely, so he'd taken a risky leap. As the words left his mouth, he'd been only remotely aware of what he was doing, but now the dust had settled. He'd formed a relationship with her. One he could very easily fuck up. And it scared the shit out of him.

There wouldn't be any room to remain detached here. He

relied on detachment. It had saved him in the SEALs, not only on missions, but when they'd turned their backs on him and severed all ties. Detachment had gotten him through two years delivering messages of a physical nature while working under his cousin. He should have seen this coming, really. No amount of willpower could make him disengage around Erin. She'd woken up something inside him yesterday. He didn't have a name for it yet, but it needed to be fed. Soothed. Unfortunately, she was the one agitating it at the same time.

Connor almost groaned out loud when Erin set her suitcase back down, awarding him with a glimpse down her shirt. Perky handfuls. He'd fucking known it. Purgatory? Nah, he'd definitely crossed the line into hell.

Don't go there, man. You want to keep her? You want to help? Do it the right way.

She cocked a hip, looking suspicious. "What do you want to talk about?"

He lowered himself onto the couch and nodded toward the other end. "Sit?"

"Hmm." She hopped onto the couch's arm and crossed her legs, making her look like some kind of punk-rock fairy. The view of her thighs did exactly zero to help his situation. "Just know that if this starts to feel like a psychiatrist appointment, I've clocked all the available exits."

"I'll keep it in mind."

She draped herself over the cushions. "Are you going to show me inkblots? Spoiler alert. I see fire. Lots of it."

"Why?"

"It erases things. Both good and bad. It's reliably destructive." She cupped her hands around her mouth. "Like me," she whispered.

He knew her game. Saw right through it. The crazy girl act she

performed to a T. While he knew it wasn't entirely a ga
it was her way of deflecting. Sort of like his savior,
only in a different form. "Erin, this is important so !
answer me seriously." He felt a familiar anger settle in his gut.
"You said someone is trying to trap you. I need to know who it is."

"Why?" She fidgeted with her hair. "I told you not to ask
me about it anymore."

"If I don't know, I can't keep you safe."

"I keep myself safe."

Connor held on to his patience. "Why won't you tell me?"

"Because if I tell you, it makes him *real*," she burst out. "I'm
just dandy pretending he's not."

"*He*." Connor's hands curled into fists. "An ex-boyfriend?"
God help the pitiful fucker.

"I don't do boyfriends."

He ignored the sweeping relief because it was pointless.
The threat still existed, even if it wasn't a man she'd been with
romantically. "Well, you have one now and he wants to protect
you."

Erin tilted her head. "You're my boyfriend?" She straightened. "Can we get matching Segways?"

God, how could she make him want to laugh and shout at
the same time? *Deep breath.* If he wanted her to confide in him,
he might have to give her a reason. *It was nice knowing you,
detachment.* "You have to be near a window, right? You need to
know how fast an escape you can make."

She propped her chin on a bent wrist. "Go on."

"Windows make me nervous. I don't like weak spots. Don't
like people looking in at what's mine." He shifted on the couch.
"If it's too early to call you mine, that can't be helped. It's a
feeling, not a mark on a timeline." Dammit, he couldn't read her
expression. She looked almost puzzled. "I understand why you

need the windows, Erin. But I'm asking for curtains. I need to know someone isn't going to see you through the window and pull you out. Away from me."

"Oh."

Patience. "Just oh?"

She shrugged. "We have conflicting views on windows. Get it? *Views.*"

"*Erin.*"

"Curtains, huh?" Her right foot started to jiggle. "You want to keep me hidden."

"Only until the threat goes away. If you tell me what it is, I can make that happen."

Erin rose and went to go stand by the window. She looked out but didn't appear to be seeing anything on the other side. The unfocused expression he'd seen last night was back, only this time she seemed more thoughtful. "You can't make him go away. I tried. He's inflammable."

Connor frowned. "How do you know that?"

Her gaze cut to his. "I set his house on fire while he was inside it. You still want to be my roommate?"

"Yes." He made sure to say it without hesitation. Should he be hesitating? Probably. She'd just admitted to arson. His only excuse was a bone-deep feeling that she'd had a driving reason. And what kind of a hypocrite would he be for judging her actions? After what he'd done, he didn't have the right to judge anyone. "Who is *he*?"

"My stepfather." She sounded numb. "Is our hour up yet, doc?"

He'd gotten more out of her than expected. He should call it a wrap for now, but he needed to know one more thing. Needed to know what physical and mental scars she was nursing, if he could potentially make it worse. If he did, he'd never forgive himself. "Almost."

She must have sensed the seriousness in his tone because she closed her eyes, pressed her forehead against the window. God, he wanted to drag her away from it. He didn't like her being exposed. He needed to resist that urge at all costs. Windows were a requirement for her.

"Did your stepfather abuse you?"

"Not in the way you're thinking." The way she'd answered so quickly, he knew she'd been expecting the question. "He might be part of the reason I don't like being touched, but it's not because he touched *me*. Does that make you feel *relieved*?"

"'Relieved' isn't the right word. I can't be relieved when you're still hurting."

She hugged her elbows close, but didn't respond. Connor couldn't watch her looking so vulnerable another second. He stood and went to stand by her, instantly feeling soothed having her within reaching distance. What sense did that make when he couldn't even touch her?

"Tell me what's off-limits, Erin." Her gaze lifted to meet his. The combination of heat and apprehension there told him she knew what he was asking. When she wet her lips, he held himself back from licking them more thoroughly for her. "How can I touch you?"

"I don't know. No one has touched me in a long time. Not like you want to," she whispered. "I love kissing you, but I don't know what your mouth will feel like...everywhere. Or what you'll feel like inside me."

They took a simultaneous deep breath. Calmly discussing his going down on her, being joined with her, made him feel anything but calm, but he ordered himself to listen closely as she spoke. "I haven't been touched like that since...before. Even then, it never felt good."

"Before what?"

His question pushed too far. He could see the second she closed him out. "I don't want to talk about this anymore. Not if it's one-sided. Not if I'm the only one revealing weaknesses."

An ache started beneath his collarbone. "There's nothing weak about you." Wondering how much he could reveal without scaring her away, he took a step toward the bathroom, but stopped. "The way you count steps to the street or need the fire. Those are things you can't control, right?" He waited for her nod, praying he wasn't damning himself. "Sometimes, Erin, I get angry. I've hurt people before and been unable to stop." His look was meaningful. "If I found the man who wronged you, I would kill him and like it. And I might not remember most of it afterward. I've learned to control myself, but it's *hard* sometimes. That's my weakness."

She appeared transfixed as she came toward him, reminding him of the way she looked at fire. Tension rolled off him the closer she got, leaving him in a rush when she laid a hand against the side of his face. "Only good men feel the weight of their burdens." She ran her fingers through his hair, making his eyelids droop. "Only good men continue to take on more."

"You're not the burden." His protest was vehement. "How could you be? They leave me when we're close."

Doubt trickled into her expression. "But I can only let you get so close."

Her scent and soft voice were fogging his senses, common sense ordering him to take a step back while they'd made some progress. "I'm going to take a shower. Tell me you'll be here when I come out."

"I'll be here."

Connor walked out of the bathroom ten min
immediately searching the apartment for Erin.
her standing at the kitchen counter cutting up the pep.
he'd brought home. In her combat boots, mussed hair, and
leather bustier, she looked vastly out of place performing
such a mundane task. Looked better suited to holding up a
convenience store or stage diving at a rock concert. She flicked
her hair back over her shoulder, then bent at the waist to
retrieve a colander from under the sink. The move showed off
her incredible ass, the taut muscles of her thighs, the sexy line
of her back. A vision of his hands pressing that back down into
the mattress while commanding she keep her bottom as high up
in the air as possible made his cock stiffen.

"Christ," he muttered under his breath, adjusting himself
beneath the towel he'd wrapped around his waist. They'd been
officially living together less than an hour and his body was
already rebelling against his resolution to go slow. Hoping he
could make it to the bedroom unnoticed, Connor turned into
the short hallway leading to their bedrooms. At the entrance
to his bedroom, he paused. They'd planned on switching, but
his things were still in there. It occurred to him that at that
moment, they were sharing a bedroom, and he swelled even
larger beneath the towel.

"Connor?"

He froze with his hand on the doorknob. "Yeah."

"Dinner in twenty minutes." Her voice sounded throaty.
Uneven. "If you're hungry."

Dammit, why hadn't he tugged one out in the shower? He
knew why. He'd rushed, worried the entire time that she'd slip
out a window and show up again when she felt like it. "Okay.
I'll be out soon."

"Did you mean what you said…about going slow?"

Jesus. "Hell yes, I meant it. I don't say things I don't mean."

A beat passed. "Can we go slow right now?"

Did he have enough willpower in place at the moment? No. Then again, he never did when it came to her. So what difference did it make? All hope of resistance flew out of his head when he felt her breath at the center of his bare back. It reminded him of their height difference. Made him picture how they'd look in bed, her petite body aligned with his bulk. Taking each thrust of his cock with a pleased cry. The kind of cry a woman gave when a man conquered her and she realized she loved it. Erin's cry would drown out all of them. Someday. Not now. He braced his hands on the door and tried to remain still, swallowing a groan when fingers traced up his left side.

"You smell so good." She laid a wet kiss on his back. "Your skin is so hot. I want to rub myself all over you. Can I do that?"

His head dropped forward with a moan. "That's not slow, sweetheart. That's fucking fast."

Her hand slowed, started to pull away. Connor spun around to stop her. Any headway, he would take it. No matter what it cost him. His instinct was to grab her hand and place it back on his body, but she wouldn't like having her wrist manacled. He found her staring at his chest, face flushed, lips rosy and parted. His arousal surged painfully. Nothing. She hid nothing when it came to her physical needs, and her honesty tore at his layers.

"You were wounded?" Her gaze was on his right pectoral, running over the puckered flesh where he'd been shot in Brooklyn, taking a bullet meant for his cousin. "It happened when you were with the SEALs?"

Not wanting to lie to her, but reluctant to talk about the past he desperately wanted to forget, he made a gruff sound and focused on her. "Do you want me to touch you?"

She made a small sound. "Not yet. I'm not ready."

"Okay." He hated the sudden uncertainty creeping into her expression. Wanted to annihilate it. "Look what you do to my body, Erin. It only wants to please yours. Tell me how I can do that. Tell me how to make you better, because I'm just as lost as you."

Her eyes cleared, heating once more. "You're a man who likes to restrain women. Tie them down and mix pleasure with pain. Aren't you, Connor?"

Just the words leaving her mouth sent lust raging to the surface. The way she spoke was almost hypnotic, captivating all five of his senses. Owning them. "Yes. I won't ever lie to you." He swallowed hard. "When I think of being inside you, I'm on top. I'm in charge. I'm so fucking *deep* I can't breathe."

Erin looked down at her right hand, looking surprised to find it holding a bottle of olive oil. He hadn't noticed it either. She must have been using it to cook dinner. "Would you let me restrain *you*?" She uncapped the bottle and drizzled a small amount of the golden liquid into her palm. His breathing grew unsteady as she rubbed it over his abs, then up and across his chest. Her palm coasted over his nipples, leaving them glistening with oil. "I'll make it worth your while."

"How?" he rasped. Could he give up control completely? He'd never handed over the power to another person. There had always been too many outside sources in his life he couldn't organize, manage, but it always stopped in bed. He was used to ruling there.

"You'll have to trust me."

No. He didn't like the idea of having his hands restrained when she could vanish so easily. Or she could panic like last night and need him. The thought of not being able to go to her, comfort her, infused him with anxiety. "The trust goes both ways, Erin. I'm telling you I won't put my hands on you. You'll have to trust me on that." He took a deep breath and let the towel drop. "Do your worst."

Jesus Christ. The hunger in her expression. It almost knocked him back against the door. Right before his eyes, her breasts swelled over the top of her bustier as her mouth fell open to suck in a raspy breath. She rubbed her thighs together in a way that told him she was growing wet just by looking at him. How the fuck could he survive this? Without any restrictions, she would have already been divested of her ass-hugging shorts and he would be banging her where she stood. Plain and simple, having her stare at his cock like it was a meal while being unable to do anything about it could very well land him in an asylum.

"Tell me you'll spread your legs for it someday, Erin. Give me that." He fisted his cock and pumped twice. "I can only fantasize about coming in your pussy so many times before I need the real thing. I bet you're fuck-tight, aren't you? Like a closed fist."

She poured more oil into her hands and rubbed them together. "Yes, I want very much to spread my legs for it someday." Her voice was throaty, sexual. "And yes, baby, I'm nice and tight."

He almost came. His erection throbbed in his hand, desperate and achy. "Fuck, sweetheart. I'm dying here."

Her slick palms dragged up his thighs, leaving slippery oil in their wake. "No, you're not dying yet. But you will be."

She reached behind him and pushed open the bedroom door, gently nudging him backward with a single finger pressed to his chest. The backs of his knees hit the bed a moment later and he sat, mesmerized by the starvation in her eyes. He might be in excruciating physical pain, but it would take a cavalry of armed men to prevent him from seeing what she'd do next. His question was answered when she dropped her shorts, leaving her clad only in a black thong with the words "You Wish" written across the front. Goddamn right, he wished. Wished he was fucking buried in her, pounding, teeth buried in her shoulder. "Take off your top for me. Let me see those sweet little nipples so I can imagine my mouth shining them up."

She ran her hands up her thighs, across her belly, making them glisten. "Would you be happy only imagining it? I'm not so sure, so I think I'll keep them covered." With that same single finger, she urged him onto his back, showing no reaction to his miserable growl. "I'll make it up to you, though. You see, I might have a problem being touched, but not touching. Rubbing. Or *sucking.*" She dragged her teeth over her lower lip and Connor's head spun. "Hands over your head."

He complied, anticipation tearing through his veins. She climbed on top of him, looking like a wicked fantasy, only no one could possibly dream her up. "*God*, I would punish that dick-tease of a body."

"How?" She came down toward him, fusing their bodies together and sliding up. Connor bit his lip to keep from shouting at the sensation of her curves slipping over him. "Would you punish me with your hands?"

"I leave bruises, but not with my fists. Never, Erin." He spoke through gritted teeth as she writhed on top of him, straddling him and running her thighs up the sides of his body. "But when I got hard, I'd be fucking you against the first available surface and your ass would bear the impact. That's where you'd bruise. And looking at what I'd done would only make me hard again."

Finally, her silk-covered pussy settled over his cock and she gave a quick buck of her hips, bringing his back off the bed with a groan. "You're a very naughty boy, Connor. I don't know if you deserve my mouth on you. Convince me."

Fuuuck. He could do it so easily with the use of his hands.

His mouth. Just spread her thighs open and lick her clit until she was begging to return the favor. Instinctually he knew that would be her way. A woman who didn't like to think she owed a man anything. *I'll make it worth your while.* As soon as they cleared a few hurdles, and he had to keep faith that they *would*, he'd cleanse her of the misconception that she was obligated to reciprocate every time he made her come. She'd never get off her knees if that were the case. They would make some headway and then he'd show her, precisely and often.

Right now, though, he'd been reduced to words, unable to communicate through the use of touch. He sensed this was important to her, showing she could give him pleasure to replace the pain of *not* touching her. To show she had something to give, not realizing he'd seen that the moment they met. But God, at the very suggestion of her pouty lips working his cock, his erection had strained hot and needy against his stomach. Dying for her to follow through. No way to be rational now.

"Come on, sweetheart. Wrap your lips around it. Give me what I need so badly." He lifted his hips to rub his erection against her core. She gasped and fell forward, catching herself by planting her palms on his chest. Her nails dug into his pecs and he gave a satisfied curse. "Put your sweet ass up in the air while you mouth-fuck me, too. Let me imagine I'm getting that next. Let me imagine I'm about to flip you around, shove your thong out of my goddamn way and fill up that tight pussy."

Erin's breath had grown labored, but she continued to undulate on top of him, running shaky hands over his chest and abs, sliding through the oil with her belly and thighs. "That's pretty damn convincing, baby."

"Need more?"

"No," she breathed. "Any more and I might let you try. It's too s—"

"Shhh." He levered himself up to capture her mouth, taking it in a slick, suggestive kiss. His tongue mimicked the act he'd just described to her, sinking in and out, pushing a little deeper each time. They moaned into each other's mouths and Erin started circling her hips on his lap like a sexy little machine, making him so hard, he questioned if he could survive it. When he released her mouth so she could breathe, her eyes were unclear, but there was a quality of desperation in them.

"I like the way you talk to me." She slid down his torso and knelt between his thighs. "Keep doing it. Don't stop." The vision of her almost sent him past the breaking point. Thighs covered in oil, lips plumped from their kiss, hair tangled around her face, she was a fucking goddess. Her gaze was riveted between his thighs, almost reverently. Her hands climbed up his legs, higher and higher until she wrapped one hand around his cock.

Connor's fingers curled into the mattress, a growl bursting free of his mouth. After that, he held his breath, waiting, begging for her to take him past her lips. "Please."

"Don't say please. You're the kind of man who demands." She pumped him twice within her fist, eyes widening with excitement when he groaned. "Demand, Connor."

Power sizzled through his body, revitalizing him, strengthening him. "Why isn't your ass in the fucking air? Don't make me tell you again."

Erin's responding whimper cleared the last vestige of doubt that this was the right thing for her. That he wasn't hurting her or setting them back by being himself. Commanding her as he craved. He watched through heavy-lidded eyes as she leaned down and put herself mouth-level with his cock, arching her back and pushing her bottom up at the same time. The little black strip of material separated two perfect ass cheeks. Ripe and taut. Flesh that would give a little shake when he slapped it.

"Good." His hips jerked when she licked up the side of his girth. "No games this first time. You're going to suck it like you can't get enough."

She gripped his base tight and let her lips hover just above his crown. "Yes, Connor."

"Show me that eager girl who rode me hard last night and came in her panties. Show me what she can do with her pretty mouth."

He fell back onto the mattress with a shouted curse as she lowered her mouth halfway down and dragged her teeth lightly over his hypersensitive flesh on the way back up. There was a wicked glint in her eye that told him she was reveling in his reaction. She knew she was slaying him, and Jesus, he didn't give a shit. She repeated the action five more times. By the time she finished, he was clutching at the bedspread and chanting her name. Her hand started to work him in time with her mouth, purring sounds in the back of her throat heightening the incredible sensation. In the distance, he could hear himself begging her to go faster, but she slowed down instead, bringing him back to the present.

"Take me to the back of your throat. Keep your eyes on mine while you do it." Again, her blue eyes flashed wide with eagerness. She might not want his touch, but she sure as hell wanted his instructions. Had even been goading him into issuing them. He watched with mounting lust as her fingers skated down her belly and dipped beneath the material of her panties. She moaned around his cock as her fingers danced behind the material.

He started to protest. No. *No.* Her orgasms belonged to him. No matter that he had limited means with which to give them to her, he would find a damn way. "Erin, don't you—"

She took him deep, deeper...all the way, his inches disappearing one by one past her lips. "Oh, God. Oh, fuck yes. Give me that hot little mouth." His body moved on autopilot, drawn to the insane pleasure she was providing like a dose of potent drugs. He dug his heels into the mattress, drew out of her mouth a bit and slowly ground himself back up into her sweet warmth. The hand that wasn't working furiously inside her panties dug into his thigh and she moaned. Loving it? Christ, he'd thought this girl was incredible, but he'd had no idea. Just as he'd told her, she kept those beautiful eyes trained on him, sending him sprinting toward his release.

"*Fuck*, I'm going to come so hard. *Erin.*"

His words seemed to ignite something inside her. She wrapped her hand around him tight and jerked him fast while her mouth continued to take deep pulls. All the while, she made these sexy whimpering noises that echoed in his head, battered his skull. His focus became her fingers, circling as she drove herself to orgasm. Something sharp impaled his chest…a need to be the one who wrung the climax out of her…unbelievable frustration that he *couldn't*. On top of it all, a rushing of pure, mind-bending pleasure blurred everything. Weak. Strong. In that moment, he felt both emotions as control wavered from his focus. In a blinding rush, it was all swept away, his world fracturing into a thousand tiny pieces. He heard himself shouting, but couldn't make himself stop. It was too fucking amazing…her mouth wouldn't stop.

"Take it, take it, *take it*. Greedy girl. *My* fucking girl."

For a brief, blinding moment, he lost track of everything. His body felt depleted and whole at the same time. He'd just begun to marvel over the singular feeling when Erin let out a cry and fell forward onto his chest, body shuddering as she came. His mind screamed in denial, hands fisting on the bedspread. *No. I'm supposed to give her pleasure. Supposed to control when and how.* Gone was the euphoria of a moment ago, replaced by shame so thick he could choke on it. Being passive was killing him. How long could he withstand this?

Erin's head came up. "What's wrong?" She scrambled back onto her heels and he bit back the need to grab for her. "Did I…did you not like it?"

He jackknifed into a sitting position, bringing their faces a breath apart. "I loved it. You were so damn perfect, sweetheart. I've never had it that good. *Never.*"

Some of her worry disappeared, but not all. "But?"

Connor turned and threw his legs over the side of the bed, scrubbing his face with his hands. "I'm not a passive man, Erin. I'm not built to watch my girl get herself off. I see to your pleasure. I *need* to." His breath came out in a rush. "I just need a minute and I'll be fine."

For a while, there was no sound in the room save their slowing breaths. When Erin's arms wrapped around the breadth of his back from behind, his head fell forward. Her body settled against his back, head tucking into the space between his shoulder and neck. "Don't give up on me already," she whispered.

His heart plummeted. Is that what she'd thought? If so, she had a lot to learn about him. "It's going to take more than damaged pride to keep me away from you." This is where he turned around and took her in his arms, reassured her the only way knew how. But that wasn't an option. Erin seemed to sense his inner turmoil, because she tightened her hold on him and tried to scoot them both back on the bed. After a few seconds of her struggling to move him, Connor went. He lay facing away from her, the exact opposite of what he wanted, while she held him from behind, face buried in his back.

It took him a long time to fall asleep, but when he did, he fell deep.

CHAPTER EIGHT

rapped. Trapped. Trapped.

Erin's body felt feverish and whip-tight. Oxygen felt like it was being sucked in through a straw to her aching lungs. Was that wheezing coming from *her*? A dense band of steel lay across her chest, her legs, making it even harder to breath. Heavy. So heavy. She couldn't *move*. Couldn't form a rational thought. One that would get her shifting, trying to get free. Useless. It would be useless anyway. Once she allowed the trap, it ruled her. How had she gotten here? Allowed this?

You let your guard down and now you'll pay. Next comes the dark box. Just like the closet. They'll throw you in, laughing while you plead. Oh God, please don't let them forget to take the handcuffs off again. Please. Tears blurred her vision before coating her temples, burning the corners of her eyes, wetting her hair. She couldn't move her hands or turn her head to get rid of them. Locust wings started to flap. Louder. Louder. A scream rose in her throat but it wouldn't release. No one would hear her anyway. The face in the whirlwind fed off her screams. They gave him more reasons to trap her. Call her crazy.

The smell of sanded wood and pine needles infiltrated

her frenetic thoughts. Tears continued to flow, breathing was still painfully difficult, but a tiny bubble of comfort found its way home through the terrible noise. Still trapped. Trapped by Connor? No, that couldn't be right. He wouldn't, would he? Had he been a trap, disguised as a magnificent mirage?

"*No*," she keened into the dim room. "Not him."

The steel bands across her chest and legs twitched. Miraculously, they yanked away and she could inhale. She couldn't move yet, but dragging in the sweet air was enough. Enough for now. She managed to turn her head and focus on the window across the room, but it was blocked by a large object. Connor. It was Connor and he was shouting at her.

"*Erin*. Ah fuck, sweetheart. *No*." He gripped the headboard in his right hand and she heard the wood creak. "I'm so sorry. *Dammit*."

"Window," she croaked. Understanding dawned in Connor's eyes and he reached for her, obviously intending to scoop her up and carry her over. He jerked his hands back at the last second and cursed, low and vilely. As she watched from the pillow, he started pacing the room like a caged lion. Terrifying and awe-inspiring at the same time. She wanted to say something, do something to comfort him, but she couldn't think past getting to the window, regaining her equilibrium. Testing her legs and arms, she was surprised to find they moved, accommodating her need to crawl across the bed and dismount on the window side. Odd, it usually took her much longer to gather the strength. The courage.

Connor met her at the glass. "You're not going out there. Don't you dare leave me here remembering how you looked—" He raked a hand through his hair. "Tell me how to make it better."

"Just stand there." She reached over and laid a hand on his

heaving chest. "Right there. You needed a minute last night and I need one now. Okay?"

After a beat, he nodded. "I fell asleep." His voice sounded far away. Hazy. "I must have…there was a minute before I woke up where I felt so relaxed. Calm. It's been a long time since I felt like that. And the whole time, you were suffering. Jesus, I hate myself for that."

A dark shadow obscured her view of the street, draping over her and folding inside her chest. His words bounced around her consciousness, damaging her wherever they struck. *I hate myself.* If this morning had proved anything, it was that she was beyond repair. Even after the kindness and understanding Connor had shown her, she still wasn't healthy enough to withstand an embrace. She never would be. Her life had been lived too long this way, and her patterns were set.

Discreetly, she watched Connor's reflection in the glass. He looked haunted. Ravaged by the need to fix his mistake, when there was no remedy. They'd only known each other for two days and already she'd frustrated him, hurt him. Made him hate himself. She needed to get away from him before she did any more damage. Really, it was selfish of her to have stayed in his magnetic orbit this long. But she could be merciful to them both now. Cut and run. It's what she did best. After he got over the initial sting of failure, he would be grateful.

She almost laughed when she saw herself in the glass. Hair a rat's nest. Leather bustier twisted above her stupid *You Wish* thong. Yeah, he probably did. Probably wished he had a girlfriend who didn't have a panic attack from being in his arms. She might as well be a ghost.

"Maybe I am."

"What's that, sweetheart?"

His sleep-roughened voice didn't fail to heat her insides.

She may have made the decision to leave, but that wouldn't make her attraction to him any less intense. "This isn't going to work." She spoke to his reflection in the glass, but it still hurt. Especially when his eyes blazed open at her words. "What were we thinking? I spend my life avoiding being tied down. You need to control and fix and manage. It's a fucking countdown until you start to resent me. Let's cut this short, shall we?"

"Don't." His voice vibrated. "Don't do this when we're both upset. Please."

She spun around with a laugh, searching the floor for her shorts. "One or both of us has been upset the entire whopping two days we've known each other. We're a couples counselor's wet dream." Having found her shorts just inside the door, she shimmied them up her legs, gasping when Connor growled at her action. *Ignore him. Move faster.*

"It won't happen again," he promised quietly. "It was an accident. We shouldn't have—"

"What? Slept in the same bed? Isn't that something you want to do with your *girlfriend*?" She realized she was shouting and reined herself in. "Look at you. You're dying to pick me up and shake me, tell me I can't leave, but you can't do it. Not without more guilt. More failure. I will *ruin* you."

"*No.*" He strode toward her, stopping a foot away. "I was ruined before we met. You didn't do that. I did it to myself." She didn't have a chance to respond to his impassioned speech before he continued. "Or maybe I don't even know what being ruined means yet. I've already decided you're mine. If you take yourself away from me, I might find out."

"You can't put that on me," she whispered. "Maybe you're too noble for your own good. Maybe you can't see it, but I'm doing what's best for us both. You need something I can't give. And I need something *you* can't give."

The wind left his sails right before her eyes, breath whooshing past his lips. She barely kept herself upright at the guilt driving spikes through her gut. "What can't I give you?"

"*Freedom*. You'll want to tie me down. Inside bed and out." She swallowed a sob. As much as it would hurt to say what came next, she had no choice. "'Don't you dare go out the window, Erin.' 'Don't get yourself off, Erin.' I can't live with the threat of my independence being taken away. I can't live with *you*."

Her words fell like a boulder between them, lodging into the floor and sending cracks to split the room in half. His half. Her half. She wanted to leap over the divide, crawl up into his warmth, and apologize until her heart gave out, but she wouldn't. This was why she didn't get nice things. She broke them. Connor was the nicest thing she'd ever had. That's how she should have known it couldn't last. Unable to witness the regret, the guilt, in his eyes another second, she darted from the room, snatching up her boots where she'd kicked them off by the couch. She shoved her feet into them and tied the laces way too tight.

"No. You can't leave right now," he said from right behind her. "It's not safe this early in the morning."

She straightened. "How are you going to stop me?"

"I'll go. You stay."

Tears threatened once again. She actually had to press both hands to her eyes to keep them from flowing. This was bad. Leaving after two days should have been easy, but her organs felt like they might rupture if she walked away from him. "Stop trying to help me. Just stop. I can't *stand* it."

He moved in front of her, eyes raging like a storm. "You don't want to end this. I see right through you, sweetheart. So guess what? I'm not letting you." His gaze dropped to her lips as if he wanted to kiss her, but she stumbled back to avoid him.

No way she could allow his kiss. It would slay her. She'd never make it to the hallway. Connor followed her, though. Slowly. "You want freedom? Fine. I can't stop you from slipping out windows or walking out doors. If I have to go insane with worry in order to keep you, I'll do it. I'll do it for how I feel when you show up again. I'm not giving up. And you insult me by thinking I can't take some frustration. Some pain. *Bring it*, Erin. I'm fucking ready."

Time slowed, but her pulse sped up. She must have been secretly hoping he would resist, because relief swamped her. Not just relief. Pride. In him. A totally foreign emotion, since she made it a point never to take pride in anything or anyone, save her escape plans. "We can't cure each other."

"*Watch* us."

Such confidence scared the shit out of her. She would let him down. She knew it. Being responsible for someone else's happiness was horrifying when she didn't even know how to be happy herself. "What if it takes a long time? Do you…will you need other women?"

His jaw flexed. "What would you do if I went to another woman?"

Red filtered her view of him. If she was standing in the kitchen instead of the living room, she would have flipped on all four stove burners full blast. Her throat tightened with the need to shout until she couldn't hold it in. It ripped out of her like a gale wind. "*I'd scratch her fucking eyes out*."

Connor didn't flinch at her ear-piercing volume. He only nodded. "Good. Don't ever ask me that again." His eyes darkened. "It goes unsaid that if you go near another man, I'll end his life."

Desire rippled in her midsection. It turned her on, that violent possessiveness. It stirred her, called to her own nature.

But this was a lot to take in all at once. She needed some distance before she could accept it. Accept him and what he was offering. Five minutes ago, she'd written this relationship off as a mistake, mostly on his end. Walking away was the right thing. This little experiment would fail. She was positive of that. And yet the thought of never touching him again, not having the right to be possessive of him…it made her want to crumble.

So she did what she did best. "I'll see you later."

She walked out the front door and escaped. For the moment.

Feeling light-headed, Erin rounded the corner at the end of the block. She'd felt Connor watching her from the apartment window, but now she was out of view. God, he must hate that. Must be climbing the walls with the need to follow her. But he wouldn't. He'd meant what he said about giving her freedom. She was grateful for it, even if she half wished he'd come with her. She'd left him only a few minutes ago and already she missed his scent, his reassuring presence.

Yeah, she was fucked.

Also, she was so damn hungry her stomach felt like it might cave in on itself. They hadn't eaten dinner last night after she'd opted for a game of Slip 'n Slide with the olive oil. Not that it hadn't been seriously worth it. The feel of him in her mouth, the things he'd said…the *growling*.

Pancakes. Focus on getting some pancakes.

Up ahead she saw an intersection with fast-food restaurants on either side. Surely there would be a twenty-four-hour diner where she could chow down and clear her head. Thinking would be easier on a full stomach. One thing she'd learned to appreciate during her short stays in prison was food. She never left a bite on her plate or complained about temperature. Hell, once you'd eaten stale granola over flavorless yogurt containing undefinable lumps, you were happy with damn near anything.

Connor's image drifted into her head. The way he'd looked with morning stubble, hair a mess on top of his head. Those loose sweatpants that hung low on his hips, but managed to hug his ass perfectly. His intensity when he backed her down in the living room. *Bring it.* A shiver coasted down her arms. Damn him. Didn't he realize she wasn't equipped to make a man like him happy?

Even as the insecurities mounted, one fact continued to make itself known. He wasn't giving her up. There was such overwhelming comfort in that, it cocooned her like a warm blanket. If he could see her in the throes of a full-blown panic attack, accept her jealousy, her faults, and still want her, maybe he truly meant it. He wasn't giving her an avenue of escape. But would this be the first time ever she didn't *want* an escape?

"Pancakes," she muttered, crossing the street toward a Denny's. At the curb, she pulled up short. Sitting beside the window inside the restaurant was Polly, all by herself, looking exhausted. Erin sauntered through the entrance, ignoring the hostess to take a seat across from her teammate.

"Come here often?" The mug paused halfway to Polly's mouth, but she didn't react otherwise. Erin studied her, wondering what she was doing up this early. Probably not an epic mental meltdown and a near breakup, unlike a *certain* someone.

Polly set her coffee down on the table with a *plunk*. "Being that I just moved here from Los Angeles, no. But the food isn't shit and they leave me alone, so I might make it a habit."

Erin studied her. Was that glitter on her neck? "Late night?"

That earned her a look that said *back off.* "I could ask you the same. I assume Connor didn't object to the roommate situation?"

"Nope. But I blew him anyway just for good measure."

Polly laughed, that girlish laugh that was unexpected every time. "And he didn't even offer to make you breakfast?"

Erin signaled the waitress for coffee. "Morning afterglow isn't really my thing."

"Shocking."

The waitress appeared with a menu and coffee. Erin waved it away and ordered a tall stack of chocolate chip pancakes. "So how does working with a computer land you in prison?"

"When you hack into the White House Twitter account." She sipped her coffee. "And you tweet screenshots of email correspondence between the vice president and his mistress."

"Hot damn."

She shrugged one shoulder. "I was paid. I couldn't give two shits who's banging who. Just needed to pay my rent."

Erin nodded once. "Did they go down, too?"

"Who? The vice president? You'll have to ask his mistress."

Her mouth curved into a smile. She'd thought company was the last thing she wanted this morning. She'd been looking for space. Room to think. But talking to Polly wasn't half bad, either. Considering she didn't have a single friend to speak of, nor had she ever *wanted* one, that realization was surprising. "No. The person who paid you. Did *they* do time?"

Polly shook her head. "Uh-uh. Just little ol' me. Three cheers for our evil justice system."

"I'll drink to that. The evil part, anyway." Erin took a healthy swallow of coffee, sighing in appreciation as it warmed a path all the way to her stomach. "The coffee isn't shit, either."

The other girl leaned forward. "Hey, I've been meaning to ask you…how did you escape Dade Correctional? From what I've read, security in that place is tighter than a duck's ass. But there's no details about your method of escape anywhere."

Erin felt a tingling in her spine. "How did you know I was in Dade?"

Polly stared into her coffee cup. "I collect information. It's something I do without thinking." She brushed her short black hair away from her face. "Sometimes I forget people see it as a violation."

Erin wasn't sure how to feel. It's not as if she ever held back when someone asked her what she'd done to get prison time. Armed robbery. That one time she'd set a police car on fire. Most of her past was an open book. It was the other, more personal remnants of her past that weren't open for discussion. Except maybe with the voices in her head. Things that weren't part of public record. No, there was something else causing the tingling that had moved to the back of her neck. Other people taking an interest in her, asking questions because they were curious, not because they wanted to interrogate. *That* had seldom, if ever, happened in her life. Yet in the last forty-eight hours, two people had tried to get to know her better.

It made her feel...significant.

She picked up a spoon and ran the smooth metal down her cheek. "First time was a cakewalk. Dade staff wears these green scrubs, like a light olive color. Ugly as sin. Ours were white." When Polly nodded with interest, Erin had the insane urge to smile. "One afternoon, I pocketed a green highlighter from the library cart. I broke it open and dyed my scrubs green."

Polly's gaze widened. "Don't tell me..."

"I almost didn't pull it off. My hair was still pink, so I needed a way to hide it." She tapped the spoon against her head. "The girl in the cell beside mine had a Marlins baseball cap. Wasn't supposed to, but her son had sneaked it in for her birthday. She gave me the hat in exchange for buying her son Marlins tickets if I made it out." Her throat tightened at the memory, so she cleared it. "The next day, I was on the schedule to work in the laundry room. We'd sort the clothes, then they were driven off-site to be cleaned. One of the wardens liked to get in my face a lot. Princess this, princess that. Anyway, I unclipped her pass from her belt and waited for her to take a bathroom break. I knew I'd have about four minutes to change into the green scrubs and pile my hair under the cap. I did it in one. Then I hopped into the laundry truck and drove straight out of that motherfucker. Ditched the truck a mile from the prison and ran for it."

"Unbelievable."

"Yes, I am."

Polly tapped a fingernail against her front tooth. "What about the second time?"

Erin's stomach lurched. The room went unfocused around her. She fumbled for the matches in her pocket and lit the paper place mat on fire, sucking in the acrid smell with a greedy inhale. When Polly put it out by dumping a glass of water over the flame, Erin frowned. "Second time wasn't as easy."

"No, I don't expect it would be after they knew what you could do." Polly watched her closely as seconds ticked by. "Did you buy that kid Marlins tickets?"

"Sure did. Took his thirteen-year-old ass to Hooters afterward and everything." She circled the rim of her coffee cup with her middle finger. "Being out in the open that day is how I got hauled back into Dade. Funny how things work, right? The baseball cap saved me and damned me at the same time."

"No good deed..."

Erin thought of Connor. His determination to help her. Would it go unpunished?

CHAPTER NINE

Connor strode into the police station and suffered through a pat-down before they would let him in to see Derek. The squad didn't have a scheduled meeting this morning because all six members of the unit had been given their marching orders yesterday. He had two hours before he was scheduled to interview Tucker May's ex–cell mate and he needed to speak with the captain first. When he walked into the main floor of the precinct and found Bowen leaning up against the pillar across from Derek's office, he greeted him with a raised eyebrow.

Bowen jerked his thumb toward the office door. "He's in there with his missus. I've been told interrupting them could lead to severed limbs. I like mine where they are."

Seemingly out of nowhere, Austin sidled up to them. "I was told the same thing, but it's been a bloody hour. Some of us have matters to attend."

"What matters are those?" Connor asked. He still didn't have a read on this guy, which bothered the shit out of him. Although he suspected any males who existed within Erin's orbit would immediately become his enemy. Except for Bowen, who'd forgotten every female name that wasn't *Sera*. Something about Austin put him on the defensive, like he might be more dangerous than his tailored appearance let on. "I thought you were sidelined until Derek found a use for you."

Austin popped a stick of gum into his mouth. "There's always a use for me. I just get to decide it for myself. I'm not a fan of following orders."

"That so?" Bowen smirked. "Then you're here to speak to Derek about what, exactly? The best place to get a spray tan in Chicago?"

"Hysterical." Austin's smile was tight. "I'll have you know my mother was Greek. If the sun worships my complexion, there's nothing I can do about it."

Connor blew out an impatient breath toward the door. He suspected the reason Bowen was here was similar to his own. Austin was a wild card. But none of them were going to get answers standing around like a couple of tools. "Two minutes and I'm going in."

A uniformed police officer walked past, whistling through his teeth at Connor's statement. "Gird your loins."

Connor exchanged a level look with Bowen and all three men fell silent. He felt itchy between his shoulder blades. Had ever since Erin left the apartment, hours earlier. This morning had almost been the end of their already-unpredictable relationship, and it was his own damn fault. He'd never been a heavy sleeper, but something about her soft body behind him, her slender arms locked around his chest like she couldn't get close enough, had induced a near-coma. He'd fallen asleep feeling *needed* by her. It was no wonder he'd had to get closer to that need, absorb it.

God, he couldn't close his eyes without seeing her in that state of panic. The fear radiating from her had reached out and choked him, guilt running him through. He needed to be careful, patient, alert. Couldn't risk her leaving again. Somehow in the space of a few days, she'd become vital. She'd crawled up inside him and put down roots that couldn't be dug up. Those roots had already grown into a shade tree that cooled him where he usually ran so hot. Only a handful of hours had passed since she'd left the apartment, and already he was desperate to see her. Be touched by her. She'd said touching him made her feel good, and he was dying little by little with each passing minute, knowing she was going without something that made her happy. Something that relaxed the monsters lying in wait inside him.

"Time's up," he muttered, striding toward Derek's office door. Just as he reached for the knob, the door swung open to reveal a petite brunette in cowboy boots and a pink sundress. She was stunning and…young. Couldn't be more than twenty-five or twenty-six. If Connor wasn't mistaken, she had a fair amount of whisker burn on the side of her face. A low growl rumbled from behind her and Connor looked up to find Derek, arms crossed, with a dark look on his face.

"Any reason you're standing so close to my wife, Bannon?"

"*Derek*," the brunette admonished before giving Connor an apologetic look. "The man doesn't have the manners the good Lord gave a goat. I'm Ginger and it's a pleasure to meet you." She stuck out her right hand, complete with sparkling diamond ring. "I had to come down here and meet the reason my husband has been working so dang hard."

Based on Derek's forbidding expression, even touching Ginger's hand was against the rules. Connor had no choice, however, and he'd be damned before he started backing down from the guy. He shook Ginger's hand. "Nice to meet you, ma'am."

"Jesus, don't ma'am me. I'm a new mama and I feel tired enough."

Austin stepped forward and extended his hand. "Well, you don't look it, that's for sure."

Another growl from Derek.

Bowen just looked anxious to get into the office, shifting back and forth on the balls of his feet. But he managed to shake Ginger's hand and give a half smile.

Derek kept his eyes trained on all three of them as Ginger went up on her toes and kissed his cheek. "Don't work too hard, sugar."

They all piled into the office when Derek stepped back, Bowen leaning against the far wall beside Connor, while Austin dropped into the single chair. Derek took his position behind the desk, arms still crossed over his chest. He pointed at Bowen. "You go first since your twitching is irritating me. What do you want?"

"I want to know who I'm working with." Bowen jerked his chin toward Austin. "Who the hell is this guy? What did those two girls do to get locked up?"

"I've vetted you all thoroughly. That should be good enough."

"It's not. Not where Sera is concerned." He swiped a hand through his hair. "I need to know who has my back while I'm watching hers. No surprises."

"I'm the only one who needs to worry about Erin." Connor stared hard at Bowen until it visibly sank in. "That's why I'm here. I need to know where she's been and I don't want an audience for it."

Derek released a heavy sigh. "Let me get this straight. Bowen is here for Sera's safety. Connor came to pump me for information on Erin." He turned his attention to Austin. "That leaves you and Polly. Is there something in the Chicago fucking water? It's barely been three days."

Austin's face betrayed nothing. "I only drink bottled water."

Connor could almost hear Bowen's massive eye roll. "Look, you can't blame us for being cautious. I think I speak for everyone when I say we've gotten this far by not giving blind trust." He ignored Bowen's sniff of agreement beside him. "If we don't know one another's weaknesses, there isn't a hope in hell of trusting one another's strengths."

"Seconded." Bowen shoved his hands into his jacket pockets. "How would you feel if it was your wife out there?"

"Don't ever say that out loud again," Derek ground out.

Austin gained his feet. "This is going rather well, wouldn't you say?" He stopped at the door. "Have fun deciding whose dick is biggest. Hint, the winner is about to leave the room."

When the door snapped shut behind Austin, Bowen pushed off the wall. "*Man*, I hate that guy."

Derek held up his hands, appearing to collect his thoughts. "Bowen, Sera is a trained officer. Treat her like one." He turned to Connor. "As far as weaknesses go, you already know Erin's. Otherwise you wouldn't have ripped the plywood off that window yesterday."

"She mentioned a stepfather. I need his name."

The captain actually looked impressed. "She told you that already? Took me months to figure out which card to play to get her here."

"I don't understand." He took a step toward the desk. "And I need to. Now."

"In front of Bowen?"

Connor considered the former underground Brooklyn criminal whose relationship with him had started off as ambiguous, but had developed into a mutual respect. Bowen bunched his shoulders and glanced away uncomfortably, but Connor could see his answer would matter. A lot. "Yeah, in front of

Bowen. If there's anyone here I trust, it's him."

Derek looked between them and nodded. "Most of you are here to avoid prison time. Erin is here to avoid being locked up as well. But not behind bars." He lowered his voice. "In a mental institution."

Bowen blew out a slow breath. "You two sure know how to pick 'em."

Connor gave him the middle finger. "Who's trying to put her there? Her stepfather?"

"She'll have to tell you the rest." Derek sat down at his desk, effectively dismissing them. "I'm done gossiping for the day. Get out there and do your jobs."

Connor checked his watch again and saw that only a minute had passed since the last time. He scanned South California Avenue looking for blond hair and combat boots. Listened for the sound of tinkling bells. Anything that might signal Erin had decided to show up for their prison visit. On his drive over, he'd still been reeling from the information Derek had provided. No, "reeling" wasn't the right word. He was livid. A lot of that stemmed from helpless fear. Even now, she could be in trouble and he was standing here unable to help her. *Unacceptable.*

Even if she showed, what could he say? It had gone unspoken between him and Derek that Erin's situation was told in confidence. If he came right out demanding to know why someone, most likely her stepfather, wanted to lock her away, she might split. She wanted her freedom; it was important to her and he imagined that extended to the right to privacy. To tell him things about herself when she was good and ready. Too bad he didn't share that sentiment. Whatever he had to do to e would be done, come hell or high water.

where the hell was she?

Connor turned just in time to see Erin step out from behind a parked car. He tried not to let his relief show, but on the inside, he felt like a parched desert experiencing its first rainstorm. Jesus, she looked sexy in those skintight jeans and black crop top. She'd traded her combat boots for some red high-top Converse that matched her dark lipstick. He wanted to drag her back behind that parked car and wipe it off with one hand and finger her with the other. Watching her battle outrage and arousal from a front-row seat might make up for the morning he'd spent going out of his mind.

She sauntered toward him, hands clasped behind her back. "Looking for someone?"

"Maybe," he answered. The closer she got, the less he cared about holding back, giving her space. The closer she got, the harder his pulse pounded. "Where did those clothes come from? More importantly, where did you change into them?"

"The mall." She rubbed a palm down her denim-encased thigh. "I keep a locker there, too. In case I can't go home to get what I need before I—"

"Run?"

"Yeah." She raised a hand as if to lay it on his chest, but hesitated. "Does it make you feel better that this is the first time I don't really want to?"

"No."

"It should. It should make you want to kiss me."

Christ. His cock swelled, pushing against his fly. The word "kiss" coming from those plump red lips shot him full of lust. His body remembered all too well how they'd felt smoothing down his length last night, drawing hard on their way back up.

"You and I will never be able to kiss in public. Both times I've tasted your mouth ended in us both coming. I don't see that changing any time soon."

A breath shuddered out. "So much for me distracting you."

"Why would you want to do that?"

She glanced toward the massive stone structure that was Cook County correctional facility and shook her head frantically, blond strands flying around her face. "Too many doors closing behind us. Too many people looking. They'll check me for weapons with their sweaty cop hands."

Connor experienced a wave of self-disgust. Since they were going into the prison as guests, not inmates, it hadn't occurred to him that she'd get spooked. Idiot. Of course she would. He'd been so focused on the more immediate threat to her, he hadn't even thought of it. "You don't have to do anything you don't want to. I'll come back a different day without you."

"No," she hurried to say. "I'm going to help in my own way, all right? I'll meet you back here in an hour."

Denial speared him. He couldn't let her out of his sight this soon. Too soon. Already the calming effect she had on him had started to dissipate. "Erin…"

"Go, Connor." She gave him a look that said, *please trust me.* "It'll be okay."

Lead in his stomach, he looked her over one final time before heading up the walkway toward the prison. He'd only taken three steps when she jumped onto his back, wrapping her arms around his neck. His eyes slid closed as she nuzzled his neck with her mouth. Her weight felt so good. Like he'd been walking around untethered all morning until that very second.

"I went to a diner and had chocolate chip pancakes with Polly, who I think maybe has a secret life after dark. One that involves glitter lotion. After that, I took the bus to the mall and carved my initials into a tree waiting for it to open." Connor knew what she was doing, and it made his chest hurt. Feeding his need for control, for peace of mind, simply by telling him where she'd been since leaving him. It comforted him like crazy. "I shopped in the junior's section of Macy's and rode the kiddie train because the girl running it gave me the evil eye. You would have been so proud." She planted a kiss on his neck and inhaled deeply. "I'll see you in an hour, baby."

She slid down his back. He groaned at the feel of her breasts dragging over his muscle, needing to breathe deeply and get a handle on his desire before facing her again.

But when he turned around, she was gone.

CHAPTER TEN

The first time Erin was in Dade Correctional, one of the guards had taken a shine to her. If groping her every time he did a bed check counted as "a shine." Greasy Gunther, the other inmates used to call him. It would have eventually gone further if she hadn't blown that Popsicle stand when she did. Gunther had even warned her he would find a way to get her alone. That warning had been an impetus for her to plot escape. She hadn't known how she would react if a man forced himself on her. Would she freeze up at the sensation of hands on her body? Would her fight-or-flight instinct kick in? The unknown wasn't good enough, so she'd gotten out of Gunther's reach before he could extend it.

Even the other guards had been aware of his fascination with her. They would rib him every time she passed by in the yard, elbowing him and reminding him he was married while he ogled her, adjusted himself in his trousers. One afternoon in the cafeteria, Gunther had gotten bold and pinched her ass while she stood in line for food. His guard buddy had come up behind them and muttered, "Man, you've always had a thing for crazy pussy, haven't you? It's going to get you into trouble someday."

She hadn't been offended, mainly because she'd erected a shield that caused everything the guards said to bounce off. But she'd never forgotten that statement. She'd let it settle in her mind and she'd played with it, wondering if it were true. If her personality, which seemed to send most men packing with a quickness, could attract a different type at the same time. If a certain amount of them sensed something inside her and were attracted by it, rather than repelled. When she'd experimented with sex *before*...before she'd been cast into the darkness... she'd learned the answer quickly enough. Three men had approached her at a bar, one asking if he could buy her a drink. Her reply had been, "Sure. Petrol, please. Unleaded."

Two had walked away laughing and shaking their heads. The third had stepped closer.

She was still waiting for her Nobel Peace Prize to show up in the mail.

The handful of men she'd tested herself with hadn't been turned off by her strict instructions not to touch her during sex; they'd been turned on. There wasn't anything too odd for these guys. They soaked up crazy like a sponge.

There had been a brief moment when she met Connor where she wondered if he was one of those men. The kind who seemed to get off on the experience of a girl who could either blow your mind or blow you away, depending on her mood. She hadn't wondered for a second since. Connor didn't look at her as if she were an exhibit at the zoo. A strange and exotic bird. No, he looked as if he wanted to climb into the exhibit with her, find out how to adapt.

Erin felt a sudden dose of yearning as she approached the entrance to Hanover's Tavern. She wished she'd been strong enough to walk into the prison with Connor. Wished he stood beside her now, warm and steadfast. Instead she was getting ready to go another round of testing on her Crazy Pussy theory by walking into a bar and seeing what information she could glean through the prison workers she'd been told frequented the place. Being that Hanover's was only four blocks from Cook County DOC and screamed *dive* with its neon beer signs and rickety awning, she knew the type who would be on the other side of the door. Greasy Gunthers aplenty.

She took a deep breath before opening the door, focusing on the smooth feel of the switchblade in her high-top. The matches in her pocket. If she concentrated on those comforting objects, maybe she could block the foreign guilt over walking into a room very likely full of other men. Men she would flirt with to get information. Connor's head would explode. But she couldn't sit around and be useless to the squad. If she didn't have the steady job and Derek to vouch for her sanity, her stepfather would pounce. What Connor didn't know wouldn't hurt him.

Erin ignored the certainty that he would somehow know what she'd been up to and pushed open the door. Every head in the place turned in her direction before she'd taken two steps inside. Oh yeah, she'd come to the right place. Half of them were still in their uniforms, nightsticks and all. The other half had the tired, jaded look sported by most corrections officers. If anyone knew how Tucker May had escaped Cook County, these guys would. Secrets didn't stay secrets over too many beers and a desire to stay away from their wives, lives, and responsibilities.

Lights, camera, crazy. She giggled and ducked her head, beelining for the bar. The bartender froze in the act of changing the channel on the ancient television over his head and looked her over with a mixture of curiosity and trepidation. She hooked her foot in the rung of a stool and leaned over the bar, knowing every set of male eyes was trained on her ass. "Hey, mister." A

Southern twang, huh? Why not? "I got separated from my tour group. Would you let me use your phone? I left my purse on the bus. As far as tourists go, I'm hopeless."

His mustache twitched. "You got ID?"

"No, sir, I don't." She bit her bottom lip and tilted her head. "Wouldn't help much if I did. I'm not old enough to drink just yet. Two more years."

Two low curses behind her. A few chairs scraped back, probably to get a better look. God, how predictable. She wanted nothing more than to turn around and give them the double middle finger, but she had a job to do. Phase one of which was to convince the bartender to let her stay. Obviously he was the type who ran when he saw her kind approaching.

Smart man.

He sighed and reached behind the cash register, closing his hands around a black cordless phone. "Make your call. You want a soda or something?"

She scrunched up her shoulders like she couldn't believe she was getting a drink in such a fine establishment. "A Shirley Temple, maybe?" She tossed her hair and sent the four men behind her a conspiratorial look. "Something with a cherry."

With that blatant innuendo, she thinned the herd by half, several men suddenly enthralled by their pints of beer. Weird. Usually more men folded under the pressure of a virgin, worried about the cling factor. Must be the tight jeans.

Time to up the ante. She dialed seven numbers on the phone, making sure the last button she hit was "clear." No reason to traumatize some stranger who had the misfortune of answering this call. She reached into her pocket to pay the bartender for the Shirley Temple he'd just set down in front of her, but he waved her off, indicating a burly man who'd just sidled up to the bar a few seats down. Burly Dude winked to let her know he'd bought the drink. *What a high roller.* Erin smiled back at him, drumming her fingernails on the bar as she waited for her imaginary call to connect.

"Henry, is that you?" She said into the phone. "I can't believe you ditched me again. Don't tell me it's an accident. It's the third time this week you've gone off without me. With *her.*"

Burlykins moved a little closer, inching his rocks glass full of amber liquid across the bar. He feigned interest in the baseball game playing on the television, but she could tell he was listening to her conversation. Hanging on to what probably used to be a decently handsome face, she put him in his late forties. A white tan line on his ring finger indicated he was recently divorced or removed it with the sole intent of approaching her. Fucking with him ought to be fun.

"This is because I won't put out, isn't it?" Erin whispered furiously into the phone. "She's easy, isn't she? Are you back at the hotel right now getting ready to—" She wiped at her eyes. "Fine. Maybe I'll give it up to someone *else*... Yeah, today is a good a day as any. Maybe even the next man I see. Think about that while you're with her. I hope it was worth it."

She ended the phony call with a flourish and sipped at her Shirley Temple. Under her breath, she recited back both ends of the conversation to herself, complete with hand gestures.

"Boyfriend trouble?"

Ahhh, right on cue, douche bag. "Yeah," she answered sullenly. "Actually, I doubt he's my boyfriend anymore. Think maybe he's found someone else."

He sucked in a breath through his teeth. "He must be blind."

She pressed a hand to her cheek as if to hide a blush. "Or just stupid."

They shared a laugh and he moved closer, right to the point she could handle. Any farther and she'd have to make an excuse to distance herself. The switchblade felt heavy against her ankle. His gaze lingered on her exposed belly as he sipped his drink. "You want to talk about it?"

"Oh, you know." She fished the cherry out of her drink. "He thinks because he's loaded and lives off campus that every girl should fall at his feet. Give it up on the first date. I told him he had to work a little harder for it." Slowly and deliberately, she bit into the cherry. "I guess I'm kind of a tease."

His Adam's apple bobbed. "That so?"

She lifted one shoulder and let it drop. "Maybe this is a sign that my methods aren't working." Her lips spread into a smile. "Maybe I'll try something else to keep a boyfriend next time. Like kidnapping or blackmail. Although I've tried both before. So messy."

Burly's laughter was halting, as if he didn't know whether or not she was joking. "Or you could just—"

"Give it up?" Erin let her eyes dip below his belt, trying not to grimace when he sucked in his gut and tilted his hips up. His pants were already tented. Lovely. "You look like the kind of man I should take advice from, too. Are you an officer of the law?"

She knew her dazzled expression had paid off when his chest puffed up. "Corrections officer. Supervisor, actually."

He leaned ever-so-slightly closer and she ducked back, wagging a chastising finger in front of his nose. To make up for it, she tucked a finger into her shirt collar and moved it back and forth, giving him a peek at her cleavage. "At Cook County?"

"Huh?" He turned toward the bar a little, possibly to hide his growing erection. "Yeah."

"Wow." She ran her hands up her thighs. "On my tour this morning, I heard there was a prison escape not too long ago. It must have been on someone else's shift. Can't imagine anyone getting by you."

"Damn straight it wasn't my shift. That shit wouldn't have happened on my watch, baby."

Her breath caught. "Oh, mister. Tell me all about it."

CHAPTER ELEVEN

Connor mentally played back the interview with May's cell mate in his head. A distraction to keep his mind off Erin. Technically, she wasn't even late yet, but that didn't seem to matter. After the way they'd left things this morning, he'd needed time with her and hadn't gotten it. He wanted it now. Layered over that pressing desire was the need to know where the hell she'd gone. Erin might hold back about her past, but she was blunt and honest in every other respect. The fact that she hadn't told him where she was going, had actually looked prematurely guilty, cloaked him in anxiety.

Letting her pull these disappearing acts whenever the conversation got tough was going to be goddamn difficult. She'd been right that morning. He was the type who needed organization, structure. It's why he'd excelled with the SEALs—until he'd gone and fucked it all up. He wanted to fight off her demons while keeping his own at bay, but how could he do it when she kept running away?

Think about the interview. She'll be here.

It had been like riding a bike. Even if May's cell mate hadn't been entirely helpful, the simple act of questioning someone was familiar. A ritual that had brought him back to his time overseas. His training. To when he'd been a valued member of a group. Until the day he'd made a massive error in judgment, he'd been on his way to a respectable career. Instead, he'd landed back in his hometown with dishonor on his back. Dishonor he'd only increased exponentially.

Today felt like the first time he might be able to get back some of his honor. But he needed to be cautious. Needed to keep his head. For so long he'd been existing one minute to the next. Living in Brooklyn, making an illegal living so he could support his mother and her medical bills. One split-second decision—a momentary loss of control—had landed him there. He'd numbed himself as a way to cope, but as Erin's presence thawed him, he found those skeletons wouldn't be ignored. It had been a long time coming, but now he had to face them head-on. Find out their names and extract them, knowing he'd be stronger on the other side. Strong for *her.*

He heard the jingling of bells and felt a rush of relief. It was short-lived, though, because she was running her hands up and down the sides of her jeans, murmuring under her breath as she came toward him. Her fingers were black with soot, telling him she'd been lighting matches, letting them burn. She looked jumpy, and he didn't like it. He opened his mouth to request an explanation, but she spoke first. "I was thinking Chinese for dinner tonight. Any objections?"

She's trying to distract me. Why? "How'd you do?"

"You first."

Irritation zigzagged through his sternum. *Patience.* "May's cell mate didn't have much to say, the bottom line being May didn't act or do anything out of the ordinary leading up to his escape." He rubbed the back of his neck. "Something was definitely off, though. His answers felt rehearsed. I didn't have enough time."

She took a step toward him, bringing their bodies close, and loosed a little sigh of pleasure. Was she cold? The idea bothered him, especially considering he couldn't warm her in his arms. "And there wasn't much you could do on the other side of the glass, right?"

Connor couldn't deny that he'd had the same thought. His interrogation style had transformed greatly during his time in Brooklyn. While he hated the memories that fact conjured, he liked not having to pretend with her. Pretend he wasn't a man who'd seen and done bad things. A sudden vision assailed Connor. Him. Tying *Erin* up and demanding she answer his questions. Her arms were suspended above her head, body stripped of clothing, writhing as she tried to get free. The blood in his head rushed south, obviously taking his ability to reason along with it. Dammit, he couldn't play those types of games with her. She wasn't able, and it was selfish and inexcusable of him to want them.

He came back to himself with a jolt, realizing he'd been staring at Erin's mouth. Unbelievably, she didn't look unaffected, lips parted to receive her dragged-in breaths. Had she read his mind?

A low sound tripped out of him. "What's happening inside that head?"

She fell back a step, giving a tiny headshake and breaking their spell. Before he could press for an answer, she skirted past him. "The bus stop is this way."

He ate up the sidewalk separating them in two strides to walk beside her. "My car is parked in the garage around the corner." When her step faltered, he cursed his own lack of foresight. "Are you all right to drive inside a car?"

"Yeah." Soulful blue eyes flashed up at him. "No seat belt,

though." Connor didn't like the idea of her in a moving vehicle without being strapped in. Not at all. He started to object, to say they would take the bus instead, but she cut him off. "So the cell mate's answers sounded rehearsed. Do you think Stark got to him?"

This constant avoidance wasn't working for him, but he sensed if he made an issue of the small stuff, he'd never get to the bigger ones beneath the surface. With a sigh, he followed her lead and changed the subject. "The prison manifest doesn't show any visits from Stark or any of his closest aides. If he got to May, he was careful."

"Or someone on the inside didn't record the visit." She appeared to be bracing herself. "In fact, I know Stark got an assist from someone in Cook County. The way he escaped was too convenient."

Connor's blood heated. Dammit. He didn't like where this was headed. Had sensed something coming and wasn't sure he could handle the rest of what she had to tell him. Already, the muscles in his neck were vibrating, his senses sharpening. "You want to tell me how you know that?"

She visibly shivered, probably over his tone of voice. "I'm working up to it."

He jerked his chin toward a two-story parking structure, indicating that she should follow, using the time they spent ascending the two ramps to attempt to compose himself. His instincts were buzzing that he wouldn't like the information he intended to get out of her. He kept seeing her nervous expression when she approached him, his intuition that she'd done something to make herself vulnerable. *Stay calm. No matter what she says, stay calm.*

They reached the roof, which was mostly deserted except for a half dozen cars. The notorious Chicago wind picked up her hair and streamed it out behind her, making her even more achingly pretty than usual. That same wind plastered her already-tight shirt even more provocatively against her body, highlighting the perky nipples standing at attention beneath. His gaze dipped to her belly and thighs, remembering how they felt sliding over his muscles with the aid of oil.

Connor stopped at a navy-blue SUV and waited, hands on hips.

Erin plunked down on the bumper. "There is a bar called Hanover's a few blocks from Cook County. I took a wild guess that there would be some CO's inside reliving their glory days." She brushed her hair over her shoulder. "I went in and talked to one such working-class hero who'd had one too many whiskeys and he spilled the beans. It was actually kind of boring."

"You think I'm going to buy that version?" He laid a hand on the car and leaned down toward her, his mind attempting to roadblock his anger, but a need for information drowned out his voice of reason. "I might not have gotten answers today, Erin, but I'm a trained interrogator. I've had terrorists where you're sitting before, so don't insult me."

She frowned up at him. "Shouldn't you care more about how May escaped?"

"I don't. I *don't* care more." He felt a punch of satisfaction when her blue eyes widened. "There's your answer. Now give me mine."

"I flirted with the guy. Is that what you want to hear?" She shot to her feet and paced away. Connor just about caught himself before he could grip her shoulders and pull her back against him. Something hideous took up residence in his stomach at what she'd just revealed. He'd seen it coming and still hadn't been prepared for the image. "I let him think he was going to take me home so I could get the information we nceded, then I crawled out the bathroom window."

His hands started to shake. It wasn't only the flirting that maddened him. He loathed knowing she'd smiled at some fucker, teased the guy with the same body she teased him with. But it was so much more. He knew what men were capable of. Some men, *especially* men who'd had a few whiskeys, weren't always satisfied with flirtation. It gave them the false assumption they were owed something. Which could lead to them trying to take it. That line of thinking might be extreme, but when he'd lived his life, seen women around him get taken advantage of or mistreated, the possibilities crashing through his brain weren't out of the question. Not by any stretch.

He massaged his forehead for long moments, trying to bring his boiling temper back down to a simmer, but it didn't work. It needed to be released or it would remain and fester. Without thinking, he hauled back with his fist and slammed it into the SUV's rear window. It cracked, glass crunching into a curved impression of his closed hand. *Goddammit.* This part of himself was disgusting. This trait he'd inherited. The need to be destructive when everything built up and required a place to go. "You don't know what it does to me, Erin." He pushed the words out between clenched teeth. "Knowing you were all alone in a bar *full* of men. You don't *know*."

Based on the stunned look on her face, she now had an inkling. "You *do* know that they can't touch me. I wouldn't let them. If I can't even have *your* hands on me, you think I could stand *theirs*?"

"*Theirs.* That's my point. How many of them, sweetheart? And only one of you." He bunched his fist, pondering full-on demolishment of the window. *Needing* to see it break. *Dying* to hear the crunch and feel his knuckles being abraded. "What if they didn't give you a choice? Any of them could have followed you to the bathroom or out of the bar—"

There went the window. Aware that his show of anger had to be alarming her, he inhaled through his nose and squeezed his eyes shut. When he opened them again, she was standing in front of him, not a hint of fear on her face. Only concern for him. He mentally sagged under the weight of her confidence in him, her obvious faith that although his fist broke windows, it would never come near her. Jesus, he'd rather die.

Connor held his breath as Erin locked her wrists behind his neck, rubbing her cheek against the center of his chest, his hammering heart. She started to sway side to side, like a lapping ocean, and he was powerless to do anything but move with her, getting lost in the unhurried rhythm. Inside him, the chaos turned from a bright, blazing red to a tranquil blue. It happened so fast, it dizzied him. All it took was her touch, her being there. "You're back now. You're back," she murmured, her voice almost carried away by the stiff breeze. "Anyway, that window had it coming."

It all came pouring out, his words tumbling over themselves in an effort to reach her and be accepted. "It felt good sometimes. Maybe all the time."

"What felt good?"

"Beating on scumbags back in Brooklyn. Sometimes I... wanted to do it." He swallowed the knot in his throat. "I started to like it too much. It was like a reprieve from thinking."

"Like my fire." She nodded against him. "I understand."

"Tell me you know I'd never hurt you," he begged her quietly. "Especially out of anger. Tell me."

"I know that," she whispered.

The frustration in his chest had eased, but as he leaned back and looked her over from head to toe, it took a different shape. A possessive one that, unlike the anger she'd soothed

away, wouldn't allow a similar fate. He let his gaz
down her exposed stomach to end between her thigh
a room full of men with what's mine? You show me
were tempting him with. I need to be the only one who sees."

Adrenaline sparkled, adding to Erin's arousal. "Here? Outside?"

"*No.*" Connor closed his eyes and took a deep breath.
"If anyone else looks at you today but me, Erin, I won't be
responsible for my actions."

Her heart rate tripled. Look. He just wanted to look, not
touch. It was so freeing, knowing he was aware of her limits.
That he'd embraced them. She wanted to reward him for that.
Wanted to ease the jagged edges she sensed she'd created inside
him. So when Connor strode to the driver's side and climbed
inside, Erin followed with zero hesitation.

Already she could see the outline of his erection in his
jeans. He followed her gaze to where it pressed against his fly
and squeezed it while she watched. Her breath escaped on a
moan.

"Climb up here on my lap and face the front." He moved
the seat back, giving them more room, before tucking his hands
safely behind his head. Erin curled her fingers around the
steering wheel and hefted herself up. She draped one leg over
his farthest thigh and sank down into his lap. Connor growled
into her hair. "Lose the jeans, sweetheart. Show me what those
men were thinking about. Tight thighs that lead to a little pink
pussy." He bounced her on his lap once, twice. "They'll all go
home tonight and think about you bent over and pouting while
they fuck their wives."

Erin felt like she'd been pulled under by a tidal wave. Wind rushed in through the open door, whipping throughout the car in a symphony of white noise. She shouldn't be turned on by his words, but there was a naughtiness to them that stirred her up like nothing in her memory. Connor's thickness pressed between her legs and she needed it closer. She unsnapped her jeans and leaned back onto his shoulder, pushing them down her hips.

"That's it. Good girl." They both groaned when she sat back down on his lap, this time wearing only panties. "Now give me a dance. Tease me like you teased the men."

"No, I didn't, I…" She braced her hands on the steering wheel and worked her hips in tight circles, contradicting her words. A whimper fell past her lips as lust winged her below her belly button. Her gaze strayed to the rearview and she saw that Connor had his bottom lip between his teeth. His hands were still tucked behind his head, making his arm muscles strain. *Breathtaking man.*

"Enough. You're the only one who gets to come today. If you keep that up, I'll break that promise." He jerked his hips beneath her. "Turn around."

Erin turned in his lap to straddle his hips, her breath catching at the sight of him. So intense. So commanding. Darkly sexual. "Why won't you come?"

"Punishment, Erin. It's going to drive you crazy knowing how hard I am for the rest of the day, but I won't let you do a damn thing about it." A muscle ticked in his cheek. "This is for yesterday when you touched yourself in my goddamn bed. And it's for today when you put yourself at risk."

Denial made her head spin. He was right. It would kill her. "Connor—"

"Your shirt comes off next." His gaze tracked down her

throat and lingered on her tightened nipples. "I know they were looking at your tits. God knows I can't take my fucking eyes off them."

An idea formed in the midst of the storm taking place within her. Right now, as close as they were, Connor had thrown up a barrier and she hated it. He might not allow her to give him pleasure, but what about the opposite? It might not work, it might end in disaster, but she had to try. With shaky fingers, she grasped the hem of her shirt and drew it over her head, tossing the garment onto the passenger seat.

Connor's attention was immediately captivated by her braless breasts, breath racing in and out past his lips. "Jesus, Erin. Could you get any more fucking beautiful?"

The expression on his face was a mixture of awe and need, so potent it reached out and grabbed her by the throat. "Touch them with your mouth," she whispered, ignoring the stabs of fear in her belly.

His erection swelled against the inside of her thigh, making her gasp. "Sweetheart, no. That's not what this is about."

"Don't tell me no. I can feel how bad you want to." She took her breasts in her hands and lifted them like an offering. "*I* want you to."

"*God.*" A masculine groan filled the car. "I spend every minute of the day wanting to touch you, Erin. If you get hurt or scared, I'm not going to handle it well when I can't hold you. It's going to fuck me up real bad. Please be sure."

Erin swallowed her doubts and anxiety, focusing on healing what had been damaged between them. She leaned close and dragged her right breast across his damp lips. Something broke inside him. His hands freed themselves from behind his head and turned to fists in midair. He licked his lips once before fastening his mouth to her breast and sucking, moaning roughly in his throat.

The dreaded sound in her head stirred, like she'd poked the nest with a stick. It was quiet, though, tentative. Watchful. She couldn't deny the reactions going off one by one throughout her body, muscles stiffening with the need to propel herself out the door. Her hands shot out to grasp both of his wrists. If he attempted to touch her now, it would be too much.

Connor watched her through eyes bright and feverish. His lips moved sensually as they sucked, like waves lapping against the shoreline. He released her nipples with a pop, rolling his lips together as if to savor the taste. "It's too much for you. I can see it."

"No, it's not." Her voice shook with determination, but she could see that Connor wasn't convinced. Dammit, he hadn't given her enough time to get used to it. He didn't appear willing to try again, either, as much as he appeared to want it. She would have to convince him. Keeping their intertwined hands poised at their sides, Erin rose up on her knees and let her breasts hover in front of his face. Connor growled, his hips rolling beneath her, nudging her core with his erection. Slowly, she pressed her chest against his face and swayed, essentially burying his face between her peaked mounds. "Did you like being in my mouth last night?"

His breath shuddered out, sending hot puffs of air over her sensitive skin. "You know I fucking loved it. I've never come that hard in my life. I shot off between those sexy lips, didn't I?" His intense gaze collided with hers. "You took it just like a good girl is supposed to."

"Yes." She whimpered when his open mouth raked over her nipple…and there was no noise inside her head. No fear. Only thick, decadent heat. Her pulse started to hammer, echoing in her ears. She needed him to use his mouth on her, but he was still holding back. "Can you suck me that good, Connor? Or maybe you don't want to return the favor."

Her back hit the steering wheel, blasting the horn in a cut-off honk. Connor's body didn't pin her, but the fierceness radiating from him kept her rooted against the wheel. Still, there was only a minimal amount of panic. His wrists were still manacled by her hands and he was making no move to extricate himself. "I try to go slow, to protect you, and you challenge me in return? That's a dangerous game to play with me, sweetheart."

"You're not dangerous," she breathed. "Not to me."

"No? It depends on your definition." He brought his mouth over her left nipple and gave it one long lick. His voice was even, but his pupils had dilated and blocked out all the green. "Let me show you mine."

Erin moaned as he drew her nipple into his mouth, pulling on it hard. He released it and flicked it with rapid strokes of his tongue, before moving his attention to her other breast. An insane throbbing started in her belly and spread to the flesh between her legs. As if he could sense her sudden burning need for friction, he widened his thighs, forcing hers to do the same. The move left her aching core suspended over his ready bulge, hardness she knew would slake the growing pain if she could only reach it, but she couldn't. Connor's mouth worked her nipples, tugging, sucking, licking, even raking his teeth over the delicate buds.

"God, I've been starving for these perky handfuls. I wanted to sit you down on my lap in that conference room and suck them in front of everyone." He drew quick circles around one nipple. "I thought about how they would shake when I pounded the ever-loving fuck out of you. How they'd look dripping with my come. I'll find out someday soon, won't I, sweetheart?"

"Yes," she sobbed. The tug in her stomach had turned into a

ueeze, making her damp center clench, *clench*. The
lease had never been so overpowering. Her body
er the effort to withstand it. If she could just bring
together or get closer to his lap… "Please, I-I need
your lap—"

"I don't want to return the favor, is that right?" He repeated
her words back to her, before blowing on her nipples, shooting a
bolt of shimmering pleasure to her midsection. "If you sit down
on my hard cock right now, when I can finally taste your tits on
my tongue, I'll come in my jeans, Erin. And we're not allowing
that today. You'll have to suffer with me."

"No," she cried out, but the denial over the thought of his
self-imposed suffering got lost in her desire to climax. One thing
at a time. She needed to assuage the relentless throb…couldn't
think straight until she did. "Connor, I need you so bad."

His answer was to suck hard enough on her nipple that his
cheeks hollowed. And then he pushed his thighs even farther
apart on the seat, leaving her more exposed than before. Erin's
vision dimmed, then went achingly bright. Her heart beat
like a tribal drum, thighs shaking violently. *Need something.
Need something to touch me.* Before she could decipher her
own intentions, she brought Connor's hand between her legs,
shoving it against the damp seam of her patnies and pressing.

Connor's body jolted beneath her, a loud growl ripping
from this throat. The heel of his palm ground tightly against
her, bringing the delicate seam into contact with her clit. "Oh
my *God*. Right there. Please, don't stop. *Please*."

"You're goddamn right this pussy is the first place my hand
touches you. I'm its owner, Erin. That's why it feels so good."
He searched her face from beneath weighted eyelids, rough
groans falling from his lips. "Come on, sweetheart. Work your
sexy pussy on my hand and come in that tight thong. I need it

as bad as you do."

His hand squeezed her. Hard. Erin screamed as the orgasm blasted her, bombarding her from all sides. She tried to ride it out by pumping her hips, but it had a mind of its own and it couldn't be controlled. Connor's mouth sealed over hers and instantly, a thread of calmness pervaded, even as the flesh between her thighs continued to spasm and weep. She focused on his mouth, the confidence in every stroke of his tongue, and it was glorious. But reality started knocking on the door, demanding to be let in. The beautiful afterglow of his touch, his taste started to set off alarm bells. She was getting too complacent. Never secure. Not even with him…security was impossible.

She released his mouth on a gasp, taking in her position in one panicked glance. Pinned to the steering wheel, a big masculine hand between her legs. Keeping her there. The driver's side door being open saved her marginally, but she couldn't prevent her instincts from intruding, making her scramble off his lap into the passenger seat.

"Erin, everything is okay. You're here with me. *Safe.* Always safe."

Don't trust him. They lie. Her fingers hammered at buttons, attempting to lower the window or unlock the door, but it wouldn't work. The car roared to life beneath her and she stamped a hand over her mouth. *Caught. I'm caught.* Cool wind hit her in the face as the window rolled down and she sucked it into her depleted lungs. She buried her face in her hands, peeking out at her escape through parted fingers, trying to focus on it.

"*Look at me.*"

She jerked her attention back to Connor and felt some of the riotous tension flee from her chest. The stark misery etched into his face is what did it. What brought her back. Oh

God, she'd fucked it up. Again. She took the shirt he offered her gently and dragged it over her head, wishing it covered her belly. When she glanced back at Connor, he was no longer in the driver's seat. *Gone. He left. I don't blame him.*

After tugging her jeans back into place, she sank down further into the seat, wishing she could curl up and never move again. Before her pity party could turn into a full-blown barn burner, Connor appeared at the passenger door and opened it only after her nod. "Come on, sweetheart. Let's take the bus home."

CHAPTER TWELVE

Connor had never been out of the Bronx for longer than a couple hours until he enlisted with the navy. At first, it had been because his family couldn't afford vacations, or hell, even a trip to Ellis Island, on his father's disability check. Connor couldn't remember a time when his father hadn't sat on their living room couch, bitter and disgusted with the world. Demanding meals, arguing with his insurance provider on the phone, drinking. Always, the drinking.

His father's penchant for imbibing too much whiskey and turning violent had been the latter reason Connor hadn't strayed too far from the Bronx. Maybe at one time he'd been too young to protect his mother, but around age thirteen, that had drastically changed. Over the course of a summer, he'd outgrown his father in every way possible. He'd started to meet the fists that had been flying at his mother since he could remember with blows of his own. He could still remember the first time he stopped his father's fist in midair and felt bones creak in protest against his palm. Connor felt no shame admitting there had been ample satisfaction in seeing his father's shock.

By age sixteen, Connor thought he'd had his father handled.

There was an unspoken threat that if something happened to his mother ever again, Connor would make him sorry. His father had even cut back on the drinking, even attending the odd AA meeting. It had been a rare snippet of time in their household where it had felt almost peaceful. His mother, Joanna, had started to smile again. Started going back to church since she didn't have to hide the black eyes anymore. He'd gotten comfortable, even dating a couple girls in his sophomore class.

The night his father died, Connor had walked into the house after one such date and stopped cold in the entryway. It wasn't even late, but all the lights were off, except for in the kitchen. He could see it emanating from beneath the still-swinging door. Silent. So silent. He'd known before he even entered the kitchen that he'd find his mother. She sat with her back against the refrigerator door, knees pulled up to her chest, pressing a bag of frozen carrots to her eye.

"How was your date?" she'd asked him, words muffled because of a busted lip. Then she'd promptly burst into tears.

Connor could remember mentally checking out, almost as if there'd been an audible *click*. He'd left his mind in the kitchen and taken his rage-filled body elsewhere. Operating on pure testosterone, he'd stormed back through the house to find his father attempting to sneak down the stairs with his jacket. They had both frozen for a split second, long enough for Connor to communicate what he was going to do. But his father fell out the door first, fast on his feet despite his obvious inebriation. Connor had sprinted after him out onto the sidewalk.

What happened after that remained clear in his head. It might as well have happened last night. Or this morning. It was his greatest shame and yet only the beginning of what the following years would bring.

He turned his attention to Erin, who sat beside him silently, pressed up against the window of the bus. So petite, yet so bold. Some of the time. Her sadness was seeping into his bones with every passing moment, and he needed to fix it. There was a part of him that wanted to shout and put his fist through more glass, but it would only confirm to her that they'd failed. And he didn't think they had. Not by a long shot. How could he when she'd shaken from pleasure on his lap? It was a sight he'd be replaying in his head for a long, *long* time. What happened afterward didn't have to take away from it.

"I want to take you somewhere."

She met his gaze in the window. "Okay."

Just like that. She trusted him not to take her somewhere she'd be uncomfortable. It made him even more determined to prove today had been amazing. Because, Jesus, he was still hard as fuck in his jeans just thinking about it. Suspected he would be for a good, long while. Sex wasn't the answer right now, though, badly as he wanted it to be. Badly as he *needed* her. No, she'd been vulnerable in front of him this afternoon, and for people like them, that was a tough pill to swallow. So he'd make sure she didn't have to do it alone. Even if the thought of exposing himself made his head pound.

"I was discharged from the SEALs for beating a civilian."

Very slowly, Erin straightened. She blinked a few times, as if trying to figure out why he would reveal something like that. On a bus. Out of nowhere. "Why?"

Connor fought the urge to yank her onto his lap, bury his face in her hair while he told the story. "We were on a mission. I can't tell you where." He cleared his throat. "For days, we were in a safe house, waiting for our target. Just...waiting. Not moving or talking. We couldn't."

"I'd go crazy." She frowned. "Crazier, I mean."

He shook his head at her. "My vantage point overlooked a

school. This teacher, she…reminded me of my mother. Always fussing with the kids' hair or making sure they had enough to eat. I didn't need to speak the language to know they all loved her." The view from the window was still painted on his memory. "One day, she wasn't smiling when she got there. She limped into the damn building. During recess, I saw that she had two black eyes. I just knew." He met her gaze, but couldn't hold it. "And it was like seeing my mother like that all over again. I couldn't…separate it."

As if she could sense he needed contact with her, Erin scooted closer and pressed the sides of their bodies together. "Your dad hit your mom," she said, not asking a question.

"Yeah." It felt hard to swallow. "He did. And then he couldn't anymore."

Erin seemed to process that, her face solemn. "What happened to the teacher?"

"We got orders to move that night. Just to the opposite side of the village. Our target had become paranoid and changed locations." He closed his eyes and remembered that night how it happened. "We were on the move when I heard a man yelling. A woman crying. We all wanted to investigate, even if it countermanded orders, but I was the only one who couldn't make a decision one way or another. I didn't think. I just went. I saw him beating my m—the teacher, and I just reacted."

She stroked a hand up the side of his face, into his hair. He leaned into her touch like a lifeline, comforted by the sound of her humming in her throat, her massaging fingers. "The fucker deserved to have the situation reversed, baby. You stood up for that woman when no one else would. I hope she holds on to that when things get rough. I hope she remembers her husband can be beaten just as easily."

He felt weightless. Like he'd been carrying around sandbags

on his shoulders for the last two years and she'd just slashed them open, allowing them to empty their contents onto the ground. Nothing could excuse what he'd done or how he'd gone about it, but knowing she didn't judge him was a potent relief.

"What about your dad?"

For some reason, he felt no anxiety anymore in revealing this to her. Even though he'd never told a single soul in his life, save his mother who was there that night. At that moment, in the back of the dim, rumbling bus, they were the only two people in the world and no ugly memories could touch them. "When I was sixteen, I came home and found my mom. He'd hit her." Connor shook his head. "He'd stopped for a while, straightened up, but…this time was bad. She needed stitches, a cast. It was like he'd decided to make up for lost time." His hand fisted at the image of his mother bleeding on the kitchen floor. "I chased him out of the house and he got hit by a cab."

Her breath hitched. "I'm sorry that happened to you. So sorry."

"That's not the worst part. I was—"

"Glad. You were glad he couldn't hit your mother anymore." She tucked her head into the crook of his shoulder, nuzzling his neck in a way that somehow healed a broken part of him. "You're human. Sometimes advantages present themselves through death. We can't beat ourselves up for recognizing them." A few beats passed before she met his gaze. "You think whatever your father had inside him made its way into you. Maybe it did. But it's no match for you, Connor. It's an ember and you're a beautiful house fire."

Humbled by her vehemence, her *confidence* in him, he didn't know what to say, so he just concentrated on the feel of her. Savored it.

"My mother died, too," she mumbled into his neck. "I'll tell you about it when I can."

"You can't tell me now?"

"No. But only because this was your time to tell a story. We have to let it settle."

Unbelievable. He felt like smiling. After all the ugly shit he'd dredged up. "One more thing, then we'll let it settle."

She mushed her nose against his skin and inhaled. "Fire away."

"Today was incredible, Erin. Maybe we got there because I was, *am*, a jealous man. And maybe it didn't end the way we wanted." He turned his head and kissed the corner of her lips, ordering himself not to do more. Not to sink in the way he craved. Too soon. "But you let me touch you and you're still here. You're fine. We're a damn sight better than we were yesterday. We're going to keep getting better, too. I want you to stop doubting."

"You sound so sure," she murmured.

"You're damn right." Connor released a slow breath. "Sure enough that I'm taking you to meet my mother right now."

Joanna Bannon barely reached Connor's shoulders without her high heels. The last time he'd seen her without them had been the day she was released from the hospital, following his father's final beating. She'd clicked out of her bedroom the next morning in four-inch pumps, hefted her purse over her shoulder, and walked out the door without her sunglasses on. Connor had stood at the window holding a bowl of cereal, watching the neighbors turn and stare. He'd stopped her on the way out to ask if she wanted him to come along, but it had been something she needed to do by herself. To show her battle wounds and proclaim herself a survivor. He hadn't known until that morning what it meant to be proud of someone. The feeling had been like a bowling ball sitting on his chest, but it was a good weight. A welcome weight. He'd wanted someone to feel that way about him.

When he'd been approached by the cops the previous month and asked to cooperate in bringing down his cousin, he'd told them to go fuck themselves. His cousin might be a murderer. A thief. A liar. But in his world, a snitch ranked even lower. But they knew his weak spot. They'd offered to take his mother out of her dilapidated house in the Bronx and move her to a brand-new high-rise in Chicago. They'd offered them both the chance at a new life. Most importantly, they'd secured insurance for his mother that would cover the bulk of her radiation treatments.

He'd been overseas when the doctors diagnosed her with breast cancer. True to form, his mother continued to fight like a warrior and made progress with each treatment. His military benefits had been canceled, however, leaving them holding the bag on her medical expenses. Thus, the NYPD had made him an offer he couldn't refuse. His mother needed the best treatment available and he'd had only one way to get it for her. If his admissions regarding his cousin had saved Bowen's life and earned him a friend—*two* friends including Sera—he considered that an added bonus.

Erin appeared shell-shocked as they walked into his mother's building, but smiled at him gratefully when he automatically bypassed the elevator and went for the stairs. Since his mother lived on the twelfth floor, maybe it would burn off some of his sexual frustration. Maybe, but not fucking likely. Not with Erin's gorgeous ass swaying in front of him with every step she took on the way up. Or the space between her thighs. Thighs that had been splayed over his lap less than an hour ago as he'd sucked her delicious pink nipples.

She tossed a saucy look over her shoulder. "What are you thinking about, baby?"

"Fucking your insane body."

Her steps faltered, but she kept going. On the next landing, she turned and pressed her back against the cinder-block wall. He knew he should bypass her and resist the temptation she presented, but he couldn't. Even looking at her sent his heart rate skyrocketing, made his hands curl into fists with the need to touch. It was more, though. The simplicity of her words on the bus, her acceptance of his past, the vulnerable girl he saw underneath the punk-rock getup. God, he wanted her so bad. All of her. Needed her to be his.

When she snagged a finger into his belt loop and tugged him closer, he growled. "What are you doing?"

Mischief lit her eyes as she smoothed a hand over the growing bulge in his jeans. "I can take care of this for you." Her voice sounded smoky and full in the silent stairwell. "Please, let me."

"No," he panted. "I meant what I said. No relief for me today."

She squeezed him in a devastating rhythm, going up on her tiptoes to whisper in his ear. "How tight do you think my pussy is, Connor?" Her hand gripped him lightly. "This tight?"

"Tighter," he ground out. "I know it's tighter, goddammit."

He gritted his teeth as her grip closed around him *hard*. "Like this, baby?"

"*Yes.*"

Her breath heated his neck. "You just say the word. I'll get on my knees and suck you until you can't stand."

"*Fuck.*" It would be so easy. Push her onto her knees, brace his hands against the wall and fuck her sweet, pouty mouth. He already knew she could take it into her throat. It would round off the sharpest edges of his need, allowing him to concentrate. No, dammit. He wouldn't do it. He gave in too much where Erin was concerned. Gave up too much of the control he *craved*. It was important to him that she realize that when he made a promise, he kept it. If in this case, that promise was to torture her with his own suffering, so be it. Stranger things had happened. "Not today, Erin. No matter how bad I want your mouth on me. I won't do it. Learn to take my words seriously."

Some of her bravado slipped. "I don't like it when you hurt because of me."

"I can take it." He took a deep breath and smiled through the agony. "Besides, I know you're just trying to stall on meeting my mother. Nice try."

"Caught me," she mumbled, pushing off the wall.

Connor forced himself to watch his feet as they continued to the twelfth floor. They exited into the hallway and came to a stop in front of his mother's door. Erin's cheeks were red, but he didn't think it was exertion. More like nerves. Hell, he didn't blame her. It was early in the game to be introducing her to his mother, but then again, they hadn't exactly been following the new couple guidelines, had they? They already lived together, for Chrissake.

"The first time I was in Dade, the television got stuck on one channel for an entire day. Some girl had swallowed the batteries for the remote, so she could get transported to the hospital." She shifted on her feet. "We watched a marathon of *Boy Meets World*. Have you seen that show?"

Connor nodded. "Once or twice."

"I'm just going to pretend I'm Topanga. Cory's parents loved her."

He started to say *to hell with Topanga*, but his mother threw open the door. "My son, I thought that was your voice." She patted the sunflower-patterned scarf on her head and gave Erin a friendly once-over. "You bring home a girl and I get no warning. Were you raised by wolves? I could have baked."

Connor ignored her tongue clucking. "Can we come in, Mom?"

"You've never been one for warm greetings, but I am not even *trying* to hear that noise. Give your mother a hug."

Unable to keep his smile hidden, Connor enveloped his mother with his arms, wishing Erin could experience the same thing without feeling debilitating anxiety. Cheeks flushed with pleasure, Joanna stepped back to let them in. Connor took the opportunity to step between his mother and Erin. Joanna might be perceptive, but he hadn't had a chance to tell her about Erin's aversion to touch yet. A simple handshake could spell disaster.

He guided Erin to the opposite side of the room without touching her. She followed, but her gaze was darting around the apartment, looking for exits. When she finally noticed the fire escape attached to the living room window, her shoulders sagged.

"Mom, this is Erin. Erin—"

"Call me Joanna, please." She clicked across the floor in her heels, pausing on the threshold to the kitchen. "I have lemonade and tap water. Yes, I'm a shitty host."

Erin fidgeted. "Nothing for me, thanks."

"You'll have lemonade," Joanna decided. "You need something to do with your hands."

When his mother disappeared into the kitchen, Connor turned to Erin, surprised to find her studying him. "This is what they offered you, isn't it? A place for your mother."

He nodded once and glanced away, taking in the renovated apartment, so unlike the shabby house in which he'd spent his youth. "Cancer treatment."

Her eyes softened. Before he could ready himself, she curled her fingers in his collar and tugged him down for a soft kiss. "I'm sorry I tried to blow you in the stairwell," she whispered against his lips.

"Jesus." A pained laugh escaped him. "Please don't apologize for something like that ever again."

"Okay."

They shared a smile. He couldn't seem to break eye contact with her. She seemed just as content to search his face. For what, he didn't know. In his peripheral vision, he noticed that his mother had reentered the room. How long had she been standing there? Reluctantly, he straightened, turning his attention to his mother, who had a strange expression on her face.

She visibly shook herself and came forward to hand them their lemonade. Erin cupped the bottom of the glass to avoid their fingers brushing and murmured her thanks.

"So, do youse two work together?" Joanna asked, her familiar Bronx accent in full effect. "Let me guess, Erin is the queen in your deck of wild cards."

Erin's brow wrinkled. "Your what?"

"That's what I've been calling it," Connor explained while tugging at the collar of his shirt. "Since we're all…"

"Cuckoo bananas?"

"Different from one another," he amended. "Yeah, Mom, we work together."

Joanna took a sip from her own lemonade and Connor could see the wheels turning in her head. If Erin worked with him, she had to be a criminal. He could sense Erin's discomfort and knew she'd picked up on the subtext behind her mother's question. God, maybe he'd overstepped by bringing her here. She'd had a hard enough day without this criminal version of

Meet the Parents.

Before he could deflect any more questions in her direction, Erin squared her shoulders. "It's okay to ask me what I did. I can't even say I paid for my crimes, because I didn't. I got out of prison faster than a whore in a convent." She drained her lemonade. "I'm sorry. I'm not Topanga. Your son deserves a Topanga."

His mother arched a meticulously plucked eyebrow at him. "Who the hell is Topanga?"

"It's not important," he said firmly. Christ, this conversation had gotten away from him. "Neither is what Erin did. *She's* important. That's it."

"Fine." His mother held up both hands. "Keep all the fun details to yourself. Don't entertain a single woman with something interesting for once." She sucked her teeth. "All I got is Dr. Oz, son. You can't blame me for wanting the gossip. Damn."

Erin's lips twisted, but Connor could see the smile underneath. "You want to hear about the time I rented a limousine to be my getaway driver?"

Joanna leaned forward. "Now we're talking."

CHAPTER THIRTEEN

Erin glared at Connor from across the squad meeting, twirling a Bic lighter between her fingers. She'd purposefully sat as far away from him as possible. His day of zero pleasure had passed and he still wouldn't give in. Last night after they'd returned from Joanna's apartment, she and Connor had traded bedrooms so she could be near the fire escape. Every time they'd passed in the hallway while transferring their things, she'd brushed a hand over his ass or planted kisses on his neck. *Any minute now*, she'd thought, *he's going to beg for me. Beg for me to take away the visible ache in his pants.*

Nope. Nothing.

So she'd slipped into bed behind him one minute past midnight and trailed her hand down his stomach, her palm already lathered with lotion. Her body had been humming with the anticipation of stroking his heavy length, feeling his big body shudder against her when he finally came. She thought he'd welcome her, welcome the pleasure he so obviously needed. Instead, he'd turned over onto his stomach and growled at her to go back to bed.

This morning, he'd been dressed and ready to leave before

she'd even stumbled out of her bedroom. He'd handed her a cup of coffee. And winked.

Someone really needed to remind him he lived with a pyromaniac with a social disorder.

It probably didn't help her street cred that she'd failed to shock his mother last night. She even kind of sensed that Joanna...liked her. As if her son bringing home a convicted felon was right up there with winning the lottery. She'd sensed no judgment. Only a desire to know her better. She couldn't really describe how that made her feel. Nervous she'd end up being a letdown. Kind of hoping she *would* be so she could pretend not to give a shit. Relating to other people whom she didn't stand to gain anything from monetarily was confusing as all get-out. Especially when the man she was *doing* it for refused to let her touch him—

Ohhhh. Her teeth clenched. *Clever motherfucker.*

Giving her a taste of her own medicine, was he? That kind of...hurt. The best part of meeting Joanna had been the way Connor looked at her afterward. Like he wasn't ashamed or regretful over bringing her home to Mom, the way she'd assumed he would be. Knowing he'd been plotting to turn the tables on her sucked. Hard. It made her trust in him waver ever so slightly. God, in the last twenty-four hours she'd dealt with so many unfamiliar feelings, her periscope had sunk below the surface. She couldn't see where the hell she was headed anymore.

One thing she could do and do effectively was formulate a counterattack. As soon as they got out of this pain-in-the-ass meeting, she was going to institute it. She'd already gotten a head start by wearing the shortest skirt in her closet. As Derek called the meeting to a start, she hopped up on a waist-high file cabinet and crossed her legs, pretending not to notice Connor shift in his seat.

"Thank you all for being on time. Isn't progress a beautiful thing?" Derek scanned the room, his mouth tightening when his gaze landed on Austin. He looked like he'd been out the night before, his head buried in his hands as if they were holding his skull together. Polly sat beside him shaking her head primly. Derek turned his attention to Sera. "How was your first day at campaign headquarters yesterday?"

"Pretty uneventful. Stark didn't make an appearance." She consulted her notes. "There was one thing, though. Around two o'clock, a silver Hummer pulled up to the curb and honked. One of the staffers ran out and handed something to the driver. I couldn't see through the tinted windows, but I got the license plate number."

"Great." Derek waited as Sera handed him a piece of ripped-out notebook paper. "I'll run this back at the station. If it happens again today, I want you to follow him, Bowen."

Bowen's smile was stiff. "As long as there's someone to take my place watching Sera."

"I wouldn't leave her exposed," Derek assured him, showing a rare patience. "Polly, did you get anything useful from Stark's financials?"

"Other than him having an expensive appreciation for European orgy porn? Not really." Her voice was serene, as if she weren't admitting to hacking into a man's bank records. "He's got his money somewhere else. Tied up in assets listed under a different name...maybe an offshore account. I'm working on it."

"Keep working." Derek aimed his pen at Erin. She propped her hands under her chin and fluttered her eyelashes. The captain only shook his head. "I know it was a long shot, Erin, but did you have any luck finding out how May weaseled his way out of Cook?"

"Yessir, I did. But before I begin, I'd like to request coffee at these meetings." She flicked the lighter on, drawing an invisible pattern in the air. "Maybe some doughnuts. Aren't you cops lousy with doughnuts? Sharing is caring."

Derek ignored everything but her first sentence. "Did you say you found out how May got out of Cook?"

"Everyone doubts a blonde." She refused to look at Connor, even though his gaze burned into her thighs, her face. "Okay, my *ass*-essment would be that May had help. The kind you buy with lots of crispy bills."

"We already thought that might be the case."

"Yes, but did you know May cut through three separate fences with a pair of bolt cutters?" She leaned back on the file cabinet, supporting herself with both palms. "It's not easy to come by tools like that inside unless you have a serious connection. He hadn't been there long enough to make friends like that without a little help. The kind of help that cuts electricity to the entire prison exactly when you're making a break for it."

"Power outage?" Derek narrowed his eyes. "So he went through perimeter fencing without it being caught on the security feed. Why didn't the guards on watch sound the alarm?"

"They were a little occupied preventing a riot. Anytime the routine is thrown into jeopardy, all hell breaks loose." She noticed Polly's subtle nod, before the brunette went back to casting censure at Austin. "Cell doors were left open, rooms full of prisoners were in the dark with no supervision. There was panic. May had about a twenty-minute window to cut through the fence." Erin shrugged. "My source didn't know how May came by the bolt cutters, but it would have been easy for a guard to leave them by 'accident.'"

Derek tipped up his chin. "Speaking of sources, who was yours?"

"I didn't get his name, but I stole his wallet." She reached into her tattered canvas bag, closed her hand around the leather billfold, and tossed it to the captain. "There's probably some ID inside."

"You got close enough to put your hand in his pocket?" Connor's voice was deceptively quiet. "Left that part out, didn't you?"

Bowen whistled quietly through his teeth. "Suddenly feeling pretty good about Sera working in an office."

"At least *someone* let me touch him." Erin swung her legs off the file cabinet and stomped to her feet. "Boyfriends are *bullshit*. Can I go now?"

"No." Derek didn't lift his head as he riffled through the burly sap's wallet. "I'm going to need to bring him in to confirm the story. Be sure he wasn't just making it up to impress you."

Austin finally lifted his head. "You know, we're all failing to recognize the real tragedy here. If *I* could disguise myself as a hot girl, we'd have this case solved by tea time."

"Don't call her hot." Connor leaned forward. "Don't even look."

Austin rolled his eyes and went back to holding his skull intact.

Derek eyeballed what looked to be a driver's license. "Where did you meet the source?"

"Hanover's. It's a dive around the corner from the prison, so bring Purell." She picked up her purse, not sparing Connor a glance when he stood. "Oh. I called the three closest fencing companies near Cook. The last one, Windy City Fences, confirmed that they sent out a technician to repair the fence the day after May escaped. Just in case he denies the story."

The captain looked impressed for the first time since she'd met him. "Nice work."

She scowled at the warmth she encountered at the unexpected praise. Too many feelings were being leveled in her direction, and she needed a break until she learned how to handle them all. Pretending not to see Sera's smile and Bowen's thumbs-up, she turned on her booted heel and ran up the stairs.

Before she could clear the exit, Connor was blocking her path. "Hey. Wait just a damn minute."

"No, *you* wait." She shoved him, but he didn't move an inch. "I know I have a problem. Believe me, I'm aware. But *fuck you* for punishing me with it."

His eyebrows drew together. "What are you talking about?"

Erin laughed without humor. "You can't touch me, so I can't touch you either?" She was furious at the pressure behind her eyes. "I can't believe you turned this into a game."

The color drained from his face. "*No.* That wasn't my intention."

"Get out of my way. I need to *move.*"

"Listen to me first. You'll kill me if you walk away crying."

"I'm not crying."

"Okay." His throat worked. Erin wanted to slap him for looking so devastated. It would be so much easier to block everything out and be mad as hell for a while if he didn't look like he wanted to sweep her up into his arms. "It feels good to be in control of something, Erin. Even if it hurts. I'm not used to having no plan. No power. It keeps me sane." He dragged in a breath. "It's a need I have and I found a way channel it, since I can't touch you the way I need. *Yet.* Hurting you didn't enter the equation. It never would."

She had the crazy urge to jump into his arms and see if she could stand it. The fact that she could be this mad and still crave the feel of him disgusted her. Another emotion to add to the Molotov cocktail exploding inside her. "*Dammit.* I'm not having an easy time with any of this."

"I know. I *know*." He dropped his head so he could speak at her ear. His breath on her neck sent a shiver racing down her back. It sounded shallow, urgent. "Come home with me now. We'll make each other feel so good, sweetheart. If you want to cuff me to the bed, I swear I'll fucking let you. Torture me any way you want, just don't cry."

"I don't *want* to feel good right now. The hurt is reminding me why I don't trust anyone." She booted him in the shin, but his jaw merely went tight. "Move out of my way or I'll just find another way out, Connor. There are three exits on this level, all of them with street access."

"Tell me you'll come home today or I'll have to follow you." His gaze tracked over her like he was memorizing her clothing, her body, her face. "Give me that, okay? I give you space and you give me the chance to apologize. I used your weakness against you, but I didn't mean to. I'm sick over this, Erin."

"*Fine.*" She refused to acknowledge the stark relief that she had a plan to see him again. God, this was so damn *complicated*. "Life is just a series of prisons anyway, right? If I moved out of yours, I'd just get locked up in another one eventually."

He didn't move a muscle as she skirted past him and launched herself into the daylight.

Erin had no idea how long she sat in the booth at Denny's, turning piles of shredded paper napkins into mini bonfires, but when Polly sat down across from her, she guessed it had been quite a while. She ignored Polly's quick intake of breath when she snuffed out the flames with her palm.

Streetlights had lit up outside, illuminating the table and the dark-haired girl who worked with her and lived across the hall, but whom she knew nothing about. It circled her thoughts back around to square one, reminding her that she knew nothing. Everything was a mystery. Nothing was solid or permanent. Weird how that used to comfort her. Now it made her nauseous, jumpy.

"Listen up, O'Dea. I can tell you want to be alone, but I found this place first." Polly straightened her silverware with a dainty finger. "If you want to be alone, find your own fucking hideout."

"It's a Denny's," Erin said without lifting her head. "Look around. They turn away no one."

"Yes, but it's an unspoken honor system. I have squatter's rights." She sniffed. "You didn't even find a different table."

"Take it up with management."

Polly snorted, shifting in her seat. "That was pretty impressive this morning in the meeting. I think you might be Derek's new favorite. And I'm *always* the favorite."

Erin batted her eyelashes. "You're *Austin's* favorite."

The other girl narrowed her gaze. "If so, it's because I'm the last available female on the squad. I like my men a little more discerning."

"Nah. He'd go for me or Sera, too, if he wanted to." Another pancake decimated. "I doubt your Facebook relationship status means dick to him."

A smile flirted with the edges of Polly's mouth. "Solid point. Still not interested."

Erin shrugged.

"So." Polly picked up a menu and flipped it open on the table. "Trouble in paradise with the dishonored SEAL? After moving in together the same day you met. Imagine that."

"Are you trying to annoy me just to get your table back? It might work."

"No, I'm genuinely curious." The waitress sidled up to the table. Without breaking eye contact with Erin, Polly stabbed her finger down onto the picture of a fruit salad and the woman left. "The whole situation might have been rushed and…unusual, to put it bluntly. But you and Connor…it's like watching two people walk toward each other from opposite ends of a tightrope. It's intriguing."

Not a bad comparison. Except Erin's side of the tightrope was on fire and rapidly fraying at the edges. She cast a look out the window, but couldn't get past her reflection. Exhaustion lined her features. Proof of her restless night. More than that, she looked on edge. She knew why, too. Connor's presence had become a comfort and a source of hurt at the same time. Just like fire, he burned and enticed her, drawing her closer despite the promise of pain. How she could yearn for his company even knowing that at the end of their encounters, only one of them could walk away completely sated, leaving the other anxious. Unhappy. Wanting to please the other, but incapable of doing so.

Her reflection wavered and she caught sight of Sera walking down the sidewalk. Alone. She'd never once seen her new teammate without Bowen at her side. The graceful way she usually carried herself was absent, replaced with a heavy tread and slumped shoulders.

Polly hummed and followed her line of vision. "It would appear you're not the only one with man troubles."

"I don't feel like being one-upped. Let's ignore her."

"I was planning on doing that anyway."

They watched as Sera dropped down onto a bench and

scrubbed her hands down her face. A man passing by on the sidewalk tossed his Big Gulp into the trash can beside Sera, sending liquid splashing out to spray her. She didn't even flinch.

Polly cursed.

Erin slid out of the booth. "Fuck it. We'll find a new place tomorrow."

"We could use a buffer anyway."

Erin marched out the Denny's and stopped in front of Sera where she sat on the bench. Apart from the tensing of Sera's shoulders, she showed no reaction to Erin's approach. *Damn. Must have been some fight.* Erin was surprised to feel a pang of sadness. Bowen and Sera had kind of given her hope that total dedication to another person was possible. "So, anyway, Polly and I are in Denny's if you want to come in and shoot the shit."

"No, thanks."

This *is going well.* "Look. I didn't spend a lot of time in the high school cafeteria, but this is basically an invite to sit with the cool kids."

Sera stared straight ahead. "I went to boarding school. The cool kids were assholes."

That surprised a laugh out of Erin. "Oh, just come in. They love people with stained shirts at Denny's."

Her lips twitched, but she went right back to looking sad. She gave Erin a considering look and stood with a shrug. "Fine. I need some caffeine."

Erin led the way back into the restaurant and they joined Polly at the booth. Erin took the seat closest to the aisle so she wouldn't get boxed in, leaving Sera by the window. Polly stirred her coffee, looking bored. "God, I've never been happier to be single."

Sera lifted an eyebrow. "Why is that?"

"You two look miserable."

"Bowen asked me to marry him." Sera crossed her legs and wedged herself into the corner of the booth. Her gaze bounced around the table, reminding Erin of Bowen. Obviously he'd started to rub off on his girlfriend. Or potential fiancée, as the case seemed to be. "I have no reason to be miserable."

Erin hid her goofy smile. The Virgin Mother and the gangster were getting married. She wanted to toss sugar packets up into the air like confetti. Which was odd, since she'd never given a shit about this kind of thing before. Other people's relationships. What they represented. It really shouldn't mean a damn to her. "What did you say?"

"I said yes. *Of course*, I said yes." Sera closed her eyes briefly. "Then I realized I had no one to tell. No one, no family, to be happy for me."

Polly saluted her coffee. "Hooray. Mazel. Felicitations."

Sera ignored Polly and flipped open a menu.

Erin gave the dark-haired hacker a sour look. "If it makes you feel any better, people usually just pretend to be happy for other people. They don't really mean it."

"No. That doesn't make me feel better."

Erin shrugged. "Worth a shot."

"So." Polly gave a heavy sigh, probably annoyed at having been dragged into a conversation. "You have no family?"

Sera shook her head. "None that I can call. No one I would invite to a wedding." She smiled her thanks at the waitress when she arrived with coffee. They sat quietly for a few minutes before Sera seemed to realize they were both staring at her, waiting for her to continue. "I don't know if you've noticed, but Bowen is a little intense."

"Yup."

"Yeah, I picked up on that," Polly confirmed.

Sera breathed a laugh. "Anyway, he didn't understand why

I was upset. Didn't understand why I wasn't thrilled over a city hall wedding tomorrow afternoon."

Polly leaned forward. "*Tomorrow?*"

"Yeah." Sera took a shaky sip of her coffee. "I saw this coming. He needs to know we're permanent and there's nothing I can say to reassure him. It has to be everything. Words, papers. Rings. I want that, too. I want him forever. It's just all so fast and I...I just wish my mother were around to talk it out with." She frowned. "So strange, since we weren't even close."

Erin shook the weird urge to put her arms around Sera. Too risky if she tried to hug her back. Which led to thoughts of Connor. Of his reaction when she tried to move out. How he'd begged her to come home tonight. She understood his passionate nature, because it existed inside her as well. What was he doing right now? Was he staring at the door waiting for her to walk through it? Thinking of him made every part of her ache, so she focused on Sera. "Your family isn't the one marrying him. You are." When Sera looked at her thoughtfully, Erin shifted on the plastic seat. "Who's going to be the witness?"

"Connor." Sera watched her closely. "Bowen asked him this morning."

"Oh."

Sera nodded toward Polly, but kept her eyes trained on Erin. "She implied you have man troubles, too. I guess I've been distracted by Bowen and the new job. Is it Connor?"

Uncomfortable with the turn the conversation had taken, straight into girl chat, Erin shrugged. "He buys me orange juice."

Polly snorted. "Don't make him *work* for it or anything."

"Oh, he's working for it," she muttered. "Believe me."

Sera stirred another packet of sugar into her coffee. "We spent some time together back in Brooklyn. When I was undercover."

Every muscle in Erin's body went stiff, her pulse skittering.

Jealousy. Thick and humid, like the lick of a flame. "What do you mean by time?"

"He was shot while I was undercover. His crew wouldn't take him to the hospital, knowing it would draw attention." She sighed after a sip of coffee. "So I nursed him back to health."

Shot in Brooklyn? Hadn't he told her he'd gotten the wound overseas? No, she realized. He'd distracted her without giving an actual answer, damn him. Polarized by the image of Connor with blood pouring from his strong body fought against jealousy that still burned hot. She didn't like the idea of any woman's hands on him. It should have been her taking care of him. No one else. No one else ever again.

The need to see him whole and powerful made her want to sprint out of Denny's at full speed, but a dose of anger kept her rooted to the seat. "Who shot him? I'd like to know now-ish, please."

Sera gave her a sympathetic look. "We don't know. If it makes you feel better, the bullet was meant for someone else. He just got in the way."

Rage clawed at her. *This is how he feels about my stepfather being out there, walking around free.* Dammit. She had no place to channel the anger. It needed somewhere to go. "Did something happen between you two?" The question shot from her mouth like a cannon. Wouldn't be contained. She'd come to this stupid restaurant to clear her head, but it felt ready to burst now.

"You might want to lie," Polly said to Sera.

"Nothing ever happened. *Ever.* He's like a brother." Sera shook her head. "It was always Bowen for me. He's…"

"What?" Erin asked without looking at her.

"Bowen *is* my family." Sera's eyes filled with tears. "Excuse me. I have to go."

Erin scooted out of the booth quickly before Sera could touch her. She and Polly watched in silence as Sera jogged down the restaurant aisle and out the door. Going to her man. It was so obvious. Exactly like Erin needed to do. She needed to see Connor. With the image of him shot still fresh in her mind, the day she'd spent away from him felt criminal. For people like them, time was precious and she was squandering it. Like a coward.

She wouldn't be a coward anymore.

Touching might be painful for her. But the pain would prove she was real. It would prove that despite what she'd been through, she'd come out on the other side. Battle-scarred, but *alive*. She never felt more alive than when she was touching Connor. If she took a leap of faith, if she let him touch her, would it magnify that feeling or crush it?

Only one way to find out.

"I have to go, too."

"Aaand I have my table back." Polly flickered a serious glance at her. "Hey, uh…good luck."

"Thanks."

She would need it.

CHAPTER FOURTEEN

For what seemed like the hundredth time that hour, Connor paused in his research, swearing he heard booted footsteps coming down the hall. After a few seconds of hopeful silence, he went back to reading the web page he'd pulled up on his laptop screen and resumed scribbling notes. At first, he'd started researching Erin's condition as a way to distract himself. If he could focus on something else, maybe he'd have a chance in hell of staying put. Not slamming out of the apartment to walk the streets shouting for her like a goddamn lunatic. At least, that's how it had started.

About five minutes after typing "fear of being touched" into the search engine, he'd realized this was where his time could be better spent. Erin had said she would come home, and he had to trust her on that. He'd abused her trust, albeit on accident, and now he would atone. Based on what he'd learned since sitting down in front of the laptop, he had a lot of fucking atoning to do. Yeah, his using her condition against her might have been inadvertent, but it didn't excuse his withholding himself. She'd found a way to ease her demons and he'd yanked it away. Remembering the way he'd turned her away last night made him sick to his stomach. An empty triumph that had only succeeded in pushing her away after they'd taken two steps forward. After she'd charged straight at him and held him, only seconds having passed since he'd shattered a window with his fist.

It had felt so good, just to regain some vestige of control after losing it at the parking structure, but it hadn't been worth it. Not even close. He doubted Erin even knew what she was dealing with. Haphephobia. The fear of being touched that often presented itself after a traumatic event. Touch from another human being often felt like fire burning the sufferer's skin. The fact that she got pleasure from contact with his body was a rare miracle and he'd squandered it. God, if he could go back to last night, he'd let her hand wring every ounce of pleasure from his body and beg for more. He'd been a selfish motherfucker.

So he couldn't touch her with his hands. Yet. Would he trade the connection he had with Erin for someone who allowed his touch, but didn't make him *feel* anything? No way in hell. Now he had to prove that to her. If it meant setting aside his overwhelming compulsion to pin her down and put his mark on her, if it meant putting himself through torture by going slow, he would do it. A significant factor in his thirst for control came from satisfying the woman. For the first time ever, the woman was *his* woman. Knowing he was the only one Erin could stand to touch might just be the most powerful piece of control he'd ever experienced. Too bad it had taken her almost walking out on him twice to figure it out. Now that he knew, his veins were pumped full of might.

Touch me, woman. If she walked in the door right now, he just might shout it at her.

But not tonight. Tonight they would talk. If a traumatic event had led to her phobia, he wanted to know every last detail, even if it might send him off on a rampage to avenge her. At least it would be out in the open. At least he would know what memories they needed to conquer. After he knew the full scope of what they were dealing with, he would take the steps to ensure her stepfather couldn't hurt her. When Erin had run out on him this morning, he'd been restless with the urge to do something proactive to help her, but he had nothing to go on yet. So he'd settled for research. For now.

Footsteps.

Connor pinched the bridge of his nose and tried to ignore the sound. It was just his imagination. She would come home when she was ready. He couldn't conjure her up by his will alone.

When the door opened, his hand clenched so tight that the pencil between his fingers snapped. She stood outlined in the entrance looking so heartbreakingly stunning, he couldn't form words. Her eyes were heavy with so many emotions, he couldn't capture them all before she was striding toward him. Sex pounded in his ears. There was no other description for it. Her hips snapped side to side with every step, breasts swaying beneath her shirt. Erin always threw off sexual energy in waves, but she'd turned it up, daring him not to look at her tight thighs, her exposed belly, her parted mouth.

Talk to her. You have to talk. Out of self-preservation, Connor stood and started to put some distance between them. But he stopped. He couldn't reject her touch again. He *wouldn't*. Not when she needed it. Jesus, he needed it, too. With her standing in front of him, the desire was practically eating him alive, stripping him down until all that existed was her first touch. Where it would land. How it would wrangle the chaos inside, getting him hard at the same time. How she'd get aroused just by pressing her hands to his skin.

First, he needed to apologize. Needed her to know he understood what she went through on a daily basis now and things would be better. He'd make it so. "I'm sorry, Erin. I didn't know."

Her steps didn't slow. "Know what?"

"What it feels like." He swallowed the knot in his throat. "When someone touches your pretty skin. My frustration is nothing compared to that. Nothing. I'll never use it to hurt you."

She came to a stop, her booted toes bumping his. "But I was counting on it."

Confusion hit him. "What?"

The seductive way she looked up at him through her eyelashes caused base lust to swirl in his gut. Christ. What the hell was her game? Keeping her gaze locked on him, Erin started to undo his belt buckle. "I want you to fuck me, Connor."

His cock swelled so severely, he groaned through his teeth. "You don't mean that. It's too fast." He watched her lower the zipper of his jeans and reach inside, palming his erection through his boxer briefs. *Oh God*, it felt so fucking perfect, it took all his willpower not to thrust shamelessly into her grip. "Put your hands all over me, Erin. I'll never ask you to stop again. But I won't hurt you. I refuse."

"Please." She went up on her toes and nipped at his neck. "I'm feeling brave. Don't tell me no. I might not feel this brave tomorrow."

"There's no ru—" She found his mouth at the same time her hand started to stroke his cock, making his breath shudder out against her lips. "I don't want you brave. I want you ready."

"I'm both." A small sound escaped her. "What if I lost you?"

That plea had the effect of an air horn going off. He pulled back from her next attempt at a kiss. "Jesus, Erin. You think you'll lose me if we don't fuck?"

"No." Her eyes were mesmerizing, her voice velvet. "You were shot and I wasn't there. Someone else fixed you when it should've been me. I need to feel you alive, moving inside me. Maybe it's too late, but this is my way of healing you. Healing me. I need that, Connor. Give it to me."

His insides felt razed, his chest wide open. Resisting wasn't possible. She needed him, and he had only one goal in his life at that moment. Giving Erin what she needed. If someone tried to take that honor away from him, he would kill them where they stood. And sweet hell, he wanted to fuck her. His body was crying out for the comfort of her pussy, the sound of her moans. Minutes ago, he'd sworn he could live without sex as long as necessary, but now, as she reached into his underwear and squeezed his throbbing arousal, he couldn't sustain his willpower. All he could hope was that he did this right. Took her in a way that wouldn't cause her too much pain. Or any at all, if he could help it.

"Go face the window. Brace your hands on the frame."

Giving the order felt good. No, not good. *Amazing.* But he needed to focus on her. Every breath, every movement would be important. He'd damaged her trust today, yet somehow he'd earned another chance and he wouldn't screw it up. If she needed to stop, he'd force himself to stop even if it killed him. As Erin went to the fire escape window and did as he asked, Connor let himself feast on the sight of her. That skirt, the one that had driven him crazy in the meeting this morning, molded to her ass like wet leather. His hunger demanded he rip it off, bend her over, and thrust home, finally take what had felt like *his* since day one. No, she *was* his. His to keep and care for. He needed to keep himself in check.

If you want to rule her world, learn to rule yourself first.

Connor came up behind her and placed his hands just

below hers on the window frame. He didn't allow their bodies to touch. Not yet. He kept his gaze trained on her reflection as he breathed, slow and easy on her neck. Her eyes closed, head falling to the side, the tension visibly draining from her body. She pressed her ass into his lap, but he didn't move, just let her circle those hips against his aching cock. No moving until she was ready.

"I'm not going to use my hands this time, so I need your help. I need you to wet your pussy up for my cock. Can you do that for me, sweetheart?"

With a gasp, one of her hands dropped from the window to trail up her thigh. "How can you be inside me without touching me?"

Dammit, he wanted to touch her so fucking bad. "I'm going to give it to you right where you need it, Erin. When we're finished getting you ready, you'll be begging for inches. I'm going to give you ten. Right between your fuck-me thighs." He growled as her hand disappeared underneath her skirt. His mouth watered at the thought of removing her shirt, baring her delicious, pink-tipped breasts, but he wouldn't allow her naked in front of the window. There might be a method to his madness, but it didn't involve passing strangers seeing what was meant for his eyes alone. "Pet yourself, Erin. That's what I would do. I'd stroke your pussy with my fingers through that silk. Nice and gentle. I'd give it a soft kiss and apologize for the fact that I'm about to destroy it."

The remaining hand she had braced on the window frame went white-knuckled, her lips falling open on a moan. "Connor…"

"Stroke yourself like you've been told. I need you ready." He dipped his knees slightly and dragged his hard dick up between her ass cheeks on the way back up. "Feel that? You're not ready for it yet. That's a problem when I'm aching to fuck you. Isn't it, sweetheart?"

"Y-yes."

He picked up on the hesitation in her voice and forced himself to calm down. There was no way to control the words falling from his mouth, but his actions were his own. "Close your eyes and imagine it's my hand reaching inside your underwear." He hummed low in his throat. "Ah, Jesus, sweetheart. You're drenched. That's what happens, isn't it? When you know you're about to be filled up so damn tight. You'll go up on your toes and tilt your ass trying to give me more room, but I'll already have taken every last bit. That'll only happen if you're ready, Erin. Are you with me?"

"*Yes*." Her body shuddered against his. "Tell me what to do."

His knees nearly buckled under the weight of that permission. It was made ever stronger by the sureness in her voice. She was right there with him, facing her fear. It made him want to kiss every inch of her, tell her how proud she made him, but their mutual needs trumped everything at that moment. "Dip your middle finger inside, right where my cock is going to sink in, wide and deep. Use all that slickness to tease your clit. Tease it until your pussy starts to want more."

In the window, he watched her hand move beneath her skirt, watched her thighs widen, her eyes glaze over. He couldn't help but press his hard lap to her backside so he could feel every writhe of her hips, every tremor that went through her body. He breathed into her ear, telling her how good she felt, how pleased her wetness made him. "I want more," she finally whimpered.

"How much more?" he demanded.

"All of it. You. *Please*."

"Soon." It was becoming exceedingly hard to keep his hands glued to the window frame. His mind screamed at him to lift her skirt and work his lust out. Fuck her until she couldn't remember life before he was inside her body. *Pull back. Don't ruin it.* "Three fingers, Erin. We're almost there. Finger yourself like a good girl who's about to be turned bad." Very slowly, he removed his hands from the window frame and unbuckled his pants, desperate to free his heavy erection. Keeping his attention on Erin, he dispensed with his clothing in record time. The chance of someone seeing Erin naked through the window might make him see red, but he had no such modesty when it came to himself.

Erin sucked in a breath when he rose again, towering behind her in the glass wearing no clothes. Her thighs started to shake around her hand. "Connor, please."

"Did you use all three fingers?"

"Yes. *Yes.*"

"Good." He fisted his cock, pumped the hard flesh, and released a ragged groan that wouldn't be stopped. Two days wasn't usually that long a time for him to go without relief. But it was now. Now that Erin kept him aroused around the clock, just by existing. "Take off your panties and bend the fuck over."

She moved quickly, dragging the silk down her legs and planting her hands on the sill. Her pussy peeked out at him from beneath the hem of her skirt, just a flash of pink, but it was enough to send hot, mind-blowing lust tearing through his system. It felt primal, ancient. *I'm about to claim my woman.*

He circled her clit with the head of his cock. "We both took the full physical to get this job. We're both clean. Are you on the pill?"

"The shot." A shaky exhale. "I'm on the shot."

Wet, smooth female flesh. *Erin's* flesh. "You want me bareback, beautiful?"

"Yes, please."

Fuck yes. Nothing between them. He would have resented anything that kept him from feeling all of her. Connor inhaled deeply, grappling for control. Somewhere deep down, he found a reserve of restraint and delved into it. He led his cock to her entrance and encountered the source of her perfect heat for the first time. When she whimpered and arched her back, his careful discipline almost fled. He grabbed on to the final thread in his possession and thrust deep.

Jesus. Jesus. So hot and tight. Can't stay still. Have to stay still and make sure she's all right. How can I stop? Want to fuck her. Need to fuck her. Now.

Erin's stillness cut through the raging impulses commanding him to take. Take hard. He searched the reflection of her face and found her eyes closed tight, her hands trembling on the window still. *Not okay. She's not okay.*

"Sweetheart, listen to me." His voice didn't even sound like him, but thankfully her eyes opened anyway. Trained on him with a trust and hope that called to the protector inside of him. *Her* protector. "Focus on the fire escape. Look. It's just beyond the window. How many steps would it take you to get to the street?"

She licked her lips. "Twenty-two."

"That's right." Her inner walls clenched around him and he bit back a curse. There was nothing he could do to stop his hips from rolling, pushing deeper. She moaned, but the sound of pleasure was tinged with an apprehension that tore at his chest. "Erin, I want to be your escape. Can you let me be that for a little while?"

"What if I can't?"

"Then I stop." His words were spoken beside her ear, concise and firm. "No matter what. No matter how far we get, I'll stop. You're more important."

Their gazes held in the window for a few beats, the uncertainty draining from her expression to be replaced with awe. She pulled away slightly, then worked herself back down on his cock with a gasp. "Oh my God, Connor," she choked out. "You feel so good."

His hands squeezed the wooden frame until blisters abraded his palms. *Don't touch, just feel her. Let her feel you.* Already, he wanted to erupt, could have come just from the sight of her gorgeous, upturned ass and splayed thighs, so he closed his eyes. Big mistake. It only amplified the sensation of her slowly riding up and down his length, testing him, getting used to his size. It only made her little sobs of surprise and pleasure sound like cannons firing off around him. He couldn't stand still anymore; the animal he kept leashed inside wanted to roar to life and take over.

"Are you ready for the rest of it yet?" he rasped.

She slid halfway down his cock and back up. "The rest of it?"

Connor growled as he plunged the entire way inside her. "Goddammit, Erin. That's what you asked for, now you'll take it." He pulled out and drove home again, drowning in her cries. "Jesus, you fuck-tight girl, I can't even move. Open your legs wider for it."

Erin only hesitated a second before sliding her feet wider on the floor. "Don't stop. Don't stop."

"I'll only stop if you ask me to." He gave her a hard thrust. "But I'm going to make sure you don't want to. Going to make sure you come so hard you crawl back *begging* for it next time."

With his hands braced on the window frame and Erin bent forward, the only part of their bodies that touched was where they connected. It didn't feel like it, though. Christ, not at all. If she was plastered against him, he couldn't have felt any closer.

Her gaze found his in the window as he increased the rhythm of his drives. She looked overcome, delirious. It made him want to complete that phase and send her straight into oblivion.

"*Harder*," she screamed. "Please."

Afraid if he went hard as he could, her head would go through the window, he gave her a sharp order to stand up. As soon as her back hit his chest, he walked her to the wall just beside the window and shoved her up against it, his cock still buried deep inside her. "You're still right beside the window, sweetheart. You just have to say the word."

"Okay." She released a shaky breath, shifted her hips. "M-move, Connor."

He laid his palms flat on the wall so she could see them, let his mouth hover just above her ear. "You feel how hard you made my dick? It's been craving this tight, wet heaven between your legs." He pushed high and deep, bringing her up on her toes. "Tell me it's mine. Tell me it's. All. *Mine*."

She clawed at the wall, thighs writhing against his. "Yours," she grated. "*Yours*."

"That's it, sweetheart. Wiggle around and make it harder." His palms slipped on the wall as they were starting to sweat. He couldn't hold back anymore. A growl ripped from his throat as his hips started to piston of their own accord. Her feet came completely off the ground as he slammed into her, again and again, pushing her higher against the wall. "Listen to me, Erin. I'm about to drain myself into your hot little pussy. And I will *still* stop. Because I don't want to fuck you like this once. I want to wreck you over and over again. I'll do whatever it takes to achieve that." He wedged her against the wall and dropped his hips to thrust at a different angle, memorizing the way she cried out in response. "Is it too much, Erin? If it is, you tell me. That's a goddamn order."

"If you stop I'll die," she breathed, seconds before her muscles tightened against him and she began shaking. "Holy shit, holy shit. *Connor*."

Her hands flew backward to wrap around his neck, dragging his face down for a kiss. The way she stroked his tongue with her own, body still rocking on his cock as she orgasmed, sent him spinning into climax. He moaned loudly into her mouth as his own relief blasted through him. He pressed her to the wall one final time, pushing his draining erection as deep as it would go. Giving her everything.

CHAPTER FIFTEEN

Erin existed inside a kind of stunned void. Her breath sounded like wind funneling in her ears, her pulse pounding in so many parts of her body, she felt like she might break apart. But that would be impossible because she'd already done that. If she looked down, her body would be lying in a broken heap on the floor. Floor. The floor. She couldn't feel it. Was she floating?

Can't run. Wall in front of her...*and* behind her? Can't move.

Wood rubbed with fresh pine invaded her consciousness. A sweaty mass of muscle pressing against her back. It wasn't a wall behind her. Connor. Just her Connor.

What he'd done to her body...she could hardly comprehend it. Her entire life she'd gone without receiving actual satisfaction from another person's body. God, "satisfaction" was such a weak word for what had just happened. He'd changed her. Introduced the two sides of herself to each other, like one might do with two strangers. There had been anxiety in the beginning, but he'd obliterated it with lust. Heat. Understanding. It was so much to comprehend when her body felt drained and exultant at the same time.

She still sucked in oxygen so quickly that her throat burned.

Relief had begun to filter in, but not enough. She needed to touch down. Stand on her own feet. Without the thrill of pleasure to distract her, the feel of Connor moving inside her, awareness started to take root. "L-let me down. Just…"

Immediately, the warm strength of Connor went missing. It left her so cold, she had to fight the urge to order him back. Her body slid down the wall, allowing her to stumble toward the window. She pressed her cheek against it and continued trying to catch her breath. Heat at her elbow told her Connor was standing there.

His concern was so palpable, she could feel it without looking at him. "Talk to me, Erin."

"I'm fine."

She took stock of her surroundings, waited for the impulse to flee, but it didn't come. It didn't come. This was exactly where she wanted to be. Her gaze flew to Connor's. Such intensity poured from him, she didn't know whether to soar or collapse under the heaviness of it. Soar. She wanted to soar. He'd *made* her soar. Without another thought, she launched herself at him. His arms stayed at his sides even though she could sense it took a shit-ton of restraint. She couldn't get close enough to him. Her body climbed his, reveling in the smell of his skin, the *life* of him.

"Thank God," he chanted, letting her kiss his shoulders, his face. "Thank God. Thank God."

"I'm really fine. I mean…I-I don't know when or if I'll be okay with hands. Your *hands*. But I never thought." She buried her face in his damp neck and sucked in his scent. "I never thought."

He walked backward and sat down in a chair, taking her with him. For the first time, weakness in her limbs didn't feel like a disadvantage. Or letting her guard down. No, she felt safe.

Always safe with him. She wanted him to feel the same way with her, but she couldn't form the words so she squeezed him tight in an attempt to express it. This didn't feel like her triumph alone, but something they'd accomplished together. Something she'd never thought possible.

The blinding wave of emotion carried words that wouldn't be held inside any longer. "It wasn't always this bad. The noise... the panic was there, but I could still *move*. I didn't freeze up and turn useless when someone touched me. It was like a bee sting I could ignore. Or try to." Connor had gone still beneath her, but he didn't say anything to encourage her. Just stayed silent like she needed. "My mother didn't plan on dying. If she had, I hope...I don't think...she would have left me with my stepfather. I don't remember everything, but I remember the fighting. Them acting like strangers."

Connor sucked in a breath, like he was bracing himself.

"The first time I acted out at school, he put me in the closet for two days. I don't even remember what I did...pulled a fire alarm to get out of a test or something." She threw up a mental block against the feeling of being trapped that first time. The confusion. "I stopped making trouble after that, but it didn't matter. Out of sight was out of mind for him. It took nothing... *nothing*, and I'd be in the closet. Longer each time."

She'd started missing so much school, it hadn't been worth going back at a certain point. Too many missed classes, failed tests. Catching up would have been impossible. Once, a guidance counselor had visited the house. She'd screamed herself hoarse throughout the morning so she couldn't even call out to the woman. Like one of those nightmares where your vocal cords have been cut. Through the closet door, she'd heard her stepfather explain that she'd gone to live with her mother. A mother she could barely remember anymore through the terror she faced every day. A mother who had been dead and gone for months.

"When I finally broke out…" The familiar surge of ease washed over her as it always did when she remembered her ability to escape. "I stayed away awhile. Went to prison the first time. When I went back, I burned his house down while he slept in the back room. There was this noise in my head…it drove me. I couldn't see anything but the flames and it felt so good to have that control burning in my hands, you know? I thought he died. He didn't."

"I'm glad he didn't die," Connor's hard voice broke in. Beneath her, his massive chest heaved. "I'd hate to lose the opportunity to kill him myself."

It was tempting to let herself curl up and bask in his anger on her behalf. It felt foreign yet wonderful to have someone on her side. But she needed to get the rest out. Purge it. Make him understand what he was signing on for. "After I escaped the first time from Dade and they sent me back…I had a target on my back with the guards. They left me in the hole for a long time. It could have been a day or a month. I don't know." She blew out a breath. "I don't even remember what I was like before I went in. It broke me."

"No, it didn't. You're whole. You survived." He cut himself off and Erin got the feeling he was composing himself. "I can't think of you down there in the dark. I can't."

She traced his collarbone with her lips while considering his words. "Maybe my stepfather can't be killed. Even if he can, the fear he's put in me, the fear the guards put in me, won't go away. Never completely."

"You don't know that."

Bolstering her courage, she told him the worst of it. "They have no proof I set the fire, but he knows. He wants to put me away, Connor. Institutionalize me." He didn't respond. What did the silence mean? "Sometimes I think that's where I belong."

"*No*." He pulled back, his green eyes drilling into hers. "You belong with *me*."

Her lungs emptied of oxygen. There was something in his expression. Or lack of something, maybe. Shock...horror? "You knew about this?"

"Yes, I knew. I needed to identify the threat." He stared at a spot over her head. "After you left the meeting this morning, I talked to Derek about locating your stepfather. I want to give you your freedom, sweetheart, like I know you need. But I can't sit around wondering if someone will stop you from coming back to me."

She should have been outraged that he'd gone behind her back. Should have jumped off his lap and flipped over a table or something. Instead, she stayed put. If there were a threat against Connor, she would do the same thing. Identify and eliminate the problem. It was how people like them worked. "So you've known I'm a candidate for a padded cell and wanted me anyway? Maybe you do love crazy pussy."

"Don't call yourself crazy." His voice deepened. "And don't talk to me about your pussy until I've built up my self-discipline again. We do this right. Every damn time."

Heat prickled her skin. God, she'd hooked up with some kind of man. A naughty part of her wanted to push him, knew he would find command over himself one way or another, but she wasn't finished with her story. It needed to be out in the open. "I'm rich, Connor. Really fucking rich." He frowned at her. "Your manly frown lines tell me you didn't know that part."

"I didn't."

Erin nodded. "My mother was a gambler. A shitty one. But she got a break toward the end." She slipped her fingers into his hair and ran her nails along his scalp. "Somehow she got motivated enough to put it into a trust until I turned twenty-five. And I turned twenty-five two weeks ago." She watched Connor struggle to listen while she toyed with his hair, dragged her dampened lips across his. "I haven't touched it...wouldn't know what to do with that much cash. But my stepfather would. He legally adopted me when he married my mother. He's my sole family member. If he succeeds in institutionalizing me, he'll have control of the money. That's why he won't give up. Won't stop coming for me."

Connor's gaze sharpened, along with his breath. Her nearness was getting to him. Between her thighs, he'd grown huge and hard again. He visibly shook himself, but couldn't hide the hunger. "I won't let it happen."

"I know, baby," she purred against his ear, flicking the lobe with her tongue. "I won't let anything happen to you, either."

"Erin, please." His head fell back, putting his strong throat on display. Rock-hard, solid male between her legs, naked and ready. She still wore everything but her panties, but that could be easily fixed. With steady hands, she found the hem of her shirt and removed it. Connor's Adam's apple bobbed, but he didn't look. "You picked a bad time to fuck, sweetheart. I'm feeling protective as hell right now. Someone wants to take what's mine, someone *hurt* what's mine, and my head isn't on straight yet. Might never be."

She dragged her open mouth up his throat, over his chin. "Let me do the work this time," she whispered at his lips. "You fucked me, now I'm going to fuck you back."

Connor's growl vibrated his chest. "Get to it, then. I know what you feel like now and that makes me goddamn impatient. Cram me inside your wet pussy or I'll put you on the ground and use your mouth."

His rough language kicked up a cloud of lust so thick, it almost enveloped her. She reached behind her and found his straining cock. They both cursed as she led his thickness through her sensitive folds and sank down on top of it. With gravity weighing her down on his filling arousal, all her weight pressing down, she took a minute to savor.

"*I said move*," he grated. His hand came down hard on her right buttock with a *slap*, the force of it propelling her forward. Sensation speared her and she screamed, already craving the movement again. Her skin burned where he'd spanked her, but she couldn't tell if it was the sting or something more. But it hadn't lessened her desire. Not at all. Connor's breathing had gone shallow but his eyes were grave, as if he'd done something he couldn't take back. Something he hadn't been able to control. "I warned you. I'm not in check. Mine. Someone wants what's *mine*."

His possessiveness reached out and claimed her. Made her desperate to possess him, too. Most of all, it filled her with determination to obliterate that uncertainty she saw in his eyes. Show him he'd done nothing wrong by obeying his instincts. That the violence he kept tightly leashed inside him didn't extend to her. *Burn for me, Connor*. She gripped the back of the chair in her hands and wedged her heels against the sides.

She rode him hard. After the first buck of her hips, Connor grabbed on to the edges of the seat and fell back, moaning at the ceiling. Power infiltrated every cell in her body like some mind-altering drug, urging her faster and faster. Every time she felt her body tighten and ready for orgasm, she'd switch tactics, bouncing on his rigid dick one minute and rolling at a downward angle the next. Her ass slapped against his sweaty thighs, mingling with her whimpers.

His head came up, eyes blazing with ownership as they

watched her breasts shake. "Already know what I like, don't you? When I let you lead, you lead hard." He started to pump into her with rough upward thrusts of his hips. "You're going to make me live for a single stroke of that tight pussy, aren't you? Make me get out of bed just for that hot squeeze every day. Make me work to keep it happy. I'll work. I'll work you until you cry for it."

Her flesh still oversensitive from the last orgasm he'd given her, she couldn't prevent the contractions any longer. They seemed to come from everywhere, all over her body, but centered between her thighs where he continued to enter her faster and faster until the *slapslapslapslap* sound wrenched his name free from her throat and she hurtled into relief so vast it hurt. "*Connor.*"

"Hold on to me." She clutched his shoulders a second before he stood, his hardness unyielding inside her, lengthening her climax until she wasn't sure where one ended and another began. Her ass hit the kitchen table. He rammed himself deep on a growl and held himself there, pumping his hips slowly as heat flooded inside her. "All for you, Erin. I keep it all for you. This is the only place I come now. Deep inside you where only I can reach. Nowhere else."

Her elbows stopped supporting her and she fell back, boneless, onto the table. "Yes, Connor."

When his face loomed inches above her, she had to catch her breath. So fierce. So male. "Do you have any needs I haven't satisfied? Do you need to be taken again? Are you hungry?"

She couldn't move her head to shake it. "I'm satisfied," she whispered.

He nodded once. "To bed." Somehow she found the energy to roll off the table onto her feet. Her hands automatically went to her skirt to pull it down from where it had become bunched around her waist, but Connor made a sharp sound. "Leave it up."

Sending him a confused look, Erin started walking toward her bedroom. Any second now, she would drop like a stone and he was acting arrogant enough without witnessing it. "'night, baby."

Connor muttered something under his breath and strode into his bedroom. A moment later, he walked out holding a pair of handcuffs. Her spine snapped straight. She was sure as hell awake now. "W-what are you doing?"

Without answering her, he entered her bedroom and lay down on her bed. Maintaining eye contact with her, he snapped one side of the handcuffs onto his wrist. The other side, he connected to a wooden slat in her bed frame. "We sleep *together*," he explained. "And I can't trap you like this."

Gratefulness. She'd only felt it a few times in her life. Once when that inmate had given her the Marlins baseball cap. Again when Derek had given her a chance at a life in Chicago. It didn't compare to this feeling. It was so extreme, she wilted, exhaustion overtaking her once more. Her head swam, making it impossible to come up with the right words, so she crawled into bed and snuggled into his warm side, secure in the knowledge that she couldn't be held down or kept stationary. She was free to enjoy this. Enjoy him.

"I'm really glad we were both early to the first meeting," she murmured against his skin.

"It wouldn't have mattered. It would have been the same outcome," Connor returned. "Go to sleep, Erin."

"Bossy." He was wrong, she decided. Everything they did, every action and reaction, mattered with people like them. As his breathing evened, a tiny spark of doubt caught her just before she joined him in sleep. She'd been reacting on impulse, on the need to survive for so long, without a thought for another person. No one had mattered enough to hinder her actions until now. How would she react next time a threat arose and her instinct shouted at her to run? How would *he* react? With this job, with her past, she would eventually face danger, be it her stepfather or something unseen. Would this bond that strengthened with each passing day end up being her Achilles' heel? Or worse, his?

CHAPTER SIXTEEN

Connor took the headset Derek handed him and slung it around his neck. Early that morning, while still in bed with Erin, he'd gotten a phone call from the captain requesting his presence at the meeting spot. Austin had gotten restless being sidelined and come up with a plan to make himself useful. Unfortunately, that plan required more than one person present and since Bowen and Sera were getting married that afternoon, that meant he'd had to leave Erin naked in bed. It didn't help matters that she'd stared at his morning wood like it was a gift from God as he grudgingly dressed himself in jeans and a T-shirt.

On his way out the door, she'd gotten a phone call of her own. Sera wanting to know if she'd come over and help her get ready for the impromptu wedding. He'd leaned against the front door and watched the multitude of emotions flit across her sleep-softened features. Flustered surprise, self-consciousness, irritation. He'd had to drag himself out the door or he would have kissed her right back into bed. Spent the afternoon seeing what other expressions he could put on her face, starting with rapture.

Goddamn, she made him feel things. He'd always been

dominant in the bedroom, but last night had been on a whole different level. She'd unearthed something primitive inside him, something so intense it had almost been alarming. But he wouldn't bury it again for anything in the world. No, he wanted to cultivate it and see how far she'd let him go. As she'd lain on the kitchen table beneath him, body slick with sweat, he'd felt taken over. *Feed her, comfort her, care for her.* Commands inside his head that had no known origin, but there they were, begging to be obeyed. It felt like a homecoming. Like she'd fit something together inside him that had been detached. Now it was electrified, bringing him to life.

"There some reason you're growling at me, Bannon?"

It took Connor a moment to focus on Derek where he sat in the van beside him. They were parked two blocks away from Maxwell Stark's office, waiting for Austin's voice to come through their headsets. "I didn't eat breakfast," he finally answered.

"Right." Derek tossed him a PowerBar, cleared his throat a little uncomfortably. "It doesn't get easier leaving them in the morning. Believe me, I know."

Considering how the captain had reacted when they'd simply shaken hands with Ginger, Connor was a little surprised he'd brought up something so personal about their relationship. Although he suspected Derek was a control freak and wanted to be aware of the inner workings of his squad more than anything. "Yeah, well. It's even worse when it's fucking Austin that drags me out of bed. Explain to me again how he came up with this idea?"

Derek hit two keys on his laptop and crossed his arms. "Polly was able to get Stark's meeting schedule for this afternoon. He's meeting with a corporation looking to set up shop in town, but without some red tape being eliminated, it would cost them a lot of time and money. All Austin's research, by the way. Turns out he's not as useless as you thought." He put the headset to his ears a moment and listened before lowering them again. "Austin had a hunch there would be a bribe offered at the meeting. So we called and rescheduled for first thing in the morning."

"But instead of the CEO, Austin is going to walk in."

"And offer the bribe," Derek confirmed. "I thought it might be too risky. If he fails, we could tip off Stark that we're watching him. So I had Polly eliminate the risk."

Conner raised an eyebrow. "How?"

"Put a freeze on their corporate bank accounts." Derek's lips twitched. "The real meeting will never take place, at least not until they get through Polly's firewall. So Stark won't get spooked when CEO number two walks in at the original time this afternoon."

A crackle came through the headphones, but no voices. "What happens if they call to cancel?"

"Polly intercepts it. She's got their phone lines rerouting until noon, when the meeting is scheduled. They don't have a high call volume, so it shouldn't seem too out of the ordinary."

"Austin posing as a CEO. Polly hacking into bank accounts. All before breakfast." He chuckled under his breath. "Some group you've assembled here."

Derek turned serious. "My city. My family's city. I'll protect it no matter what it takes or who it pisses off."

Connor didn't give a response because it didn't require one. He understood that mentality all too well. Every member of the squad had something they were protecting, be it a secret or a loved one. He wondered if the captain knew he wasn't so different from a ragtag group of criminals.

Derek snatched a two-way radio off his belt and spoke briskly into it. "All units hold your positions. Stand by for further instructions."

"You've got uniforms ready to move on this?"

"Why do you think you're here? If Stark takes the bribe, I'll have to go in and make the arrest, bring him downtown." He tossed Connor a second radio. "That puts you in command of three units. I'm sure his office is under orders to shred evidence if something like this happens. You'll see to it that they don't."

"And that no one leaves with a laptop or safe strapped to their back."

"Right."

It felt good, falling back into this pattern. No bullshitting or second-guessing, just getting the job done. It reminded him what it felt like to be part of a team. Until now, he hadn't realized he missed it or even gave a shit one way or another. Apparently he did. Having someone put their faith in him for something more than a money drop or gang retaliation. Maybe this was more than a job. Maybe he *belonged* here. Doing this.

Just then, Austin's voice crackled to life over Connor's headphones. He exchanged a nod with Derek and placed them over his ears. Gone was the slight British flavor to Austin's voice, replaced with a distinct Texas twang. If Connor didn't know who he was listening to, he wouldn't have believed it was the con himself.

He recognized the second voice as Stark's based on the audio file Derek had played for them in the second squad meeting. "Good morning, Mr. Caster. Can Evelyn get you a drink?"

"Nothing for me, thanks. I don't drink while the sun is up and I only trust Texas tap water." He laughed deep and hearty, voice completely unrecognizable. The sound of hands clasping could be heard, likely from a handshake. A heavy thud followed, metal on wood. A briefcase being set down. "How do you breathe inside all this concrete? I tell you, after K-Worth is up and running, I'm hiring a manager and visiting once a year. No, sir. City life ain't for me."

A smooth laugh from Stark. "I don't know how to breathe anywhere else, nor do I intend to learn. Chicago is where it all happens. And none of it happens without me." A groan from a leather chair. "Which is why you're here, Mr. Caster. Correct?"

"You don't waste time, do you?"

An amused hum. "This isn't Texas."

"Fair enough. We'll get down to brass tacks and you can get back to sucking smog."

Stark didn't reply.

"Now, currently the commercial space we have rented to house the first Chicago K-Worth shares parking with three other department stores. And that just ain't enough." Connor tried not to look impressed. Obviously he hadn't given Austin enough credit. The guy had done his homework. "I know how you city people work, carrying shopping home on trains or, hell, walking. But we want our customers going home with more than they can carry in one of them 'go green' tote bags. For that they need cars. Cars need parking."

"What are you asking for, Mr. Caster?"

Another rumbling laugh. "I'm getting there." A chair creaked, signaling that someone had come to their feet. "There is a huge lot running along the east side of the property. We were hoping to purchase it to use as a private lot, but we've run into some zoning issues. Apparently it was created for the sole use of the affordable housing across the street."

"Well." A pen tapped against wood. "Finally something I can help you with."

"I knew I came to the right place. Shall we discuss terms?"

A long pause. "Why don't you show me what's in the brief-case?"

Derek leaned forward in his seat to eye the laptop. Looking satisfied that the exchange was definitely being recorded, his shoulders remained tense. They were potentially seconds away from getting their man, only a few days into the job. What would the ramifications of that be? Would they continue to work together or be split up? His head started to ache at the idea of Erin or him being asked to go somewhere else. No. No, that wouldn't happen. This wasn't a temporary gig. They'd been assured of that.

Relax, man.

Both of them flinched when a loud crash traveled through the headphones, followed by a high-pitched squeal. "*Daddy!*"

Connor and Derek exchanged an uneasy glance. Obviously this hadn't been part of the plan.

When Stark spoke again, his voice had changed completely, going from darkly cultured to bright and enthusiastic. "Kiddo. What are you doing here? Where's Berta?"

"I am here." An elderly, Russian-tinged voice. "She wanted to say hello before school. Threatened to hold breath unless we stopped car."

"Well. Stubbornness runs in the family, I guess." Footsteps ran across carpeted floor. "But you've interrupted an important meeting. Next time, you'll listen to Berta. Understood?"

"Yes, Dad-dy," the child replied in a singsongy voice.

"This is Mr. Caster. Say hello."

"Hello!"

Connor frowned when Austin stayed silent. Seconds ticked by before he finally spoke. "N-nice to meet you." His Texas accent had slipped slightly, making Derek's head fall forward. Something had thrown Austin off in there. The kid? "I, uh…just remembered I'm needed back at the K-Worth site. We'll pick this up tomorrow."

Two chairs rolled back. "That's not necessary. They were just leaving." Stark's voice had gone smooth once more. Maybe even with a hint of suspicion. "I usually only have her on the weekends, so this doesn't happen often."

"No need to explain. I have to, um…" Heavier footsteps sounded on the floor. Austin's phony accent was back in place, but he sounded almost desperate to get out of there. "I'll call to reschedule."

"Fucking hell," Derek muttered. "We had him."

They heard a *ding* and realized Austin must have been entering an elevator. A second later, a door rolled and silence reigned. "I'm a bastard, but I won't have him arrested in front of his daughter," Austin said, his cultured tone clipped. "Not going to happen."

Static rushed in Connor's ears, telling him Austin must have ripped off the wire he'd been wearing. Derek removed his headphones and let them drop to the van floor.

"This is what I get for putting together a group of wild cards."

"You don't sound too upset," Connor observed, slinging his own headphones around his neck.

Derek said nothing, just removed his wallet from his back pocket. He took out a picture of a little girl who looked to be about two years old, holding a kitten close to her chest. He'd only met Ginger briefly, but this child was the image of her, even if she had a touch of Derek's shrewdness in her eyes.

"Some things are sacred," Derek said, before climbing into the driver's seat and pulling away from the curb. "Drop you off at the courthouse?"

"You're not coming to the wedding?"

"Jesus, no. Can't give you assholes the impression that I give a shit."

A smile tugged at Connor's mouth. "Fair enough."

CHAPTER SEVENTEEN

Erin paced the lobby of the courthouse, waiting for Connor to show. The security guard operating the metal detector kept sending Erin nervous glances over her shoulder. Although she couldn't figure out *why* since the woman had confiscated both of her knives. Knives she would be getting back as soon as Sera and Bowen exchanged their vows upstairs.

This morning, she'd been wary of Sera's request to accompany her to the courthouse. What did she want from her? Was she going to make her hold flowers or some shit? But hanging out with Sera had turned out to be surprisingly... easy. She didn't force Erin to make conversation, nor had she looked at her weird when she asked to take the bus. After her first stint in Dade, she'd spent a lot of time sitting in the back row of a Catholic church down the street from where she was staying. There'd been no expectation for her to participate in the masses. She could just sit and watch, inhale the incense, make use of the air-conditioning. That's what being with Sera felt like. Cool comfort. It didn't surprise Erin that Bowen didn't want to wait another second to marry her. When they'd shown up to the courthouse, Sera in a white sundress, he'd looked like he'd just been granted eternal life.

There had been a moment where she'd felt a tinge of jealousy. Not over the couple. Not because she wanted to be the one getting married. No, it had come when they touched. She wanted that. Wanted Connor to be able to touch her without thinking. Just a natural slide of his hands along her skin without fear or pain. She wanted so badly to give that to him.

As if her thoughts had made him appear, Connor strode into the courthouse. Her pulse started beating double time, her stomach muscles tightening. Good *Lord*, the man was a fucking panty dropper. She'd only been away from him for a few hours and it felt like years since she'd experienced his presence. In jeans and a fitted gray T-shirt that molded to his muscles like her hands itched to do, he personified confidence and authority. Hot, rugged male. His gaze connected with hers immediately and darkened. She thought back to that morning when he'd dressed in the early morning light, his abs flexing as he pulled the shirt over his head. His erection barely contained by his boxers. She'd never been one to beg for anything, but she'd been seconds from offering him her mouth. Pleading for the privilege of sucking him off.

Conner shook his head at her with a sexy half smile on his face, as if he could read her thoughts across the room. He stopped at the metal detector and walked through after the security guard beckoned him forward. When the woman grabbed her wand and instructed him to raise his hands in the air, something ugly reared its head deep inside her. The detector hadn't even beeped. There was no reason for the personal service. When the woman smiled at Connor and ran a hand down her ponytail, Erin propelled herself forward, boots echoing on the polished marble.

Erin hissed as she drew even with the guard. "If you're done feeling up my boyfriend, I'd love a turn. We were in a rush this morning."

The guard dropped the wand, letting it dangle near her thigh. "Did you just hiss at me?"

Erin hissed again.

"Okay." Connor stepped between them, winking down at her. "We should go. Don't want to keep the clerk waiting."

Appreciation spread in her belly like honey. He hadn't chided her for her behavior or apologized to the woman on her behalf. Instead he'd given the impression *they* were on their way to get married, appeasing her jealousy in one fell swoop. "That's right." She sauntered toward the elevator. "There's vows to be exchanged. Rings to put on fingers. Shit like that."

She glanced behind her to find Connor staring at her ass as she walked, so she put a little swing in her hips and savored his groan. Damn. She'd definitely never had this much fun at a courthouse.

A moment later, she and Connor stepped into an empty elevator. She hit the button for the top floor even though the clerk was on the first, and leaned back against the wall, looking up at him through her eyelashes. "How was your morning, baby? Was it worth leaving me in bed, all hot and bothered for you?"

"Fuck no, it wasn't." He crooked a big finger at her. "Climb on up here."

Erin didn't hesitate. With a tight grip on his broad shoulders, she hooked one thigh around his waist and used it as leverage to wrap the other one around, too. Her skirt rode up with the action, allowing the thick ridge behind his fly to nudge her panties. They sucked in equally shaky breaths.

Connor crossed his wrists at the small of his back, as if to restrain himself from touching her. "You didn't like someone else touching me. Say it."

She pressed her forehead against his, pushed hard. "I hated it."

"Put your hand between your legs." When she hesitated for the barest moment, he nudged her forehead back and spoke through his teeth. "Do it now."

Erin removed one hand from his shoulders, dragging her fingers over the inside of her thigh before cupping her core. Breath raced in and out past her lips, excitement a living thing in her veins. Against her palm, she could already feel the cotton material dampening.

"Give it a slap for me. An easy one, sweetheart. We'll save the harder ones for my hand." He licked the seam of her lips. "Say my name when you do it."

The elevator *ping*ed, signaling that they'd reached the top floor. Without taking his eyes off her, Connor reached over and pulled the emergency stop switch. Erin laughed, but it turned into a moan when he rolled his hips, pressing her hand more firmly between her legs. He nipped at her bottom lip, a reminder to do as she was told. Feeling overwhelmed in the best way, she slapped herself, right over the sensitive spot crying out for attention. Unexpected sensation racked her, tearing a moan from her lips.

"*Connor.*"

"I told you last night, Erin. *That's* where I come." He grazed her jaw with his teeth. "Every time you get jealous, remind yourself just like that. Slap it for me and say my name. Understand?"

"Yes," she breathed.

"I want to ask you a question." He started to say more, then stopped, taking her mouth in a hot, openmouthed kiss. She couldn't stop her fingers from slipping into her panties and

rcles over her clit, mimicking the stroking movements
gue. It wouldn't take any time at all to find the edge
herself fall. Just his voice, his body, his words were
driving her to the brink of climax.

Addicted. I'm addicted and I love it.

"W-what do you want to a-ask me?"

He ran his tongue up the side of her neck. "Ah, Erin. When
can I get my mouth on your gorgeous pussy? I want it so bad.
Want your heels buried in my back…your fingers yanking at
my hair. You have no idea what a scream sounds like until I've
been between your thighs with my tongue feasting on your clit."

The orgasm blindsided her, made her shake head to toe as
she writhed against her hand. "*Oh my God, oh my God.*"

"Good girl. That's what you needed, wasn't it?" His quick
inhales rasping in her ear, he reached over and slammed his fist
against the first-floor button. "If we had time, I'd take out my
cock and fuck you against the goddamn wall right now. Expect
to get it hard later, sweetheart."

Her legs stopped clenching as the tremors passed and she
slid down his body, landing on her feet to sway back against
the wall. She watched Connor adjust himself in his jeans and
almost groaned at the renewed surge of arousal from seeing
him touch himself. "How's my hair?"

His mouth edged up at the corners. "Pretty fucked up."

She tugged her skirt back into place. "Cool."

The elevator door rolled open and she stepped out. Before
she could make it one step, Connor's mouth found her neck
and she came to a halt. *Feels so good.* "Hey." The pride in his
voice had her turning around to search his face. He jerked his
thumb over his shoulder. "You just rode an elevator."

Shock trickled in slowly, mingling with amazement. How
had she done something usually so terrifying without even

realizing it? "Oh."

"Yeah. Oh." His smile faded into a serious expression. "Great job, sweetheart."

"Thanks. Or...or whatever." She'd done it because he'd been with her, distracting her. Making her feel safe. If she thought too much about it, she was going to cry, so she leaned forward and dropped a kiss over his heart. She turned and continued walking toward the clerk's office, but not before she saw Connor press a hand over the spot she'd kissed. And fuck if that didn't make her want to cry even more.

Connor had never been to a wedding before, but he suspected they were usually a little more romantic than this one. Fluorescent lighting and some bored government worker's voice droning the words you were supposed to recite didn't feel momentous. That is, until Bowen and Sera repeated the words back to each other. Even the clerk perked up a little at the sincerity in their speech. They might as well have been the only two people on the planet for all the attention they paid everyone else. Bowen, focused on Sera as usual, looked like he wanted the words spoken and done with so he could haul her out of there over his shoulder. Sera looked like she wanted to reach out and soothe him.

Damn. This wedding shit really shouldn't have gotten to him, but he found himself remembering how the three of them had met. How they'd all been marked for death at one point, but come out alive and better than before when any possible outcome had seemed bleak. How they'd formed an unlikely friendship even though they'd been on opposing sides, pitted against one another. For the first time in his life, he'd watched good triumph over evil. They'd come a long way in such a short space of time, and it hit home now, as they made even more promises to each other.

Not surprisingly, he found himself looking at Erin. He'd always given Bowen a hard time for his obsession with Sera and her safety. His constant vigilance and fear of something happening to her. He could understand it now. Jesus, could he ever. As if he'd spoken out loud, Erin looked over at him from her position behind Sera and stuck out her tongue. A smile transformed her face and she ducked her head, as if embarrassed she'd let the show of happiness slip. If it was up to him, he'd be seeing a lot more of that beautiful smile. He wanted to see it constantly, and he wanted it directed at him.

Before the clerk had even gotten finished pronouncing Bowen and Sera husband and wife, Bowen launched himself across the space separating him from his new wife and wrapped her in his arms. Erin gave Connor a meaningful look and backed away quietly, obviously wanting to give the couple their space. The clerk scratched his head, appearing to be at a loss for what to do with the embracing couple, but Erin didn't seem inclined to stick around and offer her assistance. Connor followed her from the room, checking the urge to rest his hand at the small of her back. *All in good time.*

Two men in suits entered the elevator with them on the way back down to the lobby. Erin scowled at their backs the entire way and he would have laughed if he weren't still feeling the evidence of what they'd done earlier. His pants felt tight, his mouth unsatisfied from not tasting enough of her. As soon as they got home, he would remedy that. Thinking of creative ways to get her off without his hands was fast becoming his favorite pastime.

He followed Erin off the elevator and out of the courthouse, enjoying the sway of her hips, the sultry looks she cast him over her shoulder. The girl wanted to get home just as badly as he did, but she had no idea what she'd unleashed. She sure as hell wouldn't be walking as gracefully tomorrow. When she came to a dead stop at a few yards from the bus stop, he almost ran into her. Connor started to ask her what was wrong, but her whole body started to tremble.

"Erin?" He circled around her to scan her face. Her terrified expression ruptured something inside him. It called to memory the night she'd broken into his apartment to get near a window. The Erin he'd walked out of the courthouse with was nowhere to be found. *Protect her. Heal her.* "What's wrong? Talk to me."

"He's here," she whispered. "The face behind the fire. I see him. Do you see him?"

"The face—" He didn't understand what she meant by that, but to the best of his knowledge, there was only one "he" who could scare her like this. "Your stepfather?"

She stumbled back a step, her hand coming up to cover her mouth. Her gaze was fixed across the street and Connor followed it. A man stood on the opposite side of the traffic. Smiling. Under his arm was a rolled-up newspaper. He would have looked like everyone else passing by, would have blended right in, if it weren't for the hatred in his eyes. Centered on Erin.

Rage tried to run loose through his bloodstream, but he fought it back. He needed to handle this calmly. Both of them couldn't lose their heads at the same time. He needed to be strong for her even though his instincts were calling for him to cross the street at a dead run and mow the son of a bitch down. "Don't look at him. Look at me. *Erin.*" She wasn't hearing him, but he couldn't touch her to shake her. Frustration dug into his gut like tenterhooks. "I'm going to take care of this. But I won't leave you until you're okay." *Until I know you won't run.*

Finally, her glazed eyes focused on him, as if his worry over her running had been spoken out loud. "I'm sorry. I have to go."

"*No.*"

Her nod was unsteady. "He found me. I don't know how he found me."

Connor shot a look back toward the man. Still there. Still smiling. He needed to get over there and wipe it right off his goddamn face, but he was glued to the sidewalk. She was going to run and he had to stop her. How? How could he stop her when he hurt her by touching her, when she was already having a panic attack and the slightest touch could make it worse? "I need you to come back to me, Erin. Look at me and *trust* me."

"I can't come back. He knows I'm here now."

She'd misunderstood him, but her response chilled him to the bone. She meant to run and never come back. Leave Chicago. Leave him. Around him, the world contorted, passersby's voices sounding unnatural. "We'll go together. Don't do this. I won't let him near you, Erin. You have to know I'd die first."

Her gaze cleared. "Exactly."

And then she ran. Until that moment, until Connor was chasing her through street vendors and harried locals, he hadn't fully understood exactly how adept Erin was at escaping. Her slight form weaved in and out of business suits and tourists with maps like an exotic jungle cat, sleek and agile. He could hear the jingling of her boots, taunting him as he followed her path. Back in the SEALs, he'd undergone training that should have made it simple to catch up with a single female, stop her from running. It shouldn't have been this difficult to track her movements, especially when people were giving them both wide berth, sprinting as they were down the busy sidewalk.

One second, he had sight of her blond hair and the next, she was gone. Disappeared.

Connor spun in a circle in the middle of a crosswalk, scanning the streets frantically. Looking for any sign of which direction she might have taken. Hoping people would turn their heads to indicate she had just run past. Hear the sounds of her bells tinkling. But there was nothing.

Gone. She was gone.

The demons she'd slain inside him regenerated...and roared to life.

CHAPTER EIGHTEEN

Erin ignored the stabbing pain in her heart as she circled back toward the courthouse. She tried to banish the devastation on Connor's face when she'd run from him, but it wouldn't go away. It wasn't helping. It *hurt*. She wanted him to go away so she could focus on what she needed to do. Just *focus*. As she'd booked it down the sidewalk, she'd fought the need to turn around and run straight back to Connor. The farther she'd gotten from her stepfather, the more her head had cleared. She didn't want to run away. Not permanently. Not when it made her feel like her insides were being shredded with every step.

Which meant she had some work to do.

This, her stepfather, was her cross to bear. No one else's. She'd left him alive and with a shit-ton of incentive to hunt her back down, although she still had no idea how he'd tracked her to Chicago. She would be finding out soon enough. She'd handle her problem and get back to Chicago and Connor. And fuck it, her friends. She had friends now. A job. People who were counting on her. If you'd told her a month ago she'd have a live-in boyfriend who slept in her bed, that she'd be witnessing weddings, she would have laughed until she turned blue. Now it was her reality and she liked it. Loved it, even.

She loved *Connor*.

Fuck, there it was again. His face. *I won't let him near you, Erin. You have to know I'd die first.*

Dammit, think about something else. Something less painful. No, *more* painful. The only thing that would stop Connor's pleas from ringing in her head would be to replace them with a harsher memory. Kind of like hobbling yourself to detract pain from a broken arm. Might as well make it something useful. Memories could be a powerful motivator if you picked the right one.

As she pilfered a Chicago Cubs hat from a street vendor and tucked her hair up inside it, she thought back to her twenty-first birthday. She'd been one week into serving her first sentence in Dade. A visitor had been the last thing she'd been expecting. An inmate had the right to refuse a visitor, but she'd been suffocating. The promise of sitting in an open room without having to watch her back constantly was too tempting an offer to pass up. So she'd sat down with the bastard and watched him smirk at her ungroomed appearance. Her limp hair and eyebrows in need of plucking. Sure, she'd been wearing a genuine *fuck you* expression, but it only had so much effect when she was the one behind bars.

"I have to say I'm disappointed, Erin. I had such high hopes for you."

She'd tilted her head back to stare at the ceiling. "Yeah? I have high hopes for this reunion being over sooner than later."

He'd clucked his tongue. "That's no way to talk to your father. Especially when you need money added to your commissary account."

"*Step*father," she'd corrected him. "Keep your money. I'll get by."

"We'll see."

Fingers drumming on the table danced through her memory. She couldn't remember whose. "Is there a point to this visit?"

"You didn't think I'd show up without a present, did you?"

Since he had no bags with him, nor did his lime-green polo shirt allow him to conceal anything, she'd only stared back warily.

He'd leaned forward and lowered his voice. "So many times you asked me *why*. Screamed it, really, from your room."

Bile had risen in her throat. *Her room.* How he'd always referred to the closet.

"Well, your gift is me finally answering your question." His voice had been full of glee. She could still hear it. "Ever wonder how your mother died, Erin? Yes, I can see that you have. Every girl does." The glee had fled, fading into a sneer. "She thought I didn't know about her extracurricular activities. She didn't care what it might do to my career." A short pause, full of anticipation. "It was a mixture of painkillers and wine. Her lover called me in the middle of the night, after the accident. The last place I saw her was in his bed."

A choked noise had fallen from Erin's lips, too late to snatch back. She hadn't wanted to know. Had wanted to go on assuming her mother had died doing something worthwhile or that her young life had been unfairly cut short. Tragic she could deal with, but not senseless. Worse, this information could have been spoken years earlier. He'd saved it up. Waited for the right time to make weapons out of it. Her twenty-first birthday.

"You're just like her," he'd continued, giving her white prison gear a disgusted once-over. "I did society a favor by keeping you away from it. Too bad I couldn't do it forever. I guess it's somebody else's job now." His smile had caused Erin's lungs to seize. "Or maybe not."

She'd watched dumbfounded as he pushed back from the metal table in a hurry. He'd jogged toward one of the guards, gesturing wildly. All she'd heard through a yellow haze were the words "threatened" and "weapon." She'd been rushed on both sides and thrown over the tabletop, the guards shouting at her to drop the weapon. They hadn't listened when she tried to explain she had nothing, their hands burning through her clothes to scorch her skin. Her protests had died with her ability to move. She'd frozen as the touches grew more intimate, searching and finding nothing on her person. Convinced the law-abiding psychiatrist had been telling the truth and she'd just found a way to get rid of the threat, they'd hauled her off to solitary with the stepfather's words still ringing in her head.

You're just like her. Weapon. Threatened. Weapon. Threatened.

That week in the dark had been her first and worst experience. The hands reaching through the slot at unexpected times, accompanied by the howls of misery around her, had fucked with her head. She'd felt changes taking place, felt darkness and irrational fear taking root, but she couldn't stop it from happening. From becoming a part of her. Sometimes the hands would grab on to her through the sliver of light, clammy and calloused. Yank her up against the steel door, tell her she'd better eat. Warn her she better stop screaming or they'd add time to her stay in the shoe.

There. Erin caught sight of her stepfather across the street in the park adjacent to the courthouse, as if he was waiting for her. He sat on a bench beneath a tree, one ankle propped on the opposite knee. Reading the newspaper. So casual, as if he hadn't just sent her newly constructed world into an epic tailspin. From her position behind a newsstand, she saw Bowen and Sera exit the courthouse. They were holding hands, but looking up and down the sidewalk, probably for her and Connor. *God,* where was Connor? She needed her stepfather to move before Connor came back or he would do something drastic. As if her stepfather had the very same worry after seeing them together, he took one last look at the courthouse and stood, heading toward the Madison/Wabash transit stop.

Could she get on a train? No way to get off in between stops. She'd be trapped. But if she wanted to follow her stepfather, she didn't have a choice. She took a deep breath and thought of Connor. Thought of his warmth beneath her cheek in bed last night. His even breathing against her ear.

He would look for her. She knew he would. Hopefully by the time he found her, she'd be one step closer to freedom.

"You have to calm down, man."

Connor's hands curled into fists, but he didn't know what their preferred target would be. Bowen's face or his own fracturing skull. Knocking himself out would bring oblivion, but he'd only wake up more frantic to find Erin than he was right now. Which might finally push him over the edge into madness. Two days. She'd been gone two days and he hadn't slept. Sera had practically force-fed him a piece of toast this morning, and it sat in his stomach like a lead weight.

At first, he'd eschewed anyone else's help. He hadn't wanted or needed anyone slowing him down. If he didn't stop, if he went everywhere he knew she liked to go, the mall, Denny's… he would find her, right? Once she saw him and realized he wouldn't stop looking, she would come home. She'd told him she had money. Lots of it. Did she have access to it? How? Would she use it to leave Chicago? Once these questions had begun to penetrate the intense panic, he'd enlisted Polly's help.

She was currently holed up in her apartment using information provided by Derek to locate Erin's stepfather. Now that he'd made a slight attempt to think clearly, he realized two possible outcomes were in play. Either Erin had taken off for parts unknown, hoping to get clear of her stepfather, or she'd gone after him. He didn't want either to be true. One took her away from him and the other put her in danger. All he could do was wait for a lead and follow it.

Waiting wasn't easy, especially in the apartment they shared. Bowen had attempted to pour himself some orange juice from the refrigerator and he'd nearly taken the guy's arm off, ordering him not to touch it. Erin's smell lingered in the air, everywhere he went. Every room he walked through. If he lay down in bed, he knew it would be more discernable, so he refused to go in there or it would wreck him. Goddammit, they'd made so much progress and in one split second, it had all been snatched away. Stolen. He missed her touch, the way her mouth parted simply from running her hands up his chest. He fucking needed her, and her abusive, asshole stepfather had taken her away.

Whenever he needed a fresh dose of anger, which was never really necessary, he thought back to the smile on that fucker's face. He thought of Erin's nightmarish expression. The need to destroy something ate at him constantly, sitting on his shoulder and whispering in his ear. He couldn't go much longer like this. Needed to see her soon. Be near her. *Now.*

"Calm down?" He repeated Bowen's words back as a question. "The way you calmed down when that rival gang tried to abduct Sera with baseball bats back in Brooklyn?"

Bowen's pupils dilated, hands clenching on the kitchen table. "Point made."

A knock on the door. Full of restless energy, Connor stood

and gave a cursory glance through the peephole before throwing the door open. Derek walked in with a stack of files. He quirked an eyebrow at Connor when all he received was a glare in place of a welcome. "Watch yourself, Bannon. It's not my fault she ran." He tossed the files on the table. "If she doesn't want to be found, she won't be. It's why I hired her."

"Really not helping," said Bowen.

Polly caught the door before it closed, breezing in with her open laptop in hand. "Greetings, menfolk."

They all grunted.

"Charming." She set her laptop down on the kitchen counter and hopped up beside it. "I have some mildly disturbing news, although not sure it'll come as a shock to all of us."

"What is it?" Connor asked, then held his breath. Come on, give him *something*.

"I know why Stepdaddy Dickhead, aka Luther O'Dea, was at the courthouse yesterday." She sent Connor an uneasy look. "He was petitioning for a conservatorship. A mental health one, specifically."

A conservatorship. Giving him control over Erin's money. Her decisions. Connor ground his molars together, wishing he'd given in and gone after the bastard when he had the chance, even though deep down her knew nothing could have prevented him from chasing Erin.

"As it turns out, Erin is filthy stinking rich and Stepdaddy D wants control over the cash flow." She glanced around the room, holding up what looked like a bank statement. "Was everyone aware of this but me? I could have hit her up for some grocery money."

"I knew," Connor muttered. It was obvious from the captain's expression that his squad member's financial status had been the one thing of which he hadn't been aware. Connor reached for the files he'd brought. "I don't give a shit if she's a billionaire, but no one is going to take what belongs to her."

"*Well*," Polly hedged. "That's where it gets sticky."

Bowen stood. "Jesus, sometimes I wish I hadn't quit smoking."

Connor crossed his arms. "Sticky how?"

Polly spun the laptop in their direction. "The petition Stepdaddy D turned in yesterday had Erin's signature on it."

"She never would have signed something like that," Derek said. "I could barely get her to sign a W-9."

"If I had to guess, based on the type of petition—"

"He could claim she signed it and doesn't have the capacity to remember," Connor finished for Polly, holding the bridge of his nose. His stomach was churning so hard, he was going to be sick. "How the fuck did the guy find her? She's smart. Knows how to avoid being found. She wouldn't have used credit cards. She doesn't have a cell phone to track. How?"

No one had an immediate answer, so each of the men flipped open a file while Polly continued to punch away on her laptop. The file Connor had picked detailed her two stints in Dade. It didn't contain any information he didn't already know...until the end.

Total consecutive days spent in solitary confinement: *seventy-two*.

Bile rose in his throat. Dammit to hell. No wonder. No wonder she had a fear of being trapped. She'd been treated like an animal so often in her life, her bravery, the way she faced a world that had betrayed her, amazed him. He thought of her smile that morning in the courthouse, the tears in her eyes when he'd withheld his body from her, and he felt himself crack. It might as well have been a visible, jagged line down the center of his chest.

"Whoa." Polly shook her head at the laptop screen. "He's a

psychiatrist? That's kind of ironic, no?"

"I've said it before." Bowen flipped a page. "Not helping."

"Wait. A psychiatrist?" Connor leaned back in his chair, remembering the other night. The first night he'd made love to Erin. *I'm on the shot.* "Would that give him access to medical records? If Erin had a physical when she reached Chicago, if she was prescribed medication, the information would have been recorded somewhere. If he searched hard enough, he'd find it."

Polly heaved a breath. "The search wouldn't have been that hard if he had any type of skill."

Derek pulled his cell phone from his pocket. "You're wrong, Polly. Those medical records are sealed. He would have had to do a lot of digging, maybe call in a favor or two. I don't leave loose ends like this."

"Will he have this address?" Connor demanded to know. "Is this address on her medical forms?"

"No." Derek shook his head. "We rented this place after she underwent the physical."

Bowen shoved a hand through his hair, looking thoughtful. "My half sister's boyfriend...he's a cop. When he was shot last year, he had to see a shrink afterward for weeks. Mandatory-like. Is there any way this guy has access to police records or a database somehow that way?"

"Like maybe he works with cops?" Polly's fingers flew over the keyboard. Her eyebrows shot up a second later. "Holy shit. He's the mental health counselor for Miami PD."

"Jesus Christ," Connor gritted out and began to pace. "If he's in contact with cops looking to skip out on mandatory counseling, it wouldn't be a stretch for him to call in a favor. Get information. If that's the case, he would find her anywhere she went."

"Well." Polly tucked her short black hair behind her ears. "Now that I have his real name and social security number, I can find out where he's…" She punched a few keys. "Bingo. I have his potential location."

Before she'd even finished rattling it off, Connor was halfway out the door.

CHAPTER NINETEEN

Her stepfather had finally come home.

Erin forced her breathing to stay even as she heard keys jingle outside the house's front door. She was crouched on top of a washing machine. Had been for what felt like hours. The laundry room included a back door leading to the garden, so she'd been semi-comfortable waiting there, bright sunshine turning to dusk and finally darkness. The only other door led into his kitchen, but he couldn't trap her from both sides. She had an out if she needed it. *Please don't let me need it.*

For almost four days, she'd been following Luther. From the courthouse, he'd gone back to a Motel 6 near O'Hare. She couldn't get to him there, though. The fear of being cornered in a room with only one escape was too intense. So intense she'd had to work through a panic attack behind the adjacent 7-Eleven with her head tucked between her knees. The lack of sleep and fuel hadn't helped, but her hunger and exhaustion had paled in the face of not having Connor.

Early the next morning, Luther had left the motel on a bus. By that time, she'd been sitting in the front seat of a Buick she'd hot-wired in anticipation of following him. He'd met a realtor at this house. The realtor had left almost immediately, but her stepfather had stayed inside for almost twenty-four hours. Had he bought the house? Rented it? It was almost completely unfurnished, apart from a few odds and ends the previous tenant had likely left behind.

So she'd waited…hoping to what? She didn't know exactly. Scare him into leaving her alone? Appealing to a man who had an irrational hatred of her because of something that happened when she was a child? On top of the long shot that he would even *listen* to her, since when was she capable of convincing anyone of anything? She didn't exactly have a reputation for being coolheaded and reasonable, especially when it came to this man.

No, she was far more comfortable in the darkness, holding a metal skillet in her hand, as she was at that moment, although she wished it were a book of matches instead. She inhaled and relished the scent of the kerosene she'd splashed strategically around the house's inside perimeter. Yeah, matches would be a *bad* idea.

Located in Park Ridge, not too far from the airport, the house had an almost identical layout to his home in Florida. Setting foot inside it hadn't been easy. Memories had threatened to breach her walls, but she breathed through them.

The weight of the skillet was reassuring. Over the course of the night, it felt like the only thing keeping her from floating up and hitting the ceiling. With each passing hour, she felt less and less real. After nearly four days without exchanging a single word with another person, namely Connor, she was beginning to feel insubstantial. The way she'd felt in solitary. A twist on the age-old question about the tree falling in the woods. If no one was around to communicate with her, did she really exist? She was slipping. Slipping back into that cave without light, and it scared her. She'd never needed anyone before, but she needed Connor now. Needed to be held and made to feel real.

What am I doing here?

That question was the only thing helping. In the past, she'd never once second-guessed her impulses. If she wanted to whack her stepfather upside the head with a blunt object, burn down his house and cackle at the moon afterward, she did it. For so long, she'd existed without a regard for consequences. So what if she ended up in prison? She'd just get herself out. So what if she got another charge on her record? Harvard wasn't exactly an option at this point anyway. Yet as she sat in the darkness, she found herself anxious. Wondering if there had been any new developments on the Maxwell Stark case. Had the squad solved it without her? The very fact that she didn't want to be in her stepfather's house lying in wait, that it felt *wrong*, told her something inside her had changed for the better. She couldn't identify it or name it. Right now, it was only a feeling. But she held on tight to it because it made her feel human when in reality, she was someone else's monster hiding in the darkness.

Ice formed in her veins when her stepfather's heavy tread moved down the hallway. She didn't have a plan. Didn't know what she would do when faced with the man who'd spawned so many nightmares. Her modus operandi had been to avoid him. He wouldn't expect her to show up. The smile on his face outside the courthouse had been smug. Secure. He thought she would run.

Not this time. If she ran, he would follow. He continued to prove that over and over. Now that the money was being released to her, he'd be twice as tenacious. It would never end. She would never again sleep as soundly as she had in Connor's bed. His specter would hang over the bed like a ghost, no matter what she did. It would smother her. Knowing him, he would find out her weakness for Connor and use him against her. *My Connor.*

Her blood went from cold to boiling. Maybe she *could* kill him.

With that possibility lingering in her head, she slowly eased off the washing machine, dropping onto the balls of her feet without a single tinkle from the bells. A light went on in the kitchen and she pressed her back against the wall beside the partially open door. Too many potential weapons in the kitchen. If she charged him, he would have time to pick one up. No, she would wait until he got close enough to the door and make her move.

What am I doing here?

Erin shook her head hard to clear the doubt. This was what she'd *dreamed* of. Confronting the face behind the whirlwind of fire. The man who'd made her helpless. Made her *beg.* She shouldn't be considering slipping out the back door and returning to safety. To a man. That was weak. Beneath her.

The thoughts distracted her a second too long. She wasn't prepared when the laundry room door opened and her stepfather walked inside. All she could do was act. The skillet rose on its own and uppercut Luther in the jaw. She couldn't deny the satisfaction his shout of pain gave her as he stumbled back, hit the opposite wall, and crashed to the floor.

Her teeth bared themselves. "Ding dong, motherfucker. Someone just got their bell rung."

He clutched his jaw, scrambling back against the wall. "You…" The pain of talking caused him to flinch. "You're here?"

Fear. There was still fear at being this close to him, but she forced it into hiding. "Didn't expect me, did you?" She twirled the skillet in her hand. "That's the thing about crazy people.

You can't predict what the fuck they're going to do."

His head moved on a swivel, searching around him. Probably for something to use as a weapon or to block her should she swing the skillet again. Too bad towels were the only things in reaching distance. She saw the exact moment he smelled the kerosene, barely suppressed fear sparking and fading in his eyes. "What do you want, you lunatic bitch?"

Erin clucked her tongue. "That's no way to talk to someone holding a weapon." She ran her finger around the metal edge. "Someone with violent tendencies. Someone who you're trying to screw out of a boatload of money."

"She *owes* me that money," her stepfather sneered. "If not for fucking around behind my back, fucking with my *life*, then at least for saddling me with her illegitimate brat."

Can't hurt me. Words can't hurt me. "It's too bad you see it that way. I don't even want the money, but I'd rather send it gift-wrapped to the government than let you have it."

"What are you going to do to stop me? *Kill* me?" There it was. The almost glowing evil that always transformed him. Made him appear to be a wax sculpture, frozen in hatred. Here she stood with the upper hand and his expression said, *you can't win.* It was almost enough to make her believe it. *Maybe he can't be killed,* she'd told Connor.

His confidence made her waver. *What am I doing here?* She tightened her grip around the skillet and battled back. "Yeah, maybe I am." She took a step closer, felt her anger rising. "Don't act so damn surprised. You don't treat a human being the way you treated me and expect them to *forget.*"

Luther eyed the skillet. "Always blaming everyone else. Me, the system. We all have choices in life. We each choose our own path."

"No. *No.*" The sound in her head started quietly, a beating

of wings, but it might as well have been a symphony tuning up.
It meant she was losing control, and that heightened the terror
of being this close to her tormentor. "I didn't f-fail. I have a job
now, I'm—"

His harsh laugh cut her off. "How long do you think that
will last? Look at you. You broke into my house to assault me.
How long do you think it'll take before they realize you're just
a broken toy?"

"No." The wings beat louder. *LOUDER*. She heard a sound
in the distance and realized she'd dropped the skillet. Her
stepfather shot forward the retrieve it, jolting her into motion.
They both grabbed on to the handle at the same time, resulting
in a tug of war. Her survival instincts roared to the surface.
Luther might be an evil man, but he hadn't been in prison. He
spent his days in an air-conditioned office, sipping Starbucks.
She'd fought for her life behind bars. When you'd done it once,
you never fought halfway again. Full throttle became your only
setting.

His hand slipped down the handle and brushed against her
skin, wrenching a scream from her throat. *Burning. It's burning.*
Erin twisted around and brought her boot down hard on his
wrist. Once, twice, three times. He howled and dropped the
handle, sending her reeling back at the loss of leverage. With the
skillet in her hand, she launched herself forward again, meeting
him halfway. She hadn't expected him to charge. He must have
seen something in her eyes that told him it was kill or be killed.

She held the skillet out of his reach, simultaneously bringing
her forehead down on his nose in a full-force head butt. The
crunch of cartilage echoed in the tiny room. He fell onto his
back, holding his bleeding nose, shouting obscenities that were
muffled by his hands. Erin came to her feet and loomed over
him. This was it. Where she'd always pictured herself when

revenge was allowed its fantasy. Standing over his cringing body with all the power in her hand. Power he'd once taken away. All she had to do was bring the object in her hand down on his skull and it would be over. No more wondering when he'd show up to terrorize her. No more threat of being locked away.

The ever-present matches in her pocket heated against her hip. She could already smell the singular scent the match strike would give off. Sultry. Decadent. So sweet. Crackles and pops sounded in her ears from the blessed fire that could take this all away. Erase it.

No more Connor. No more friends. No more team.

If she killed him...if she set fire to this house, those things would be taken away. She would have to run and leave them all behind. Even now, merely by breaking in and assaulting him, she might have damned herself to doing more time. Being put away in an institution. But she could walk away. She didn't have to do this. There were people who could help her if she just asked.

What am I doing here? I'm doing nothing. I'm...leaving.

As soon as she made the decision, it hit her that this is where the true power lay. Walking away. Not giving in to the darkness. Not eliminating her fear, but controlling it.

"Stay away from me or I'll come back and finish this." Her throat felt sunburned. "Do you understand me?"

He didn't answer. His chest rose and fell rapidly, hatred pouring off him in waves.

Erin tossed the skillet onto the washing machine with a loud *bang* and turned to walk out the back door, but his voice stopped her. "You won't get away with this."

She considered him a moment before sauntering back toward his prone body. He withdrew into himself the closer she got, making her smile. She reeled back with her fist and brought

it down once, connecting with his already-damaged nose w
all her strength. The blow rendered him unconscious.

"Tonight I will."

Erin closed the side door of the house behind her.

And ran straight into Connor.

He didn't budge an inch or try to steady her with his
hands when she bounced right off of him. His hard form
stood completely still in the darkness, except for his flexing
jaw. Frustration, anger, helplessness was evident in every line
of his strong body. His eyes were haunted. She could see that,
even in the darkness. They were focused on the bridge of her
nose where she could feel a fresh contusion, courtesy of her
head butt. She wanted to kneel down in front of him and weep.
Apologize. Tell him how much she'd missed him. Beg him not to
lose faith in her. Tell him how she'd just overcome the need to
do something bad because she couldn't imagine being without
him.

She couldn't, though. No. If he was here, he knew who was
inside. And if he went inside, he would kill her stepfather. Those
were the facts and she had to deal with them. Now. Prevent
any such outcome from happening. It would mean her restraint
tonight had been for nothing, because if Connor had blood on
his hands, he'd have to face the consequences instead of her.
He'd have to live with it when he already lived with so much
guilt every day of his life. She couldn't allow him to add to it on
her behalf. Couldn't allow him to be arrested or taken away in
cuffs. Or running for his freedom.

"I was going to come back to you."

Still, he said nothing. Didn't move. Just stared down at her

...h an unreadable expression.

She took a step closer to him. "Do you believe me?"

"No."

A pained sound slipped past her lips. Her ribs were caving in. She'd expected his anger, but she hadn't expected him to lose faith in her. He'd never been emotionless with her, through all the shit she'd thrown at him. She'd always been able to get a read on him, break through. "I'll convince you. I'll make you believe me."

His attention shot to the door like a whip being cracked. "Is he inside?"

"Connor, no." Oh, God. Her worst fears were playing out. She couldn't stop him when he was like this, could she? Her Connor wasn't anywhere to be found. Just this stiff, closed-off man who could brush her off like a fly if she tried to prevent him from going inside. "I took care of it. He won't come after me again."

The air around them thinned. "You killed him?"

She swallowed. "Yes."

His laugh was dark, unfamiliar. "That's two lies you've told me already tonight." He focused back on the door. "You're not a murderer. I know you're not."

I can't let him go inside. "Take me home. Please."

He tried to sidestep her, but she blocked his path. His hands curled and uncurled at his sides. "If you did as you say, let me confirm it. Let me see it with my own eyes."

"Don't. Don't go in there. It's not worth it."

"*You're* worth it." His voice thundered down at her. "You're worth four days of hell. Busting into a fucking motel, wondering if I'd find you dead inside. Wondering if I'd see you again. Then finding out you weren't even there…you were somewhere else when I *was not*." A light came on in the neighbor's yard and he automatically blocked her from its path. He lowered his voice but it was no less furious. "He made you run from me and I want to check the fucker's pulse. It's *worth* knowing that will never happen again. Do you understand me?"

She battled with the relief that assailed her. Nearly took her to the ground. He still wanted her. At least he still wanted her. "Show me, then. Show me I'm worth it. Trust me now."

"Oh, no. I didn't say anything about trust." He lowered his face just above hers. "After what you've put me through, I can't even trust you not to vanish when I turn my back."

He changed directions and started to move past her, sending panic tunneling into her midsection. *No.* Erin didn't think, didn't reason with herself.

She grabbed both of his hands and laid them on her face.

It burned like blue fire. It had been so long since someone had touched her face…maybe no one had *ever* touched her face. If they had, she had no memory of it. It felt like two brands had been applied to her skin. So hot and sharp was the pain that her knees dipped; a scream trapped itself in her throat. But she didn't let go. She refused to let go. Green eyes bored down into hers, dulling the pain in degrees. He spoke to her, his voice raw, so different from moments ago, but she could barely hear him.

"I trust *you*." Her teeth chattered around the words. "I trust you. See?"

"Sweetheart…oh *God*. Stop. Let go. You're making me hurt you. Please…*please*."

Miraculously, the pain was starting to lessen. Instead of a spiked burn, it turned into a rounded throb…then it dimmed. And dimmed some more. She moved his hands down her throat, marveling at the new sensation. Every new inch encountered a distinct burn, but it eased quicker the farther she went. She focused on his agonized eyes as she dragged them down, down, over her shoulders. Underneath her shirt to caress her belly.

Alive. She felt alive. Her nerve endings were singing. Connor. Only Connor could do this to her.

She must have said it out loud because he choked a curse. "Tell me what it feels like. Tell me I'm not causing you pain. I'm all fucked up right now, Erin. I can't deal with any more."

"Your hands…they're making me real. They feel so perfect. So perfect. Take me home," she whispered. "I'll let you touch me everywhere."

He dropped his head into the crook of her neck and groaned. "You feel so good. Your skin…" Erin sobbed a breath as he fell to his knees, wrapped his arms around her waist, and buried his face in her belly. "God, I missed you so much." His hands smoothed up her back and she arched into his touch, needing to feel everything. Every single stroke of his hand. "Now that I've had this, touched you, don't take it away from me. *Please* don't take it away from me."

"I won't. I can't." His hands swept down her thighs and traced the backs of her knees. A gasp flew from her mouth. Who knew she was so sensitive there? She wanted to stand there all night and let him touch her, let him acquaint his hands with every inch of her body, but time was a limited resource. Luther could stir at any time, and if he walked outside, it would be over in seconds. Connor wouldn't hesitate to act, and this beautiful moment would be lost to them.

Connor rose slowly to his feet, dragging his open mouth up the center of her body as he went. As soon as his face was even with hers, she captured his mouth with a kiss. She swayed into him with a moan and took. She'd seen him aroused before, but nothing compared to this. His erection dug into her belly, hard and demanding. Hands tunneled through her hair, making up for lost time as he seduced her with his tongue. Her primary goal of getting him away from the house blurred, but she snatched it back. She was fighting for their lives and needed to remember that.

Erin pulled away and sucked in a fortifying breath. "Let's leave." She smoothed a hand over one side of his perfect ass and tugged him against her, twisting her hips at the same time. "I need you."

He closed his eyes and cursed. "I know what you're doing. I know you're using my goddamn need for you to keep me out of that house. Even knowing I'm being played, I still can't fight it."

Before she could form a single word of protest, he swung her up into his arms and started toward the street. Tears pushed against the back of her eyelids, scalding and heavy. His words hurt worse than the initial burn of his touch. He'd belittled what they'd just shared, disregarding it as a ploy. She wanted to curl up and live within the hurt because crawling out required too much effort. She knew hurt. They were old friends, whereas hope was a newcomer, twice as dangerous.

Connor stopped in front of his navy-blue SUV and flung open the door, placing her inside. He started to buckle her seat belt, but stopped when she tensed. He closed the door and rounded the back of the car. Her gaze followed him, noting that the destroyed back window had been covered with plastic. His silhouette halted at the back of the car, illuminated by the streetlight. Hands planted on hips, he hung his head a moment, body momentarily deflating of tension. For a moment, she thought he might leave her in the car and go back to the house, but she breathed a sigh of relief when he climbed into the driver's side and started the engine.

He started to put on his seat belt, but stopped, letting it *whoosh* back into the strap holder, leaving himself unbuckled like her. When he spoke, he didn't look at her. "If something happens to one of us, it happens to both now, Erin."

Her fingers flew to her throat, placing pressure over the sudden tightness. She couldn't form a single word on the drive home, but it didn't stop her from thinking. This distrust between them, distrust she'd caused, would need to be repaired. Letting him touch her hadn't worked, obviously. Even though she'd laid herself achingly bare, he still thought she'd planned to run away and never look back. That she'd been using his attraction to her against him.

She had one last card to play, though. Even if it might kill her.

CHAPTER TWENTY

Connor prowled the kitchen, refusing to take his gaze off the bathroom door. On the other side, he could hear the shower running, knew Erin was in there, but having her gone from his sight so soon was like having a reprieve from death snatched away. She'd been silent on the ride home. God knows he hadn't been in a chatty mood with a combination of raging lust and reticent fear lacing through his insides, but when she'd walked into the bathroom without a word, alarm had been thrown into the mix. When he thought of the blood on her face, her disheveled appearance, his vision sparked with red. It took considerable effort to calm down enough to wonder just what she'd been through. The last four days had been hell for him, but he was more concerned with what they had been like for her. It had happened on his watch. Anything that happened to her, any threat she encountered, was his responsibility. As chauvinistic as it sounded, he couldn't rid himself of an instinct this strong.

Right now, his instinct was telling him to kick open the bathroom door and fuck her screaming against the tiled shower wall. It was telling him to bandage her cut, dress her, put something substantial in her stomach. Not performing those tasks was causing him physical discomfort. How long did it take to shower, anyway?

He spun on a heel toward the fridge and took out the carton of orange juice, pouring it into a glass just as the bathroom door opened behind him. Steam curled out, appearing to carry her out the door in slow motion. Oh, holy fuck. She was naked. Naked and dripping with water. Skin flushed from her shower…every inch of her glowed rosily. Temptation on two gorgeous legs. The orange juice slipped from his hands and landed on the floor, liquid gushing from the plastic cup, but he didn't even pay it a glance. He wanted to go to her, but his legs wouldn't move. Her lips spread into a tremulous smile as she turned and swayed toward the bedroom, her ass so delectable it set his teeth on edge.

He now had the ability to touch her. Jesus. It almost didn't seem real that he should have such a privilege. But had he *earned* it? Was she really ready? Or was she trying to keep him distracted when he needed to be hunting down someone who could potentially harm her?

Whatever her motive, his willpower still refused to make an appearance. His cock pressed against the fly of his jeans so insistently, he had to reach down and lower the zipper. A groan fell from his mouth as his hard length bobbed free. He could be inside her tonight without keeping his hands out of the equation. It was a heady thought, but also a worrisome one. Taking away the use of his hands had been a way to guarantee he didn't push too far. Didn't succumb to the driving urge to pin her, dominate her. They might have overcome a huge obstacle, but his darker tastes hadn't yet been addressed. After days of not knowing if he'd see her again, he didn't know if he could keep himself in check. If he went too far and injured her progress, he'd die inside.

Unable to wait a second more, knowing she was in the bedroom naked, warm, wet, Connor strode after her. He gripped his cock and stroked as he went, something he hadn't allowed himself in days, even when the pressure mounted or thoughts of Erin's perfect touch bombarded him. He'd made her a promise and he intended to keep it. When he walked into the bedroom, the scene that greeted him drew him up short.

Christ. Jesus Christ. He could hear his pulse in his ears, banging like a steel drum. "What the hell are you doing?"

Erin lay faceup on the bed, her wrists wrapped in silk above her head. The yellow silk belt from her bathrobe? The makeshift restraint had been tied around a wooden slat in the headboard, restraining her. Connor almost went to his knees for a second time that night, but her shallow breaths wouldn't allow him to succumb to the driving need. No, he couldn't want her like this. Wrong. It was wrong.

Oh, but he fucking did. Here was his ultimate fantasy brought to life. She looked spectacular, palm-sized breasts pointed straight up in the cool air, her stomach pulled taut. The things he could do to her like this. She'd cry out and try to get free, but it would be up to him.

Bastard. Think about what you're considering. Think. He didn't want her to ever hurt again, but she was doing it now on his behalf. A sacrifice. The ultimate apology. Giving away the freedom she required to keep her very sanity. All for him.

No, he couldn't let her do it. He *wouldn't*.

His willpower seconds from snapping in two, he climbed onto the bed on his knees, leaning over her to undo the bonds. When she licked her lips at his approach, wrists flexing in the restraint, Connor growled. "What are you trying to prove, Erin? *Goddammit.*"

"That I'm not leaving again." Her voice was surprisingly

strong considering the way her body trembled. This wasn't easy for her. Or him. Definitely not him. He was starving for her, and she was offering herself up to him on a silver platter. *Need her. Need her so bad.* "I'm giving myself to you. I'm yours. I won't go away again unless you make me."

His heart felt like it might jump from his chest. "*Make* you leave?" he shouted. "I've been *miserable* with you gone."

"Show me." She shifted on the bed to glide her legs around his hips. Fuck. Her damp, naked pussy was mere inches from his aching cock. He could already hear the needy little sobs she'd make as he thrust into her heat, over and over. Could feel her knees wedged against his palms as pushed her legs wide to get deeper, ride her harder. She must have seen his resolve slipping because her energy changed. Right before his eyes, she went from sacrificial lamb to seductress. Her back bowed under his hungry gaze, displaying her tits for him like a prize to be won. She touched her tongue to her top lip and let it linger as she writhed on the bed. "Will you kiss me between my legs, baby? Please?"

His world imploded. There was no more self-control to draw from. If she were showing even a fraction of uncertainty, he could have held back. As it was, she was looking up at him like a sexually deprived siren desperate for a hard fucking. His world turned a gritty shade of sepia, power roaring past his barriers and running wild. *Dominate her. She's begging you for it.*

Almost casually, he slipped his fingers into her hair, smiling as she purred under the touch. Both of them sucked in a breath as his fingers went tight, gripping her hair in an iron fist. *That's it. I'm lost.* "The next time you instruct me on how to please you, I will deny that request until you're willing to give up *everything* to have it granted."

Her mouth fell open on a sharp exhale. "Yes, Connor."

She wasn't looking at him the same as she had a moment ago. There was a new awareness. He didn't know if he loved that or hated it. Should he exult in her acknowledging this side of him or be nervous that it would change what they had? He was too far gone to decide. The line had been crossed and he couldn't turn back. Erin's gaze ran the length of him, and although he wanted to touch, to arouse her more, he waited for her to look her fill. When her attention lingered between his legs, he came up on his knees to loom above her. "I'd love to let you suck it, sweetheart. I can see how bad you want to, but I've gone four days without you. The second you deep-throated it, I'd come like a fucking freight train. I could tell you not to let it past your teeth, but you'd do it anyway, wouldn't you? You love every inch."

Her mouth looked swollen, begging to be breached. "Yes, I love it."

He fisted his shaft. "I haven't touched myself since you left. Do you remember why?"

Excitement shimmered all over her, like she'd been dusted with magic. "Because you only come inside me."

"That's right. Spread your legs and show me where."

She wet her lips as she hesitated. Only a few beats passed before her legs fell open on the bed. He longed for rope to bind her ankles to the bedposts. He also knew if this situation got any closer to perfect, it might kill him, so it was a good thing he didn't. Jesus, her thighs were enough to captivate him with their smooth lines, their slight quiver of anticipation. As he laid a hand on her right inner thigh, he watched her face for panic, but saw only trust. *Good girl. Brave girl.* His attention was arrested by the exquisite flesh at the apex of her thighs. Still wet and flushed from her shower, it begged for invasion. Begged to be mastered.

"You're going to need a safe word, Erin, because I'm about to do such obscene things to your pussy with my mouth, you're going to scream for me to stop even when you want me to keep going." He slapped her between the thighs with his weighty erection, groaning at the sound of their most sensitive flesh connecting. "Pick a word to scream if you can't take it."

"Um." He slapped her again with his cock, making her head thrash on the pillow. "S-skillet."

Any other time that might have struck him as funny, but right now he had only one goal. Taste her, fuck her. Own her. "Look at me." He waited until she complied. "I will *listen* if you say that word. I will listen and *stop*. Always."

Her eyes cleared of everything but lust. "I know."

He dropped onto his stomach between her legs and plunged his tongue inside her. Wood creaked as she screamed and begun to chant his name. His only regret was her fingers not being free to pull at his hair, but he more than consoled himself with her already-spasming flesh, the thighs that locked around his head like a vise. The knowledge that she was entirely at his mercy. Finally.

"Oh *God*, oh my God. I-I *can't*."

Yes you can. Recognizing the ecstasy in her tone, Connor kept his tongue inside her and added his middle finger, moving them in and out, devastating her with the smooth rhythm. *Christ.* The taste of her could keep a man alive in the desert. Possessiveness caught him in a stranglehold. Not a man. *Him. He* could live off her, the taste of her keeping him alive. Living to keep her satisfied. She was warm, wet woman. Ripe and delicious. He would never get enough. Never. But he couldn't get close enough because her hips worked feverishly in time with her hoarse cries of his name.

"*Hold still*," he commanded, crooking two fing
to play with her G-spot. "I need to get my lips around
I'm going to suck that little bud until you pass out. You've b
keeping her from me, but time's up, sweetheart. She's mine."

Erin started to shake, eyes going blind with her orgasm. The most beautiful goddamn thing he'd ever seen in his life. "N-no more. No more. I can't—"

He suctioned his mouth over her clit and took a long pull. She shot off the bed, heels digging into his shoulders as she moaned. He took her ankles in his hands and held her legs open on either side of him while he worshiped the most sensitive part of her body. After she'd come once more, he gave her back his fingers and worked her hard, getting her ready to be fucked. His head was swimming with her, turned on by every lithe, desperate movement of her body. He pictured her as she was, stretched out on the bed, wrists bound as he mouth-fucked her, and it drove him crazy. His hips started to roll against the edge of the bed, pushing and dragging his cock along the mattress.

Not good enough. Nowhere near good enough. Inside her. Get inside her.

He tore his mouth away with a growl and crawled over her body. The head of his length slipped through her pussy and his breath shuddered out. Taking hold of himself, he was poised at her entrance when he searched her eyes. What he saw there sent him reeling. Sent him even higher.

She looked…tamed. Owned. From the sweat-dampened pillows where she struggled to catch her breath, she was a woman looking up at her master. It humbled him. It filled him with an unbreakable determination never to live without that trust from her. That trust owned *him* as much as he could ever own her.

"I was coming back to you," she whispered.

A weight crushed down on his chest. In the crystal clarity of the moment, with her handing over her terror and doubt to him, to share, to repair, he knew she meant it. "I know."

The exhilarated smile that spread across her face reached inside Connor and mended every damaged corner of his being. It mended *him*. Made him whole. It made him want to live forever so he could see the same smile as many times as God would allow. There was no choice before him but to press their bodies together and kiss her.

Erin had lost any sense of space or time. She was everything Connor decided to give her. Everything he decided to make her feel. His to conquer and direct. Yet at the same time, she was there with him, moving in the same patterns, accepting every gift of sensation with a sureness that he would provide with it. There was no uncertainty here, only revelry. The overwhelming intensity of being tied up, trapped, had been transferred to him until he became all she could see, feel, taste. Her all. His mouth moved over hers, hard and delicious, vanquishing any reminder that her arms were bound. He was the only thing binding her now.

This kiss started out slow and savoring, but it built. Oh, it built until they were struggling to wrap their bodies around each other. Growls of desperation, bucking hips, licking skin. His hips wedged between her thighs and even without being inside her, he was already fucking her. His bulky erection slid through her wet flesh, over her sweaty belly and back down to nudge her entrance.

Instead of thrusting into her like she was physically begging him to do, he took hold of his length and teased her clit with the smooth head, jaw loosening as he groaned. The green of his eyes had turned almost gray in the dim light. His massive body hovered over her like a predator, muscles catching the light and shadows, highlighting every valley and ridge. For the first time, she wished for the use of her hands if only so she could explore that unbelievable body, touch the man who was about to take her. He was fucking magnificent. And by some twist of luck, he was hers.

His head dipped so he could close his mouth around her nipple, watching her through hooded eyes as he sucked. When she started to writhe, he moved to her other breast and licked it reverently. "After tonight, we won't talk about how you left ever again. For my sanity, Erin. We won't discuss it." With a drive of his hips, he plunged inside her and held her there, pinned, without moving. She couldn't breathe or think beyond the pressure already building in her abdomen. "For tonight, though, we won't forget." He spoke through clenched teeth. "I'm a man who lost his woman and I'm going to fuck her very hard until she knows what it did to me. I'm going to make sure she never does it again."

She wanted to soothe him. To tuck herself into the space between his neck and shoulder and croon to him. But there was another, equally poignant side to her that wanted it rough. "Go ahead, Connor. Show me." She worked her hips and his chest shuddered. "Make me sorry."

Until she said the words, she didn't know they were there, ready to spill out. It was as if some unknown part of her had communicated with Connor on a different level. As soon as the challenge left her mouth, the air around them changed. Thickened. Her heartbeat echoed in her ears as he withdrew from her and knelt beside her on the bed. She stopped breathing. What was he going to do?

Her question was answered when he clutched both of her ankles in one big hand and lifted the bottom half of her body off the bed, as if she weighed nothing. The position left only her head and shoulders resting on a pillow, hands still connected to the bed frame, the rest of her dangling from Connor's grip.

His breath rasped in and out. "Make you sorry, Erin?"

"Yes."

"*No.*" His calloused hand smoothed over her naked backside. "Use your safe word, goddammit. I'm drowning, sweetheart."

She bit her lip hard and said nothing, suddenly craving what would come next. Anything. She wanted *anything* he could give her. All of it. When the first slap came, it wasn't hard, but it knocked the breath out of her. Something akin to pleasure danced along her nerve endings, turning her nipples to tight peaks, but there was an underlying harshness to it. A harshness she was responding to. A burn. A flame-like edge. *Yes, yes. More.* "Please."

He released a sound of frustration, but it was coupled with lust. "*Please,* what?"

"Another." She could barely speak around the blanketing need. "Do it again."

Connor's growl ricocheted off the walls. His palm landed on her bare ass harder than before, sending reverberations of bliss through her middle, gathering at her core. Again and again, the firm smacks rained down, each one sensitizing her skin slightly more until she felt like a barrier had fallen. There was nothing to stop the vibrations from reaching her, the sharp licks of pain from biting her where she needed them. This was how her body was meant to be used. She'd been avoiding touch? No. She'd just never been touched by the only person who knew how.

One slap came incredibly close to the needy flesh between her thighs and she came off the bed with a cry. Oh God, if he didn't do that again, she would die of neglect. Connor's fingers dug into the cheek of her ass, distracting her from the sting. "Liked that, did you? Twisting and moaning like a greedy little girl. We know just what you need now, don't we? Is this what it'll take to make you stay put? Because I will hook you to this bed and land blows on your ass all fucking day. Do you doubt me?"

"N-no." *Slap.* "*No.*"

He dropped her lower body back onto the bed, letting her bounce once before he shoved her legs apart. "Can't wait anymore. *Want.*" He inhaled on a curse when he gripped his erection and led himself between her legs. She expected him to slide home right away, but he fell forward instead to press their foreheads together, hand still wedged between their bodies. "Where do I come, Erin?"

"Between my legs," she breathed. "Inside me."

He rammed home with a hoarse shout against her neck. Sensation spearing through her belly, she automatically tried to circle his hips with her legs to account for the pressure, but he palmed her knees and kept them open. "Don't try to limit me. I get all of you. I rule every goddamn inch of that pussy." He rocked out slightly and thrust deep again, hissing between his teeth. "All tied up for me. Thighs spread. Tits begging for another suck. I've got you where I want you, so hang the fuck on."

Erin barely had the presence of mind to reach up and wrap her bound hands around the headboard before Connor started to pound. A scream was rent from her throat, long and loud. *Oh, Jesus.* He was huge and hot inside her, filling and stroking her slick walls with merciless drives of his hips. Beneath her, she could feel the bed inching along the wooden floor, hear the accompanying scrape. Nowhere to go. Nowhere to hide from the building pleasure. It gathered like a darkening storm as he rode her body, used it in a primal manner reserved only for starving, desperate men. She'd made him this way. Driven him to this state of blind abandon, where he snarled into her neck and fucked her like he might die.

She would die, too. If he were snatched away now, she wouldn't survive it. *No me without him. No him without me.* There was no separation between their bodies, just sweat-slicked, intertwined limbs writhing together on the bed. The storm began to break, trembling beginning in her thighs and traveling up to encompass her entire body. Her back bowed to accept the rush of pleasure, and Connor, sensing her oncoming release like only he could, shoved his forearm beneath her ass to angle her perfectly. His name fell from her mouth over and over, in time with the powerful rolls of his hips.

He gripped her jaw in his hand, forced her chin up. "You look at me when you come." His pace increased until the sound of flesh slapping in the room was enough to speed her even closer. Connor leaned down and spoke very precisely at her lips. "You might escape everywhere else, but you can't escape this. Me. I'm where you *live.*"

Erin launched into her climax, floating for an extended moment in the gripping euphoria of it before time sped up again and she was back to shaking and calling out for God. Connor. Both. He panted above her, his powerful body's movements growing uneven. He closed his eyes and threw his head back, but she would have none of that. Equal measure. She would give him everything, every damn broken piece of herself she had to bargain with, but he would do the same.

She tightened her thighs around his hips and squeezed with every ounce of energy she had left over. "You look at me, too. I don't *want* to escape you." The words were choppy because she could hardly draw enough breath to release them. Connor's head immediately snapped up, eyes blazing down into hers. Something inside her relaxed and spun wildly all at once. Again she wished her hands were free so she could reach up and grip the strands of his hair. He needed her. Needed touch, even if he might think he wanted control more. "Show me where you come, baby. Show me how. Let me have it. I need it."

He fell on her with a jagged groan, hips pumping once, twice, before his entire body began to quake. When a man his size shook, everything shook. Erin convulsed right along with him; their bodies were skin to skin, so close that not a breath of air separated them. Feeling his orgasm rock him almost sent her spiraling into an aftershock. She suspected that if her arms were free to hold him, it would have happened. As it was, she could only lie there and absorb his heaving breaths, his elevated body heat. It was glorious. She never wanted to leave this spot. Could live here for all eternity, just pillowing Connor's body with her own.

Connor seemed to come back to himself, then. His head dislodged from the crook of her neck, hands flying up to disconnect her from the bed frame. "Tell me you're okay. *Tell me.*"

One hand came free, but it fell uselessly beside her on the bed. She shook it frantically, trying to move life into it. Where a moment ago, Connor's eyes held such command, now they were shadowed and she needed to reassure him. Amazing that she, someone whom *no one* had ever turned to for support, was now…needed. Even through the urgency to take away Connor's worry, she felt a burst of something like pride. She finally got her hand to work and laid it against his jaw. "I'm better than okay. Look at me."

Connor's glazed-over eyes finally focused on her. He shook

his head. "Okay? No. You're fucking beautiful." His throat worked. "I need you to promise if I ever go too far, you'll tell me. If I ever did something to scare you or send you away, I'd — "

"Baby, I'm an arsonist with extreme claustrophobia and a jealous streak." She finally ran her fingers through his hair and savored his sigh. "I think it's safe to say we're holding an even amount of scary playing cards."

His eyes crinkled at the sides, and she almost swooned over how fucking adorable it made him look. Was this really the same man who'd just spanked her? She nestled down into the pillows and held her arms out to him. He didn't hesitate to align his naked body with hers and tuck her against his chest.

"Play any card you want, sweetheart," he murmured. "I'm not budging."

CHAPTER TWENTY-ONE

Connor and Erin sat across the street from Tucker May's house, watching his wife receive a furniture delivery. Sera had managed to get the license plate number of the SUV that continued to pull up outside Stark's campaign headquarters, and a quick search had led them here. Derek wanted to know why the seemingly distraught Mrs. May continued to make her presence known at headquarters and what was being delivered to her curbside each time. Connor had a good idea, especially considering the high-end name on the delivery truck. Money was exchanging hands. They just needed to figure out why and prove it.

Erin rolled the passenger-side window down, causing a breeze to lift the blond hair from her shoulders. Her scent crossed the car to sucker punch him, and Connor's groin tightened on cue. There would be no getting enough of this girl. With each passing minute, his desire for her built like an out-of-control hurricane. He'd woken this morning to find her worshipping his morning wood with long licks and kisses, murmuring husky praise against his stomach, jacking him off in her fist. Fuck. He'd managed a strangled request to finish inside her pussy, but she'd refused to let up. Holding him down with a hand on his abs, pulling hard with her mouth, and moaning, as if she couldn't stop.

She drummed her fingers on the armrest, dragging him from the memory. "May's wife must know what happened to her husband. Taking payouts to keep quiet, maybe?"

He dragged his head out of the gutter and focused. When he adjusted himself in his pants, she gave him a sexy, knowing smile, which didn't help at all. "Yeah. She doesn't exactly appear to be the grieving widow. Derek interviewed some friends of the family, people at church. They wouldn't have won couple of the year, but staying quiet about your husband being killed is a whole other level."

"You never know what's happening behind closed doors."

Something in her voice tugged a chord in his chest. They needed to talk about her stepfather, even if it meant shattering the peace of the morning. Before last night, he'd known there would never be anyone else for him. Not as long as he lived. But the way she'd sacrificed the freedom she required in order to satisfy him, to prove she wouldn't leave again…he'd simply never be the same. He'd woken up feeling different. Weighed down with purpose in a good way. She had given herself to him, and he wouldn't take that responsibility lightly. Because he belonged to her, too. If something happened to her, they would both suffer. What he'd gone through when she'd gone missing, but multiplied by a thousand. He needed to prevent that outcome at all costs.

"If you think any harder, smoke is going to come out of your ears," she commented without looking at him. "How about I save you the trouble and just tell you what happened?"

Relief and hope warred in his mind, but he was still wary. It wasn't like Erin to volunteer information without being asked.

"I'd like that."

As if she'd heard the doubt in his voice, she turned and scrutinized his face. Her shoulders slumped a little at what she saw there. "I didn't kill him."

"I knew that, sweetheart. You didn't have to tell me."

She sniffed. "It's the *why* that matters, Connor. I didn't kill him because of this." She waved her hand between the two of them. "I can't be who I used to be anymore. Neither can you."

He knew mostly what she was trying to say, but needed to hear her clarify. "Explain that."

"I never gave a shit before. I give a shit now." She crossed her legs, making her boots jingle. "I wanted to do the right thing, but I didn't even know what it *was*. You know how pathetic that felt? Standing there with a skillet in my hand, not understanding *why* I shouldn't kill a man?"

Fury infiltrated his veins at the thought of her needing a weapon for a goddamn minute. At the thought of her scared. Needing to defend herself. He beat back the emotions, knowing he needed to listen. *She* needed him to listen.

"I need you to help me, Connor. Help me find the right way." Her blue eyes implored him. "We're better than him. What he did to me…we beat it last night. It's gone for us. I know the second I'm not looking, you'll go over there and make him pay. But I think I'm making him pay just by being happy, you know? You make me that way."

His throat constricted. "What you make me feel goes so far beyond happy, Erin."

Pleasure softened her eyes. "Good. So it's settled."

"No." He shook his head regretfully. "I'm not ready to agree to that yet."

Her expression fell. "Stubborn motherfucker."

"Yeah." They sat quietly for a while. Across the street, the furniture movers unloaded a chaise longue that probably cost a year's salary for most people. He knew they should talk more, but he needed to change the subject. If she kept flashing those blue eyes at him and saying shit that made his heart swell, he'd find himself agreeing to a promise he couldn't keep.

As much as he wanted to be strong for Erin, he didn't have it in him to let the man walk around free knowing his sole focus was on locking Erin up and taking her money. Over his dead body would that be happening. So at the very least, he would be paying the man a visit. A visit where the man would answer for what he did to Erin as a girl. Maybe that brought him down to the fucker's level, made him a villain. But the simple knowledge of knowing someone who had caused her untold agony was out there, walking around free and clear? It strangled him with helpless frustration. Erin thought it was pathetic that she didn't know right from wrong? They weren't so different. To him, wrong meant leaving her open to a threat. Nothing else.

Erin didn't give him a chance to speak. She picked up the cell phone he'd bought for her that morning and hit one of the programmed numbers. "Hey, hacker. What's the racket?" He almost smiled over the unique greeting she gave Polly, but the resignation in her voice stopped it in its inception. "We're outside May's house, watching a truck vomit fancy furniture all over her lawn. The furniture store is called Lazzoni. Can you get into their system and see how she paid? Credit card, bank account…"

Connor considered her a moment. The girl was so much smarter than she gave herself credit for. What kind of potential might she have reached if she'd been allowed to attend school? If she'd had the supportive family she deserved and gone to college?

"Yeah. We know she doesn't have it in the bank records you

pulled. If she's hiding money, maybe Lazzoni can lead us to the end of the rainbow." Erin hung up the phone and placed it back in the cupholder. "I kind of like Polly. Don't tell her, though."

"Why not?"

"It would mess with our dynamic."

His lips twitched as he considered the scene across the street. Mrs. May was directing the furniture movers with one hand, holding a Chihuahua in the other. "Even if we find out Mrs. May is receiving money, it might not be traceable. I can't imagine Stark has gotten this far without learning how to make cash invisible."

"True. Even if we trace the money to Stark, Derek needs May to testify. He's the only one who can prove Stark took the bribes." She sighed and dropped her head back onto the headrest. "Where would be the last place anyone would expect May to hide?"

"With all the suspicion over Stark silencing May?" Connor scratched his chin. "The last place I'd expect to find him is living in Stark's basement."

Erin turned impressed eyes on him. "You read my mind. Not easy to do with all the caution tape and potholes I've got scattered in there."

He bit his tongue against admonishing her. "How do we test our theory? And if you suggest climbing over the ten-foot-high gate surrounding his house and going in to investigate, let me rid you of that fantasy right now."

"I've gotten in and out of worse."

Connor clamped his jaw shut. It was either that or start shouting.

Erin winked to let him know she had no such plans, but he didn't relax entirely. She had that familiar spark of mischief in her eye, telling him there was more than caution tape unfurling in her head.

"Erin—"

She reached over and dug her nails into his thigh to quiet him. He followed her line of sight and found Mrs. May peering across the street, lifting her hand to shield her eyes from the sun. Erin moved at the same time he reached for her, settling on his lap. They couldn't be caught watching the house, and obviously were of the same mind that kissing was the best way to detract from suspicious attention. Erin's ass nestled over his already hardening dick as their mouths met in a long-overdue kiss.

What had it been? An hour? Jesus, he'd missed the taste of her. He'd taken her to Starbucks on the way over and she'd picked a peppermint mocha at random, never having been there before. Now her mouth tasted like Christmas and he couldn't get close enough. He pinched her chin between his thumb and forefinger, tugging it down so he could revel in her texture with his tongue. Her head fell back on a groan that he echoed in his chest.

She twisted her hips on his stiff lap, biting his bottom lip and tugging as she did it. *Tease.* She knew he couldn't have her here. In retaliation, he reached under her skirt and gripped her pussy. Her mouth left his, breath panting in and out. Connor squeezed her flesh, a reminder of what she'd woken in him last night. A part of him that wouldn't be denied anymore now that it had been released.

"Play fair, sweetheart. I came in your mouth this morning, but I only consider that foreplay. I haven't fucked you today as far as I'm concerned, and I'm not happy about it." He rubbed his knuckles along the dampening material of her panties, glorying in her gasp. "If you wanted my cock inside you so bad, you should have stopped sucking when I asked, but you were a greedy girl. Weren't you?"

He felt a shudder pass through her. "Yes."

"Don't tease me, Erin."

"I won't."

He released her and she slumped against his chest. Casting an eye across the street, he noticed Mrs. May had gone back inside, but the movers were sending covert glances in their direction. Breathing through a surge of possessiveness, he gently maneuvered Erin back into the passenger seat. He noted her stiff nipples pushing against the front of her crop top. Her denim skirt had ridden up, giving him a tempting view of her beautiful thighs pressing tightly together. He should find somewhere less public to ease her. God, he wanted to like hell. But she'd asked him to help her do the right thing regarding her stepfather, and he hadn't been able to give it to her. That shamed him. So once again, he would atone. Would make today special for her. Because as early as tonight, he would act. He wanted her to have a memory to hold on to when he failed to give her what she wanted, but took what he needed instead.

"Will you let me show you something?"

"Anything," she answered, without a single hesitation.

CHAPTER TWENTY-TWO

Erin marveled over the feel of her hand tucked inside Connor's as he led her toward the skyscraper's revolving-door entrance. He'd offered her his hand so casually, she'd felt silly doing anything other than taking it. She suspected he was acting that way on purpose. Aware that all these little steps they were accomplishing one by one were actually mammoth-sized leaps. The skin-on-skin contact still stung at first, but somewhere in the middle of the night last night, pleasure with a hint of pain had turned into a craving instead of something from which to escape.

As long as Connor was the one holding her hand, she could trust it. Case in point, she had no idea where he was taking her, but she followed him willingly. Something she would have chewed her own arm off before doing a couple weeks ago. On the ride over, she'd been a little shaken up over what had happened between them outside the May residence. One minute she'd been lost in their kiss and the next, he'd been in command of every cell in her body. His hand between her legs, his deep, velvet voice that only came out to play when he dominated her. It should startle her how easily he could take over her emotions, her thoughts. But she wasn't startled. He'd found a lock deep down inside her and turned a key only he held. Now energy flowed through her without the usual obstacles, reaching out to him for more. She could never be alarmed over something that felt this good, this right. And if it ever stopped feeling good and right, she also knew Connor wouldn't rest until it did. That kind of trust was as unfamiliar to her as the responses he wrung from her body, but they were hers and they were perfect.

When they had passed through the glass doors, Connor asked her to wait nearby while he purchased tickets. For what? She strolled over to a display on the wall and saw that they were in the Willis Tower, the tallest building in the Western Hemisphere. She didn't get a chance to read more before Connor placed a hand at the small of her back and led her to an elevator. They waited while a group of tourists boarded and Connor signaled that they would take the next one. She was grateful for that. While she'd taken a step toward conquering her fear of elevators, this was a tall-ass building and she didn't know how high up they were going. They might be in the steel death trap for a while, and who knew what crazy her brain would decide to dig up.

The second elevator rolled open, devoid of other passengers. She lifted her chin and stepped inside, Connor following behind her. As soon as the doors closed, she held her breath, waiting to see which button he would push.

The 103rd floor.

She gave a sharp exhale. "Guess the stairs are out."

Just as her vision started to swim, Connor walked her back toward the wall, creating an instantaneous clenching in her middle. Lower. He pressed his lips to her forehead and hummed quietly, which she found immensely comforting, although she didn't know why. Slowly, he molded their bodies together against the wall, letting his lips travel down to nuzzle her ear. "Show me what a brave, sweet girl you are."

If his goal was to lower her heart rate, this method wasn't working. Her pulse skyrocketed back to where it had been in the car as they'd kissed. Out of control. Furious. She reached out and held on to the distraction for dear life, knowing he would deliver more. Always more.

He raised his left hand, running his fingers along the seam of her lips. When her lips parted on an inhale, he dipped his middle finger all the way inside and held it there. "Come on, sweetheart. Show me how you sucked me off this morning."

Erin's eyelids fluttered, lust wrapping her up in its haze. She kept her gaze fastened on Connor as she drew hard on his finger, wishing it were the real thing. Remembering the way he'd spoken to her this morning, alternating between commanding her to stop and ordering her to *never, ever fucking stop*. It had felt different, with his hands on her. In her hair, on her chin, her shoulders. The most intimate act brought only higher.

Now, Connor's chest rose and fell heavily as he watched her mouth. He took the opposite hand and palmed her breast, making her gasp around his thick finger. Making her suck harder, lips sliding up and down as she silently begged him with her eyes to make contact with her nipple.

"So eager to please, Erin. But it's my turn." The hand on her breast trailed down over her rib cage, stopping at the spot just below her belly button. Without warning, he used the heel of that hand to pin her back against the wall, then began to massage slow, tight circles inches above her needy core. Erin moaned around his finger, the sound bouncing off the steel interior of the elevator. "Does my cock hit you here when we fuck, sweetheart?"

She nodded her head frantically, letting her teeth graze the inner flesh of his finger. A muscle in his jaw jumped in response. She'd never seen his green eyes sharper, more alert. Being preyed upon would have scared her once upon a time. Now she found herself yearning for it.

Stalk me.

He groaned low in his throat as her tongue got involved. "Good girl. Show me how well you suck me with that wet, hungry mouth."

The rhythmic massage he was performing against her lower belly was building something undeniable inside her. For what felt like the tenth time today, she squeezed her thighs together and rubbed, unsure if she wanted to lessen the ache or cater to it. If only he would go *lower*.

Connor's hand left her belly and started to descend. Erin whimpered a protest as he changed direction, though, smoothing his touch over her hip and splaying his big palm over her bottom. He tightened his fingers in a gesture of ownership, before removing his hand and propping it on the wall behind her. In degrees, he withdrew the finger from her mouth, spreading the moisture across his sculpted lips. His head dipped and he kissed her with such erotic intention that it felt as if his hands were still on her body, feeling their way down and molding her flesh. Her mind reeled under the assault, but he pulled back before she could wrap her legs around his waist and plead to be filled.

His voice was gruff and slightly rueful. "When we got on this elevator, I was going to tell you I'm proud of you. In so many ways. I'm proud of you for what you've overcome. Proud of the trust you've given me. Proud to call myself your man. Jesus, I'm more than proud of that. I'm goddamn lucky." He placed a kiss on her forehead. "I was going to say all those things, then I looked at you and it all got lost."

She felt like she'd just lain down in a giant feather bed. Utter happiness teamed with a sense of belonging. "You just said them," was all she could manage before the elevator doors opened. Connor stepped back, slung an arm around her shoulder and tugged her from the space, looking a little smug when her legs didn't work as well as they should. They walked onto an enormous open space. Out of habit, she immediately looked for the exit doors, even though that escape would be futile. One hundred and three floors had to be at least one thousand and fifty steps to the street, probably more. As if he sensed her relapse into fear, Connor pulled her protectively into his side.

And then she saw it.

Built into the wall, there was a giant glass window. But it wasn't an ordinary window. It was a glass box, extending out at least four feet over downtown Chicago. She couldn't catch her breath as she walked toward it, leaving Connor to follow. The skyline seemed to go on for a million miles before her, piercing blue sky blending together with it on the horizon. She'd never been up this high in her life. Never felt this imminent sensation of free-falling, but it blasted her with the ultimate impression of freedom. A high she'd been seeking without realizing it. This was the escape to end all escapes.

Erin stepped into the glass box and looked down at her feet. No floor. Just air. She looked from side to side. Up. No walls. No ceiling. Tears blurred her vision as her arms seemed to float up all on their own, extending and rising like a bird's wings. In the back of her mind, she knew it was an illusion, but it was a powerful one. Not a trap in sight. Free. She finally felt free. Like with a single leap, she could land on one of the fluffy white clouds passing by in the breeze and float forever.

But she didn't want that. Didn't need to run ever again.

That realization made the box seem even bigger, encompassing more of the city and its skyline through the simple fact that she could take it or leave it. She'd been wrong. The ultimate escape wasn't in front of her. He was standing behind her, ready to catch her if she fell. Believing in her to do the same for him. She wanted to do that. She wanted to be this glass box for him. His freedom. The place he ran to when he needed comfort.

She turned around to face Connor and the breath whooshed from her lungs. He was watching her with such tenderness in his eyes, such pride, she almost sank to her knees. No one had ever looked at her like that. Not a single person since the day she was born. But it didn't matter anymore, because he'd just made up for every moment of lost time with one look.

"I'm in love with you," she said. "But please stop looking at me like that because I don't know where else to put the feelings. All the cracks are filled in and there's nowhere for them to go."

"We'll make room." His voice rang with intensity. He didn't come to her, though, appearing rooted to the spot. "I'm in love with you, Erin. Get used to me looking at you like I mean it."

She swallowed the king-size knot in her throat. "Thank you for bringing me here."

He took a step in her direction, stopping at the very edge of the box. "Remember this if I ever do something to disappoint you. Remember that I'd give you everything you can see from this window if I could. Everything."

He didn't mean buildings, cars, or rivers. No, he meant a place to soar. To get away if she needed to. He'd brought her here to show her he wouldn't fence her in. He'd set aside his controlling nature to give her what he thought she still needed. Erin closed the distance between them, bringing them toe to toe. His Adam's apple worked in his throat the closer she came, eyes sliding closed. She placed a hand over his heart, trailed it up his neck and into his hair. "I don't need it anymore. I only need you."

"Christ, Erin. I need you, too."

Yes. He did. And somehow to her that meant more than "I love you." It meant she finally had a place. Someone who not only found her worthy of love, but capable of holding his heart. She took his hand and led him back toward the elevator, leaving behind the most beautiful escape she'd ever encountered without a single glance. A group of French tourists entered the elevator at the same time, but when Connor pulled back, silently suggesting they wait for the next car, she shook her head.

They boarded the elevator with the group, retreating to their own corner in the back. Instead of waiting for Connor to press her up against the wall again, she took control, feeling so empowered her blood heated and snapped in her veins. With a firm hand on his chest, she nudged him back and aligned their bodies. More people piled onto the elevator at the last minute, forcing them even closer together. Connor's eyes fell to half mast, a complete contrast to what she could feel rising in his pants.

After the words they had just exchanged, keeping her hands to herself felt like sacrilege. They should be kissing. More, their bodies should be connected. It was obvious from Connor's muttered curses, he felt the same. Remembering the way he'd taken her to the brink with only a few touches on the way up, a hint of wickedness crept into her already-rushing blood and carried her away. Hoping none of the animated tourists were paying them any attention, she reached for the hem of her shirt and drew it up, revealing her braless breasts. Because of their position, Connor was the only one who could see what she'd exposed, but his reaction could make or break the situation.

Apart from the accelerated rise and fall of his big chest, the subtle flare of his nostrils, he showed no reaction.

She reached up and locked her wrists behind his neck, lifting her breasts. Her distended nipples glided over the soft material of his shirt, and she felt his erection grow stiffer against her belly. Muscles she didn't even know she had tightened in response. This spontaneous plan to drive him crazy was backfiring. All she could think about was climbing his sturdy male body and riding his hardness until relief sent her spiraling.

Connor dipped his head to growl against her ear. "What did I say about teasing?"

"Not to do it," she whispered into his hair, smiling when his whole body shuddered. "I'm not teasing, though. I'm showing you how bad I'd like you to fuck me."

"Christ." He scanned the elevator with a glare before returning his eyes to her. Again, he spoke for her ears alone. "Put your hand on my cock and say that again."

A renewed dose of excitement assailed her. Without hesitation, she removed one of the hands locked behind his head and dragged it down his chest, over his belt buckle to cup his hard length. Breath hissed out from between his teeth. She stroked him once, twice, entranced by the way his hips rolled in perfect unison with her touch. "I'd like you to fuck me."

"You'd like or you'd love it?"

"*Love* it." She swallowed a gasp when he closed his teeth around her ear. "Please, baby."

As always, when she called him that, his eyes darkened like thunderheads. "Cover yourself, then. Because as soon as we get off this elevator, my only goal will be to find a dark place where I can get my cock beneath that skirt and fuck you blind."

On cue, the elevator doors pinged open behind her. The dark promise in Connor's eyes was so distracting, she almost forgot to pull her shirt back into place before turning around, a fact that didn't go unnoticed by Connor if his growl was any indication. She'd only taken two steps when her hand was swallowed by Connor's and he started striding toward the building's exit with her in tow. Only his profile was visible, but his rigid jaw didn't welcome conversation. Thankfully, she didn't have shit to say at the moment. She had just crossed the line from aroused to out-and-out desperate. How was it possible to need him this bad when he'd been inside her a matter of hours ago? She didn't know. Didn't care. She could only follow Connor and hope he found some way to make it better.

When they exited the building, he headed in the direction of his car, but turned a corner when they were still a block from the parking garage. After half a block of walking at a fast clip, she saw his destination. An older-looking movie theater lit up a small section of the side street, boasting action flicks from the eighties and nineties. *Die Hard* and *Death Warrant* were missing letters up on the marquee.

Connor stopped at the ticket counter and tossed a twenty through the slot. "Two for *Death Warrant*."

As soon as the tickets passed under the glass partition, Connor snatched them up and led her into the theater lobby. Apart from one senior citizen leaning against the concessions counter reading a newspaper, they appeared to be the only people with a pulse in the entire building. Connor nodded at the man and led her down a dim hallway, entering the last theater on their right.

One man sat by himself in the front row of the theater, barely bothering to look up as Connor and Erin bypassed him on their way to the back row. The movie was already in full swing, loud grunts and punches connecting with flesh signaling the fact that they'd walked in on a fight scene. Connor sat down in a seat just off the aisle and pulled her down onto his lap. She tried to capture his mouth for a kiss, but he spun her around until she faced the screen. The movement was so quick, she had to grip the seat in front of her for balance. Big hands closed around the hem of her skirt and yanked it up, leaving it bunched at her hips, before he drew her back against him. With only a thong separating her from Connor's jeans, she could feel his thickness, pressing up between the cheeks of her bottom.

"Goddammit, Erin. It's never enough." He trailed his fingers up the inside of her thigh, stopping just short of her panties. "You tell me you're in love with me, then beg me to fuck you. Are you testing me to see how much I can take?" His hand finished its ascent, cupping her womanhood like a precious work of art, kneading the flesh gently. "All of it, Erin. *All* of it. But when you make me feel so damn *much*, I only know how to channel it one way. I don't know how to make love. You deserve that, dammit."

"I don't know how, either." She turned her head to meet his gaze. His serious expression tugged on the newly minted strings in her chest, but the gathering tension centered between her legs overrode everything. If he didn't give her what she needed soon, she'd expire. Hoping to entice him, she took the hand that wasn't occupied and slid it beneath her shirt, where it immediately clung to her breast. "Maybe fast and hard is just the way we make love, baby. There's nothing wrong with that."

His breathing grew shorter as she started to work her hips on his lap. "I need to give you what you deserve. You're not everyone else. You're mine."

A thread of gravity in his tone told her to pay attention. He needed something here just as badly as she needed him. She had two people to think about now. Not just herself. "You want to try to go slow?"

The only answer he gave was to reach between them and undo his pants. He pushed them low on his hips and took out his erection with a gritted curse. Once again, he dragged her on top of his hardness and used a hand on her hip to circle her body. "Let me see how ready you are." Rough fingers slipped beneath the waistband of her panties, two pushing inside her. Erin barely managed to hold back a sob as he held them deep. "Always wet, this delicious pussy. You were made to be filled up, weren't you, sweetheart?"

"Yes," she moaned softly. "By you."

He bit down on her shoulder, just enough to make her whimper. "From now on, that's a given. It will *always* be me, Erin. Every fucking time."

She could only live in her anticipation as he hooked both arms beneath her knees and lifted her off his lap. His erection prodded the inside of her thigh, hot and insistent. So close. He was so close to being inside her. "Oh God, *please.*"

"Reach back and guide me in where I belong."

Erin was all but frantic to obey his firm command, trailing her hand down his ripped stomach to seize his huge erection. Physically incapable of waiting another second, she took his plump head inside her and slid down, impaling herself. *Completion. Finally.* Even though her body throbbed for relief in a hundred different places, demanding she *move*, it felt like she'd been reunited with her other half.

Connor let loose a string of curses at the back of her neck before wrapping her hair in his fist and jerking her head back until it met his shoulder. "Feel my cock inside you?" He maneuvered his hips back and forth. "My heart beating at your back? It's all yours, Erin. I fucking love you and it's all yours."

"I love you, too," she breathed against his bearded cheek. "So much."

"Show me." His grip tightened in her hair. "Show me with your body."

When he released her hair, Erin shot forward and anchored her hand on the seat in front of her. She found herself wild with the need to follow his instructions. Before, she'd been curious about the pleasure obeying him seemed to give her. Now, in this moment, she'd embraced it. Decided to live for it. She swiveled her hips and gloried in his groan. *That's right, baby. I own you as much as you own me.*

His desire to go slow had her setting a deliberate pace, rocking her hips up and grinding back down. It was an X-rated lap dance that caused the inferno inside her to rage out of control. The fingers digging into her waist turned bruising. But she could feel him behind her, daring her to quicken her pace when he hadn't given her permission. Clutching the seat for dear life, she tossed her hair over her shoulder and sent him a look that held nothing back. Maintaining the scorching eye contact, she danced on the tip of his arousal, lowering herself with painstaking slowness. A returned dare. At the very base, she jerked her hips forward and watching his jaw slacken.

One masculine hand dipped between her thighs, the heel of his hand placing exquisite pressure over her clit. He leaned forward to chafe her sensitive neck with his bearded jaw. "I will kill for this pussy. Kill for the right to continue ownership of it. Nod if you understand how serious I am." He made a satisfied noise when Erin nodded. He slapped her sensitive flesh, sending devastating vibrations through her core. "Now fuck me like you mean it."

She braced her hands on his knees and started to ride, rebounding off his hard thighs after each fulfilling descent. Oh God, it felt so damn perfect. The slide of hard flesh into delicate. Big into small. On the movie screen, she vaguely registered a shoot-out taking place, so loud that she gave in to the urge to moan. Her thighs slapping down on his rougher, more muscular legs joined the sound only to be drowned out by the movie's volume. "Oh please, oh please, oh please," she chanted under her breath as a quickening began in her middle, twisting with the promise of pleasure.

Connor scooped his hands beneath her knees and jerked them against her chest, leaving her body folded in half, ankles in the air. Still, she didn't stop writhing. She couldn't. Relief was too close. So close she could already feel tremors beginning at the tops of her thighs. When Connor began to piston his hips, slamming her down on his thick erection with each upward thrust, her eyes rolled back into her head and she lost all sense of the present. "If you say please, you say it to *me*. Use my name."

"P-please." Her voice shook. "*Connor*."

He licked Erin from neck to ear, making her feel dizzy. When he drew away to blow cool air on the damp trail he'd left, she turned with a shiver to find him watching her work his lap with an expression of ecstasy. "Jesus, that body doesn't quit. Hips bucking, thighs spread wide. Working so hard for your orgasm, aren't you?" His hand smoothed over her ass, gave it a stinging slap. "One stroke between your legs and I could take care of that, sweetheart. You'd come all over my lap."

Her head fell back and she stared blindly at the ceiling as she continued to ride, but couldn't help casting the occasional heated look behind her. He'd sprawled out like a king, fists resting on his head as he watched her under hooded eyelids. He was so fucking hot it made her teeth clench with the need to bite him. Every time she wrung a groan from his throat, it felt like a victory. *No one can please this man like I can.*

With release hanging so closely in the balance and him

acting so sure of himself, she felt the need to remind him of that. Her lips tilting at one end, she swung her feet up and wedged them against the seat in front of her. That added leverage allowed her to take him deeper with each undulation of her hips. Connor's hands flew to her thighs, punishing them with a white-knuckled grip as he groaned. But she wasn't finished. She reclined against his chest and reached up to wrap both arms around his neck, drawing his attention to the straining nipples beneath her shirt. One scrape of her teeth against the underside of Connor's jaw and his breath began to rasp in and out, encouraging her without words to work her hips faster.

"Oh, fuck. *Fuck*. You're killing me."

"But I only want to please you," she rasped, licking the per-spiring skin of his throat. "Fill me up, baby. Mark me as yours. Give me everything."

Her words hit their mark. Less than a second later, she found herself pushed forward and bent over the theater seat as Connor's length pummeled her wet flesh. His coarse fingers found the sensitive bud between her thighs and flicked it once, twice, before he gave her what she needed and rubbed it with tight circles. Finally, the climax crested over her and bathed her in mind-numbing sensation, drawing every ounce of energy to her surface and depleting it in degrees, leaving her shaken. Connor wasn't far behind, burying his teeth in her shoulder as he rammed home and came with a growl of her name.

She had no idea how long they stayed like that, his heaving chest pressed to her back, but she loved every moment of it. It felt like they'd been through a battle and come out stronger than before. When the air conditioner began to cool the sweat on her skin and she shivered, Connor fixed her clothing and drew her down onto his lap, both of her legs slung over one of his thighs. He tucked her head under his chin and massaged the back of her neck with his thumb.

"This is my first movie in a theater."

His thumb stilled on a curse. "No. Please don't tell me that. It's fucking *Death Warrant*."

She yawned, noting the bullets once again flying across the screen. "I don't know. I think it kind of suits us."

He sighed and closed his arms around her. "I'll do better next time. A comedy or something. Popcorn, too. All right?"

Erin fell asleep smiling.

CHAPTER TWENTY-THREE

Connor swiped a hand over his jaw and checked the urge to call Erin's cell phone. She'd left the surveillance van ten minutes ago to get coffee for the team. How long did it take? It had only been one day since he bought her the phone, but she still assumed it was someone *else's* phone every time it rang. They were working on it. He'd offered to go in her stead, but suspected she needed the breathing room. With six of them crammed into the back of the van, he could tell she'd felt claustrophobic. Not to mention, he'd needed the opportunity to catch Derek's ear. This shit with Erin's stepfather would be straightened out immediately. Tonight. But if the unexpected happened and something went wrong, he needed to make sure Erin would be okay.

His plan had been to pay a visit to Luther last night, but she'd distracted him. If he'd suspected she was doing it on purpose, he would have called her on it. But no, she'd been... glowing. Walking around the apartment in one of his old Yankees T-shirts, feeling her way through mundane tasks like they were new experiences. Cooking dinner, taking a shower. All things she had done before, but there was a noticeable difference. Her edginess had fled, to be replaced with wonder and optimism. Jesus Christ, he couldn't have pried himself away if he wanted to. He'd appeased himself with the reasoning that nothing could happen to her as long as he was there to protect her.

After they'd showered off the day and changed, he'd lain down on the couch. He'd pretended not to see her watching him thoughtfully from her perch on the kitchen counter. After a minute, she'd hopped down and prowled toward him quietly, so light on her feet he wouldn't have heard her approaching if every cell in his body wasn't acutely attuned to her. She'd looked so young and fresh with her damp hair and bare legs, his throat had hurt. Very slowly, she'd climbed over him on the couch and settled in against him, tucking her feet between his calves. He swore he'd held his breath as she relaxed little by little, sighing into his chest.

Yeah, they might have slept in the same bed before, but there had been a note of tension. Worry over how she would cope. Anxiety that he'd wake up and find her having a panic attack. This had been different. Simple human contact that would have been anything but simple weeks ago. She not only trusted him, she trusted herself, and it was extraordinary to watch. Of course, he'd only managed about twenty minutes of her mouthwatering curves nestled against his before reversing their positions and tonguing her pussy through three sobbing climaxes. Hearing her cry out that she loved him had made it a thousand times sweeter, because he knew she meant it.

He took that love seriously. It was precious and hard-won and no one would fuck with it. This morning he'd walked into the kitchen and found her drinking a cup of orange juice at the table. She'd had her game face back on and he knew. She was going to try to talk him out of meeting with her stepfather. Even though he'd known they would butt heads over it eventually, he'd hated the idea of shattering the atmosphere between them. So when Derek had called to tell them they were needed, he'd found himself relieved to put off the inevitable a little longer.

Sera had been working at campaign headquarters for a week now, but Stark had never made an appearance. The previous day, she'd managed a peek at his assistant's appointment book that heralded Stark's arrival today at lunchtime. Which is why Bowen sat beside him white-faced, leg bouncing a thousand miles per hour. Connor suspected he was mostly there to make sure Bowen didn't try to make a break for it, intent on retrieving his new wife and heading off into the sunset. They still had about twenty minutes until Stark was set to arrive. Erin would be back any minute, and he needed to talk with the team first. He didn't trust easily, didn't like discussing their private business with other people, but he'd learned something from Erin when she'd gone missing. Learned how to close his eyes and take a leap of faith once in a while. Not to mention, each of them had gone out of their way to help him find Erin. He wouldn't forget that. But they didn't know the full story. As usual, he'd gone solo the final day she'd been gone, starting his own mission.

"Erin's stepfather bought a house in Chicago." He scrubbed a hand over his beard. "He left a forwarding address at the Motel 6. It's how I found Erin."

Polly paused in the act of filing her nails.

Beside her, Austin only spared him a glance before going back to studying Polly with a slight frown on his face. "What of it, mate?"

"Erin burned the poor fucker's house down," Polly explained, taking everyone but Derek and Connor by surprise. "He's been renting in Florida since then. My guess is he thought a permanent residence in the city where Erin is dwelling would give him a better chance at the conservatorship." Her smile was tight. "Probably even painted her room pink."

Connor's stomach pitched at the idea of Erin sharing four walls with that monster. "That won't be happening. Derek, did you manage to block the request?"

The captain lowered the headset he was using to listen in on Sera's wire. "For now, yes. But I'm her employer, not family. It won't hold forever."

"Right. I want a restraining order filed. Today." Connor checked his cell phone to see if Erin had called. She hadn't. "I'll convince her to sign the paperwork, but it needs to go through immediately. It might tangle up his request to control her assets."

Austin fell back against the van wall. "We all know you control her *assets* now, hey?"

"Watch it," Connor said. "I was just beginning to tolerate you."

"That makes one of us," Bowen muttered beside him, before jerking his chin at Derek. "Has this motherfucker Stark shown up yet?"

"Nope."

Connor shook his head when both of Bowen's legs started to bounce. "So far, all the court has is Luther's account of Erin's mental state. But they have nothing from her. It needs to be on record."

"He's right," Polly chimed in. "We need to stop playing defense."

Connor nodded to let her know he appreciated her use of the word *we*.

Derek eyed him closely. "I've got a car outside his house, like you phoned me about last night. I'm not going to get a call informing me that you've shown up and gone inside, am I?"

He didn't respond. One thing he'd never been accused of was being a liar, and he wouldn't start today. Before he could discuss it further, Erin tapped on the van window. Calmness flooded his system like ice water as he opened the door for her, took the coffee in one hand and helped her in with the other. True to form for a van full of cons, not a single one of them had a guilty expression on their face, as if they hadn't been discussing her a moment earlier. Well, everyone but Austin, who never wore anything but a smirk.

Connor set the tray of coffees in the center of the van floor and watched everyone converge while he pulled Erin down onto his lap. "Okay?"

She buried her nose against his neck and inhaled. The girl loved to smell him. He'd never given much thought to his aftershave before, but it had become top priority. "Yeah."

Derek held up a hand for everyone to be quiet. Silence descended over the group as he listened to what was being said through the headphones. Bowen had gone still as death beside him. The captain hit a few buttons and removed his headset as Sera's voice filled the van for all of them to hear.

A muffled shift against the speaker. "—to meet you, Mr. Stark."

"My father is Mr. Stark. I'm just Max. Especially for the people working so hard to make my campaign a success." A long pause before the politician said smoothly, "You're so acquainted with my career, I feel like we know each other already."

"Oh, fuck no," Bowen growled, his hands curling into fists.

For the next hour, the group listened to a campaign staff meeting. From the sounds and explanations filtering through Sera's wire, it was obvious some kind of PowerPoint presentation was taking place. Even Connor had to admit that Stark was an engaging speaker. He drew laughs from his audience even as he rallied them to work harder for his "noble" cause. It was enough to make Connor sick. Hell, there was suspicion he'd murdered Tucker May to silence the man. He didn't want Sera, whose friendship he valued, to be anywhere near the sleazy asshole, either. When the meeting wrapped up, everyone in the van sat forward to see what would happen next. If Sera could get close enough to Stark, she'd been instructed to slip a listening and tracking device in his designer leather satchel. That task was what had Bowen ready to jump out of his skin. If Sera got caught, they would need to get her out immediately.

Stark's voice came through distorted for a moment, then clear as a bell, calling Sera by her cover name. "Uh, Trish. Trish, right?" The sounds of chairs rolling back and a door opening, signaling the end of the meeting. "Can I have a word with you?"

The barest of hesitations. "Sure. Something I can help you with?"

"Oh, please. You're doing enough. My assistant tells me you've brought in a record number of cold-call donations this week. How did you manage that? You're so…new."

Austin made a gagging sound. "The man is sorely lacking in anything resembling game."

"Shut up," Bowen bit off, yanking on the ends of his hair.

Sera spoke this time, sounding innocently pleased. "Oh, I was just friendly, I guess. My father always said the best way to make a sale is to listen first."

"Wise words," Stark murmured. "Listen, I'd love to take you out to lunch. Just to say thank-you."

Bowen lunged for the van door.

"*Driscol*," Derek said sharply. "You go in there and blow her cover, you don't just screw her over, you screw us all. Stay put and let her do her fucking job."

Bowen ground his head against the metal door once before denting it with a blow from his fist. "If something happens to her, I will burn this city down." He turned a look on Derek. "How do you know he hasn't already made her? She could be in danger."

"Because I know," Derek returned coldly, initiating a stand-off. "Don't question me."

Sera hadn't spoken in a few seconds, probably all too aware of how her husband was reacting to the offer of lunch. "Oh. Could we plan for another day? I'm...well, I'm seeing someone and I'm supposed to meet them for lunch today."

Until Erin slipped from his arms, Connor hadn't realized how quiet she'd been. She watched Bowen with concern, but there was something else happening behind her eyes. Plans taking shape, her sharp brain working overtime. She gave him a meaningful look and placed a finger over her lips to silence his questions before slipping out the front door of the van. Every instinct in his body demanded he go after her, but he knew what her look had meant. He recognized it too well. *Trust me.*

A third voice filled the van. Stark's assistant. She reminded him about a phone call he had that afternoon with the state education chairman before clicking back out of the room. Stark cleared his throat into the silence. "Another day is fine, I guess. Although my schedule is very tight. I was so looking forward to—"

"Honey? Did you forget our lunch date?"

Connor jolted in his seat as Erin's voice joined the conversation between Sera and Stark. Four pairs of eyes swung toward him, obviously noting for the first time that Erin was no longer in the van.

Austin and Polly both burst out laughing. He and Bowen

exchanged a speculative glance.

Derek pinched the bridge of his nose and cursed. "What the hell, Bannon?"

Fuck if he knew. But he would support Erin. She'd proven herself to be a valuable member of this group and he'd damn well have her back if she'd made a call that would help Sera. Even if it went against basic orders not to be seen while they were undercover. He hated the fact that she might have just thrown herself into a dangerous situation, but he felt marginally better knowing Sera, a damn good police officer, was there with her.

"This…is who you're meeting for lunch?" Stark's voice. There was no mistaking the blatant heat in his tone. He sounded almost gleeful. "When you said you were seeing someone, I assumed—"

"I'd be a man?" Erin was closer to Sera and her wire now. "We get that a lot."

Polly slow-clapped. "Well played, O'Dea. You are *so* getting that recorder planted today, Captain. Can we say *distracted*?"

Derek started to reply, but was cut off by the unmistakable sound of a kiss. Erin and Sera had kissed? Connor and Bowen exchanged a distinctly uncomfortable look.

Austin let out a hoot. "This shit is finally getting interesting."

"*Shut up*," Connor and Bowen shouted at the Brit.

"Lunch sounds great," Erin said with a smile in her voice, silencing the van once more. "Where are you taking us, Mr. Treasurer?"

All right, so she wasn't completely cured. That kiss with Sera had stung like a son of a bitch, but she'd managed to disguise her shock as arousal, which had probably worked in their favor. To be perfectly honest, she kind of liked knowing Connor was the only person it didn't hurt to touch, to kiss, to allow access to her body. The wickedly sexual side of her he'd woken, this side of her that liked being dominated, wanted to give him that honor. For a man like him it would be the ultimate high, knowing his woman could stand only his touch. Maybe it was wrong or fucked up that she'd found a way to be happy about her affliction, but it made her feel secure somehow. She didn't *have* to be cured completely. There was no pressure. She could still be Erin, but she'd been given an extraordinary gift to go along with all her screwy qualities. Connor. His hands, mouth... heart.

Right now, she needed to focus on the task at hand, though. That day at the courthouse, when she'd witnessed the wedding between Bowen and Sera, she'd fallen in love with them both. Not in the way she loved Connor. Nowhere close to that consuming or life-changing. But she couldn't discount the feeling that these two new people in her life had given her hope, possibly even helped her heal. They'd proven that being dealt a shitty hand didn't prevent you from folding and finding a new game. They had all done it, but Bowen and Sera had found their pot of gold at the end of a shit rainbow. No way could she sit by and let Sera go into something on her own. Let Bowen go insane with worry. These people had the unfortunate luck of being her friends now, which meant she would go to the wall for them.

Joining Sera undercover hadn't been as spontaneous a decision as she'd made it seem. Okay, the timing was a little abrupt, but she'd already been planning on lighting a fire under this investigation. When things took too long, she got antsy. That morning, she'd come to the conclusion that Connor would pay a visit to her stepfather that night. Her plan had been to plead with Bowen to go with him and make sure he didn't do anything crazy, so she could get Sera alone and plot without the men around to cramp their style. Honestly, they took protectiveness to another level. Did she like Connor wanting to keep her safe? Yes. Would she always try to find a way around it? Also yes.

Okay, maybe her plan wasn't foolproof. Bowen being sent along to play the level head? Funny ha ha. But she hadn't seen another choice. When this opportunity to help Sera had come along, doubling as a distraction for Connor? She'd jumped on it. Tomorrow she'd come up with another idea. If it meant signing over the money to Luther, she would do it to keep Connor out of it.

Sera sat in the front seat of Maxwell Stark's car laughing politely at his lame-ass jokes. The guy was good-looking, she could admit to that, but it was in a weekly eyebrow wax appointment kind of way. Too pretty. Nothing like the rugged ex-SEAL she would have to deal with later. Damn. The idea of dealing with a perturbed Connor didn't exactly seem like a hardship. Maybe he would—

Focus.

Erin draped her arms across the back of Sera's seat and played with the ends of her friend's hair. "You still haven't said where we're going. Is it a surprise?"

Stark barely managed to stop at a red light in time, his eyes were so focused on Erin's fingers. "I, uh, thought we could head to my house. I'm always being hounded by photographers downtown…figured this would be a nice break."

Break. Right. Erin smiled. "Sounds…intimate."

Sera smiled at her in the rearview, embracing the act. But there was tightness at the corners of her mouth, probably because the team, including Bowen, could hear everything being said. She hoped Sera realized they would have to separate at some point so one of them could search the house for the elusive Mr. May. Ever since she and Connor had brainstormed that theory yesterday, she hadn't been able to get it out of her head. If he wasn't there, they would plant the listening device, make an excuse and leave. If he *was* there? She'd play it by ear. And trust that Derek would have Chicago PD descending on the house if trouble presented itself.

There was that word again. *Trust.* It got easier every time.

They drove for fifteen minutes, leaving the city proper and entering the suburbs. Manicured lawns and long driveways, so foreign to her, threatened to snag her attention, but she focused on the street names and the turns they were taking. Stark finally pulled into a gated driveway, hitting a button on his sun visor to open a wrought iron gate. He winked at her and Sera, looking super pleased with himself, and continued toward the house where he parked beside a marble fountain. When Stark climbed out and went around back on his way to the passenger side, Erin snatched the gate remote off the visor and stuffed it into her pocket, keeping an eye on the rearview to make sure Stark didn't see.

When Erin was in prison, she'd always imagined the correctional officers sharing a big house like Stark's when they were off the clock. They would play paintball and munch on giant turkey legs in front of the television. Common sense had told her they probably lived in one-bedroom apartments devoid of reading material or color, but it had made her feel better somehow. Making them characters in a cheesy reality show instead of the assholes who watched her use the toilet or treated her like cattle.

Erin turned in a circle in the foyer, which had two carpeted staircases ascending to the second floor on either side. "Wow."

She placed a hand over her heart as she spotted the gaudy chandelier. "This place is amazing."

"Designed it myself." *Douche.* "It's the one thing my wife didn't take in the divorce."

Erin made the pouty face she knew he wanted to see. "Some people are so greedy."

Sera nodded. "It would have been a shame to lose something you worked so hard on."

If she could have high-fived Sera at the moment for her subtle insertion of the phrase "hard on," she would have. Instead, she reached up and gathered her hair on top of her head, letting her belly button peek out as she perused the art on the wall. Sera did the same across the room, although Erin knew she was looking for much more. Stark stood between them with his hands in his pockets, checking each of them out in turn.

Erin turned back in time to see Sera smiling over her shoulder. It was an innocent smile, but there was a hint of daring. *Nice.* "Is there a bathroom I could use?"

"Sure, just down the hallway—"

"Ooh, can I see the kitchen?" Erin asked, cutting him off as Sera slipped from the room. Great. They were on the same page. Now all she had to do was keep Stark distracted while Sera did her thing. Only problem was, Sera wore the wire. She didn't have squat. Wait. Except for the cell phone in her pocket. Guess the electronic handcuffs Connor had foisted on her would come in handy after all. As Stark led her toward the back of the house and through a giant archway, she pulled out the cell and dialed Connor's number before quickly stowing it away once more.

The kitchen looked like *Architectural Digest* had thrown up in it, and Erin was willing to guess the expensive-looking, stainless steel appliances were never used. It looked too clean, like it hadn't been lived in. She would take her and Connor's tiny eat-in kitchen over this place any day of the week. Not bothering to hide her smile over the spark of pleasure the phrase "her and Connor's kitchen," she pretended to be absorbed in Stark's explanation of how much everything cost and how hard each piece had been to come by.

When he turned his back on her, gesturing to the crown molding decorating the ceiling, Erin slid open a few drawers. If her hunch proved correct...*bingo*. Beneath a stack of take-out menus, the butt of a Glock peeked out. A nice one, too. It would make too much noise to check if it was loaded, but she shoved it into her jeans' waistband at the small of her back anyway. Stark circled back on her, obviously finished with his explanation of the finer things in life. She knew his expression from experience. It said *enough with the small talk bullshit*.

Backing away from him under the guise of wanting to look out into the backyard, she slowly dragged her fingers along the cool granite countertops. A pool...a garden. The high gate extended around the entire perimeter of the property. No way out but through the front. Good to know. *Now stall.* All she had to do was stall for a while. Easier said than done when dealing with a presumptuous dickhead who assumed he was moments away from a threesome. "It must get lonely in this big house with no one to share it with."

He grinned cockily. "I get by."

"Oh, I bet you do."

"How long have you and Trish been together?"

"A long time." She sent him a sly grin. "Since college."

"Jesus." He cocked a hip on the counter. "And do you do this kind of thing often?"

She smirked. "What kind of thing?"

After a long pause, they both gave a slow laugh. Stark began his prowl toward her again. Reassured by the piece at her back, she started to skirt around the kitchen island with a teasing look on her face. Just as she passed the kitchen entrance, Sera entered.

She wasn't alone.

With her arm extended in a shooter's pose, Sera backed into the kitchen with her gun pointed at none other than Tucker May. Who also had a gun pointed at Sera.

"Are you out of your mind?" May shouted. "Bringing people here with no warning? I'm a fucking fugitive, Max."

To her left, Stark cursed vilely and threw open the drawer. In the blink of an eye, Erin removed the gun from her waistband and pointed it at Stark. "Looking for this?"

"*Bitch*."

Erin clucked her tongue. "So unoriginal." She edged toward Sera and pressed their backs together, ignoring the sharp pain that zinged down her limbs. "Here's how this is going to work since we have two guns, you have one...and Chicago PD is already on the way."

"Also, my husband and her boyfriend are coming," Sera chimed in with a steady voice. "And they're mean as hell."

"Almost as mean as we are." Erin was just starting to enjoy herself when an angry voice distracted her. It was coming from her pocket. Keeping the gun trained on Stark, she drew out the device. "Sorry, boys. I have to take this." She put the phone up to her ear. "Hey, baby."

She felt Connor's rushed exhale down to her toes. "We're on the way. Please just tell me you're okay."

"I'm fine." God, it felt great to have someone concerned for her. Fucking great. "Tell Bowen his wife is a badass, too."

Sirens split the air and Stark's eyebrows hit his hairline.

Reflected in the stainless steel refrigerator, she saw May drop the gun and run for it.

Erin grabbed Sera's arm when she started to give chase. No. Too big of a risk. There could be more weapons stashed around the house. "Let him go. He doesn't have a bolt cutter or a convenient power outage this time." She let go of Sera's arm, reached into her pocket and removed the remote control for the gate. "There's only one exit and our boys will be there to meet him."

The sirens were right outside the gate now. Sending Stark a wink, she pressed the button to let them in. "Honey, we're home."

CHAPTER TWENTY-FOUR

Connor watched Erin lick salt from her wrist, followed by her plump lips closing around a lime for a long, hard suck. *Jesus H. Christ.* A bar was the last place he wanted to be tonight. He didn't mind the licking and sucking, but he wanted it done at home. Privately. His girlfriend, however, had kind of saved the day and she deserved to celebrate. That didn't make him want to drag her home and reassure himself of her well-being any less. He wanted to praise her in his own way and it didn't include Austin, Polly, and Derek, who shared the booth with them in the Brass Monkey, a bar two blocks from the police station. Bowen had scooped up his wife and vanished as soon as she and Erin had given their statements. He'd wanted to do the same with his girl, but he hadn't been able. This was another new experience for her. Having a drink with friends, listening to music during happy hour, bullshitting. He would never take that away from her.

He'd even invited his mother to celebrate with them, although she hadn't known if she could make it on short notice. It took his mom a good three hours to get ready for the supermarket, let alone a night out.

The restraining order against Erin's stepfather had been filed this afternoon thanks to Derek's pulling a couple strings. Hopefully it had already been delivered to Luther O'Dea's door. It would have to be enough for tonight, knowing the man knew Erin wasn't vulnerable anymore. That she had people who cared about her. That she wasn't going to stand for his terrorizing behavior anymore.

Erin tilted her head back and met his eyes, her expression one of exhilaration. Damn, her beauty hit him square in the chest and he couldn't even draw a breath. Every time she looked at him, he remembered dying a thousand deaths at hearing the word "gun" come over the loudspeaker that afternoon. They'd still been en route to the house, and his universe had flickered, then darkened at the possibility that he might never see her alive again. Her voice had been the only thing that kept him sane. She'd been so confident, so sure of herself. Enough for the both of them. It hadn't stopped him from falling at her feet the minute he entered the house and saw her. True to form, she'd gone down on her knees, too, and met him halfway.

"You should have seen this poor fucker's face when you kissed our Sera." Austin waved a lime in his direction. "Priceless, it was. He didn't know whether to be turned on or pissed off."

"We know which one you were," Polly commented. "You were like that horny cartoon wolf, eyes all bugged out. *Awooooga.*"

"Ah, now." Austin tilted his head at Polly. "Don't be jealous, love. You know I'd be your love slave if you'd only let me."

She rolled her eyes. "I can barely contain my feminine arousal."

"Maybe I have it backward." Austin chewed his red cocktail straw a moment before leaning in closer to Polly. "Maybe you prefer to be the love slave, hey?"

Polly flushed. "If you can switch it up so easily, I'm not

interested. Other girls might not realize you only know how to play roles. But I do."

Austin's expression turned hard. "Are you calling me inauthentic?"

Thankfully, Derek chose that moment to return with a round of beers. After an afternoon with those two, Connor had enough bickering to last himself a year. Another reason he wanted to get out of this godforsaken dive and take Erin home to bed. The captain seemed to have the same idea, because he'd only dropped four beers off at the table.

"Heading out?" Connor asked.

"Yeah. My wife saved me a piece of chicken potpie for dinner. It's the worst." Funny, he didn't look displeased by that at all. He looked like he couldn't wait to get home and eat it. "Take a couple of days off. I'll let everyone know when the next meet will be."

Polly picked up a pint and saluted Derek. "To our fearless leader, who is turning out *not* to be an epic asshole like his brethren."

"Give me time." Derek leveled them all with a look. "And stay out of trouble."

Erin reached for her beer. "What if it finds me first?"

Connor shook his head at the same time as Derek. "You're my star pupil so far, O'Dea. Don't screw it up."

She turned her face into Connor's shoulder but not before he saw her smile. The four of them sat quietly for a while, mostly speculating on what their next assignment would be and if Bowen would be twice as crazy now that Sera had seen some action. When Erin excused herself to go to the bathroom, she was forced to crawl over his lap to get out of the booth. His dick had already been hard from the way her hand rested on his thigh, but now it grew demanding behind his fly. Yeah, he wouldn't last much longer in here. Time to let her know.

Erin glanced back in surprise when he rose from the table to follow her to the bathroom. "I don't need a babysitter. Haven't I proven myself to you yet?"

The way she glided away and let the question hang in the air told him she didn't mind him following her one damn bit. Her hips snapped side to side with every step, those painted-on jeans wrapping up her tight body like a sexy birthday gift he didn't deserve. They entered the dark hallway that led to the bathrooms and Connor wasted no time halting her in her tracks and wedging her up against the closest wall. When he nudged her belly with his erection, those blue eyes darkened and her mouth fell open on a gasp.

"Is this your way of telling me it's time to go home?"

"Caught that, did you?"

He gritted his teeth when her smoky laugh vibrated her curves against him. "What's wrong with right here?"

"This place isn't good enough for you." He gave a downward roll of his hips, satisfied when her head fell back and hit the wall. "I just wanted to pass on a warning."

The inside of her thigh slid up the outside of his leg. "A warning about what, baby?"

Connor ran his tongue along her bottom lip, bit it gently. "I didn't like hearing you flirt with Stark. Let him think he was going to get what only I take. My head knew you were doing it for a job, but the rest of me didn't care." He drew her leg up around his waist and ground his hips against her, drawing a whimper from her lips. "It's going to be sweet reminding you all night that no one gets you but me. That includes Sera." He petted her rounded ass with one hand, ending with a hard squeeze. "We'll be dealing with that kiss later."

After a long, deep delving of his tongue that left her clinging to his shoulders, he stepped back. Any more of her mouth and they would never make it home. Erin fell against the wall, breasts rising and falling. "Get the check."

Connor knew he wore a self-satisfied grin as he turned to leave the hallway, but he didn't give a shit. If you could make a woman like that moan, what the hell else did you need in life? Feeling the sudden urge to say something, he turned and found her staring after him. "Hey, sweetheart?"

"Yeah?"

"I'm so fucking proud of you, I can barely stand it. You know that, right?"

Her laugh was pure joy. "Yeah."

He stood there and watched her disappear into the bathroom, boots tinkling the whole way. Returning to the table with a smile on his face, he spotted his mother at the entrance, going up on her toes to scan the crowd. When she saw him, her face transformed with relief and she met him halfway across the bar.

"Son. This place could use a mop. You bring our girl here?"

"Hey, Mom." He kissed her cheek, inordinately happy to hear his mother refer to Erin as theirs. "Late as usual, but you made it."

"So." She ignored his teasing and patted her neon-yellow head scarf. "Where's the guest of honor?"

"In the bathroom. She'll be right out."

Erin stared at the wooden door of the bathroom stall, reading the various scrawlings that had been done with everything from Sharpies to knives. *Megan loves Paul. Paul is a dick. Dick is a dick.* She stood and used the toe of her boot to flush the toilet, felt the switchblade shift at her ankle. Experiencing the familiar urge to leave her mark, she embraced it, removing the blade and flipping it open. She thought for a moment, then carved the words, "Be the fire and you won't get burned."

The bathroom door opened and closed, bringing her back to the present. How long had it taken her to carve the words? Connor had probably sent Polly in to check on her. She shook her head even as it gave her a thrill of pleasure. Being cared for. Caring for someone else. She hoped she never took it for granted.

With one final glance at her handiwork, she shoved the blade back into her boot and pushed open the door. "Peeing is kind of a one-woman jo—"

Terror took root in her veins. Just inside the bathroom door stood her stepfather. He still had an abrasion on the side of his head where she'd clocked him with the skillet, but that wasn't what chilled her most. It was the intention on his face. She was used to his disdain, but this was different. He was here to kill her.

She dropped into a crouch and snatched the blade from her boot just as he pulled a gun from his jacket and pointed it at her, forcing her to freeze before she could even flip her weapon open. Anger rose in her so swift and furious, she choked on it. She'd only just figured out what it meant to be happy and this man, this nightmare, would not stop coming at her. Would not just leave her in peace.

"You want the money? *Take it*," she spat. "It will be a small price to pay for never having to look at your face again. I don't need it. And I'll sleep just fine knowing you'll run out someday and be miserable all over again. Just take it."

His laugh was almost indulgent. "That offer is late in coming, I'm afraid. Your little goon squad has closed ranks around you, so it's not just you I'm contending with anymore."

Dammit. The restraining order. It had set him off, just as she'd known it would. "What's your other option? I've got a captain in the Chicago PD to vouch for my sanity. You're nothing but a bitter, lonely man." She already knew his plan. In his convoluted brain, he thought if he killed her, the money would go to him. Her next of kin. But she needed to keep him talking. Connor would find her. He'd be wondering what was taking her so long.

"I know you're stalling, but I would advise against it." His expression turned gleeful. "You didn't think I'd come without leverage, did you? Oh no. You're going to walk with me right out the back door without a problem. I promise."

Her teeth started to chatter. "What is it?"

"More like *who*." He started to speak faster, sounding more impatient. "That day at the courthouse wasn't the first time I saw you in Chicago. No, I'd been following you longer than that. Saw you go into a building down in Lincoln Park." Erin tried to show no reaction, but his sickening grin told her she'd failed. "I watched the building a while. Saw your boyfriend coming and going with his mother." His hand flexed around the gun. "Drop the knife and the cell phone in your pocket. Get your ass up and come with me now, or I make a call and she's gone."

Erin's heartbeat pounded in her ears, her mouth dry as dust. He could be lying. As far as she knew, her stepfather had always worked alone, and this plan would require another set of hands. But she couldn't chance it. It was too in character for him to prey on weakened women. Goddammit. She couldn't allow her life to affect the ones she cared about. She wouldn't.

"Fine." After letting the knife clatter to the dingy floor and digging out her cell phone to drop beside it, she stood with her hands up, tightening the muscles in her legs so they wouldn't shake. "Lead the way."

Luther cracked open the door and looked out before pulling back. "Ladies first."

Erin swallowed hard as he shoved her through the open door. The hallway was a funnel of noise captured from the bar, but it was deserted of people. She thought of Connor kissing her there just minutes before and wanted to wail at the ceiling. The cold muzzle of her stepfather's gun dug into the middle of her back, directing her in the opposite direction of the bar. A gated back door stood partially open, just beside the kitchen. The cook's back was turned to them as they passed, his focus on a tiny television screen above a giant fryer.

They walked through the door and into a dim alley, music and laughter from the bar following in their wake. She peered through the night's freshly fallen darkness for Luther's car, but only saw a white panel van with no windows. He shoved her toward it so suddenly that she stumbled.

As if she'd never made an iota of progress, the wings started beating in her head, drowning out rational thought. Trap. He was going to lock her in that airless van and trap her. *No, no, no.*

When they reached the van, he threw the back doors open. And she saw it.

A cage.

"Get in."

CHAPTER TWENTY-FIVE

It was an odd feeling, being exasperated over the amount of time your girlfriend took in the bathroom. Was it stupid that something so typical felt…good? Sure, there was an invisible countdown clock over his right shoulder, tick-tick-ticking away the seconds since the last time he'd put eyes on Erin. It would always be that way, because looking at her erased the bad in him. She was a signal of peace he need only think about, and the rapids inside him became a still pond. She'd turned his constant craving for control into something positive, because she'd given him the power to be in control of *himself*. A feat he'd had to accomplish to be with her.

And that made it his life's accomplishment. This internal head-shaking versus pacing the floor was a healthy change. They would build on small milestones, like allowing her out of his sight for extended periods of time, until they had a fucking city.

"Erin must have fallen in," Polly remarked with a smile and a good-natured elbow in his side.

Connor put the kibosh on his tingle of nerves. "She needs her space sometimes. Needs to…"

"Feel unfettered?" Polly nodded. "I get that."

Connor picked at the beer bottle label with his thumb to avoid glancing toward the bathroom. *Baby steps.* "You don't think it's possible to actually *fall in*, do you?"

Polly's answering chuckle cut off when her gaze fixed on something over his shoulder, the smile leaving her face in degrees. Connor pushed back from the table and jumped to his feet before his brain registered the command. Derek stood just inside the entrance. The captain held a cell phone up to his ear, speaking into it sharply as his razor-like gaze raked the table. He looked over and locked eyes with Connor.

"Where's O'Dea?"

Connor was running for the bathroom before Derek had even finished posing the question. Knives twisted in his gut as he careered through the door and turned in a circle. Switchblade. Her fucking cell phone. On the ground. Bathroom empty. No Erin.

Gone. I let my guard down and now she's gone.

Fear tearing at his insides, he turned and lunged at Derek, grabbing him by the shoulders. "How? How did you know she was gone?" His voice cracked. "*Where is she?*"

Derek pried Connor's hands off, but there was a hint of empathy in his eyes. "We've been following Luther's car since yesterday. He ditched it in a lot. Best we can tell, he picked up a different vehicle." He checked his phone and cursed. "We don't know for sure he took her. It's just a hunch. You know her, she likes to take off once in a while." Even as Derek said the words meant to calm him, his eyes were grave. He knew what the ditched cell phone and knife meant.

"No," Connor felt the need to reiterate. He swiped a hand through his hair, denial over the entire situation coursing through him like bolts of electricity. "No, she wouldn't have left like this. She doesn't need to. Not anymore. He has her. Jesus, he fucking has her."

Connor shot toward the exit, intending to drive like a bat out of hell to the bastard's house. If she wasn't there, he'd turn over every block in the city until he found her.

Derek stepped into his path. "Look, you're not going to help her by flying off the handle. I've got a guy at the lot questioning the owner. We'll find out what he's driving."

Connor had lost the ability to reason. All he could think of was Erin, scared and alone. Wondering why he hadn't come to check on her sooner. *God.* Before he could bypass the captain and leave the bathroom, Derek's cell phone rang. He answered it without delay. "Captain Tyler." He listened for a moment before his gaze locked with Connor. "White panel van. License plate number?" He nodded once. "Put out a BOLO on the vehicle. Do it now."

It was the laughing that snapped her out of it. Luther's high-pitched chuckle coming from the front of the van. Erin had no idea how long she'd been lying there, caged on the floor, listening to her thoughts deteriorate into a vacuum of noise. Her fingers were curled around the thin metal crisscrosses, but she hadn't made the futile attempt to shake them, nor could she work up the wherewithal to scream. One thought went round and round in her head, sounding like it was being spoken inside a cave.

She'd done the right thing. She'd let him live. And she still didn't get to win.

"Fair" had never been an active word in her vocabulary, because the concept had never really existed for her. But right now, as the van took her farther and farther from the life she'd only just managed to get a foothold in, she wanted to shout and rail at the unfairness of it. Unfair. *Unfair.* She'd regressed back to the child in the closet, screaming for a mother who would never come. A savior who would never save her.

Connor.

His name whispered through her mind like fog.

The maelstrom of noise eased a little…receding like a wave. She pressed her open mouth against the back of her hand and sobbed. He'd told her he was proud of her, but he wouldn't be proud if he could see her now. Curled up like a weeping baby, lamenting the past. Maybe she had never been that girl he was proud of. Maybe she'd only been pretending.

No. *No.* Fuck that.

She wouldn't give up, and neither would he. If she didn't believe in him, then she'd been lying all along, and that trust she'd claimed to have had never existed. But not just in him. In herself. She would fight and bargain and scrape her way out of this and back to him. She loved him too much to give up.

The van stopped and she forced her breathing to even out. *In, out. In, out.* Her stepfather knew what small spaces did to her, hence the cage. Hence his ploy that long-ago afternoon in the prison to send her to solitary. He wouldn't expect her to be lucid, let alone ready to rumble.

Think.

With renewed determination, she reached out and examined the lock with her fingertips, unable to see in the nonexistent light. No go. She fumbled through her pocket until she found her ever-present matches, striking one and breathing deeply as it flared like a beacon in the dark. *Focus.* Okay, standard lock. Not a padlock and nothing fancy enough to keep her from picking it, if she only had something to use. Normally, she kept a bobby pin handy for occasions like this, but with her newfound confidence in herself, she'd grown complacent. *Dammit.* She tried to remember what she'd seen upon entering the van, but nothing came to mind except for the cage.

No…there had been rack against the wall. Had there been tools? Something. There had to be something. Erin crammed herself as far as she could into the corner of the small cage and rammed her body against the other side, hoping to scoot it toward the rack. It didn't budge.

So she did it again.

And again.

"Come on, come on."

Connor's stomach lurched violently as Derek took a sharp turn off of Lake Shore Drive toward the water. DIVERSEY HARBOR, the sign said. Police personnel fanned the expressway about a mile behind them, but he and Derek were closing in on the van. An off-duty cop had spotted the van seconds after the BOLO had gone out and followed. The cop's voice buzzed though the radio on Derek's dashboard, steadily updating them on the van's progress toward the harbor.

A throbbing had started behind his eyes, matching his wild pulse. If he let himself picture the scenario in which Erin's stepfather required a body of water, he wouldn't hold it together, so he closed his eyes and tried like hell to breathe. Told himself that as soon as this car stopped, he would find her and hold her. Tell her how sorry he was for letting this happen. He had to believe he'd be given that chance.

The chill of metal against Connor's arm had his eyes opening. In the driver's seat, Derek held out a gun to him without comment and he took it gratefully, holstering it beneath his jacket. At the end of the expressway off-ramp, Derek took a hairpin turn and slammed on the brakes just beneath the overpass.

Connor looked upon his worst nightmare.

The white van was parked at the very edge of the water, doors flung open. A man Connor assumed to be the off-duty cop had his gun aimed at Luther. Luther, pointing a gun back at the officer, had his foot propped on the side of a cage, as if he were in the process of shoving it into the water. Erin was inside that cage. Alive, thank *Christ*. But in a fucking *cage*.

Rage leached his body of reason. Flashes of light compromised his vision as he threw himself from the van and raised his gun. *Don't look at her.* He couldn't look at her or he would lose it. Her fear would rip him wide open.

The only thing that kept Connor from firing his weapon at that moment was her stepfather's obvious panic and Erin's proximity to the water. One wrong move and she would be sinking to the bottom in a tiny prison. Surrounded by pitch black. That image socked him in the gut and it took him a moment to inhale through the denial of such an outcome. The off-duty cop demanded Luther drop his weapon, but had no luck. His foot inched the cage closer to the water.

"Don't do it. You'll be dead before she hits the water," Connor rasped, slowly moving closer, once again fighting the need to reassure Erin. "Or you give us Erin and we give you what you want in return. Seems like a pretty easy choice to me."

"You must think I'm an idiot, trying to talk me down like an average perp," Luther sneered. "Don't insult my intelligence. I'll never see that money now, so I might as well give her what she has coming."

Terror turned his blood to ice. *Don't talk about what she*

deserves, he wanted to shout, but forced himself to keep a level head. "You willing to die for that?"

Beginning to look indecisive, Luther glanced down at the cage and Connor couldn't help it any longer. He made eye contact with Erin and almost fell to his knees. She was…serene. Like she'd already accepted what was going to happen. There were tears in her eyes, but love crowded them out. Love for him.

When he spoke again, his voice wavered slightly. "The one who wronged you is dead. You're taking it out on the wrong person. But you can make it right if you just give her back to me now. Get in your car and drive away."

Everything happened so fast. Too fast. Erin's stepfather's foot slipped off the cage, edging it closer to the water. Connor, Derek, and the off-duty cop raised their guns, causing Luther to jerk his weapon back up defensively and fire off a round. Connor didn't wait for any more encouragement, but unloaded his weapon at the same time as Derek.

Just as the cage…and Erin…went flying backward into the water.

"*Noooo!*"

Ah, fuck.

Erin's head slammed into the bottom of the cage. Or was it the top? She'd anticipated the bastard trying to send her to a watery grave, but being upside-down and not knowing which direction the surface was hadn't entered the equation. Her head connecting with the cage had disoriented her, making it twice as bad. Even now, she could hear Connor's bellow echoing in her skull. Could see his anguished face. She'd tried to calm him, telling him she had everything under control, but he hadn't been in a very interpretive mood. She didn't blame him. If someone put him in a cage, she would unleash unholy wrath on whoever had made such a mistake.

After an effort that had left her sweating and the beginnings of quite a few bruises, she'd found a bent nail in the van's storage rack. It had only taken her seconds to pick the lock, but the van had stopped, her stepfather throwing open the back doors before she could climb out of the cage. Her plan had been to wait for an opportune moment to take him by surprise. Jam the nail into his foot and bust free of the cage while he howled in pain. Then the cop had shown up and forced Luther to draw his gun. No way could she make her move when he held a weapon. When Connor had shown up, it became an even bigger impossibility. She wouldn't place him in the line of fire for anything in the world.

Beneath her in the water, she heard a splash. No, wait, it had to be above her. She was upside down, which meant the cage door was to her left. Erin felt along the metal crisscrosses and pushed open the door. A moment later, she was through it, but her legs had cramped up from being in the fetal position for so long. Dammit. She swam with her arms and twisted her hips, trying desperately to bring life back into her dead limbs. There it was up above. The surface. She could see a glow of headlights, streetlights lining the expressway above. Blood rushed to her feet, making them prickle, but she welcomed the discomfort and began to kick. How long had she been under the water? Her lungs were starting to burn. Jesus, she needed to breathe. Needed Connor.

Almost there. Almost…

Erin broke the surface and sucked in delicious air.

Once her vision came back into focus with the resurgence

of oxygen, she expected to see Derek and Connor at the edge of the concrete drop-off, ready to pull her from the water, but she saw no one. Using her kicking feet, she turned in a circle and saw a male head break the surface of the water before it went back down. In the near-darkness, she couldn't tell who it was. She kicked toward the rock piling at the edge of the water and waited. Above her, she heard tires squeal to a stop and doors slamming.

"Hey!" she screamed when another head came up. She dragged in long pulls of air to compensate for the scream. "I'm here. Over here."

Derek. It was Derek. He gave her an incredulous look and started to say something, but a second head surfaced a few yards away. Connor.

"The cage is *empty*." His voice was so hoarse, her heart splintered. "Why the fuck is it empty? Could there be more than one down there? I don't...*Jesus*, she can't *breathe*. I'm going back—"

"Bannon," Derek shouted. "Turn around. She made it out."

Connor spun around, hands flying to his drenched head. A choked sound left his mouth when his tortured gaze found her against the rock piling. He swam for her, so fast his muscular arms were a blur of water and flesh. Before she could launch herself halfway across the distance separating them, he was there, pulling her into his arms. "Erin, Erin, Erin," he chanted into her wet hair. "Oh God. I saw you go under. I *saw* it and—"

"Your mom," she interrupted him. "I-is she okay? He told me he had her, that he would kill her. I had to go. I didn't leave you again. I *had* to go."

His breath released on a heavy exhale, head dropping into the crook of her neck. "Ah, sweetheart. She's fine. I could kill him all over again for making you think that."

Tears fell from her eyes, fusing with the salt water on her cheeks. "I wasn't scared. I thought of you and I wasn't scared."

"Don't ever look at me like that again, okay?" He shook her. "Like you know it's over. Please."

Erin pushed the wet hair off his face and waited until he focused on her. "I already had the cage beat. That's what I was trying to tell you." Connor's harsh exhale warmed her face. "I know you would have gotten me out. I know." She gave him a cocky wink. "But I have a reputation to uphold."

His laugh sounded pained. "I love you so much."

"I love you, too." She kissed him hard. "I just want to go home."

"Ah, sweetheart. Me, too." His expression changed, grew more serious. "I'm sorry. I had to...he's gone. I know you wanted me to do the right thing, but he's gone. I—"

"No." Derek's voice brought them around. He was halfway up the rock piling, looking down at Connor meaningfully. "You never had a weapon, Bannon. I fired the shots."

Connor shook his head, a frown marring his brow. "I'll face the consequences of my own actions. I don't need you to shield me."

Derek climbed a few more feet and glanced back over his shoulder. "Who's going to shield me when they find out where you got the weapon?" He rubbed the back of his neck. "A man died on my watch and I'll own up to it. Frankly, taking credit for this one won't keep me awake at night." Erin watched silent communication pass between the two men. Connor's expression was a struggle between reluctance and gratefulness. Derek's was firm. "I'll see you both at work next week. Don't be late."

Erin took Connor's hand and started to follow the captain, but he pulled her back. "Wait until they cover his body up. I don't ever want you to look at me...and see that."

"I could *never*." She glided back into the water, wrapping her legs around his waist. They both let out a shaky breath when his hands molded to her backside and drew her closer. "I only see one thing when I look at you. I saw it the first day. I see it now. Hope. You made me hope."

"You don't have to hope anymore, Erin," he whispered at her lips. "Hope implies you might not get what you want." Their tongues mingled in a kiss. "If I'm what you want, hope is futile, because I couldn't belong to you any more completely than I already do."

Heart overflowing, she laughed through happy tears. "If that's a challenge, I accept."

EPILOGUE

ONE MONTH LATER

Connor bent Erin back over the kitchen counter and swirled his tongue inside the hollow of her neck. She tossed her head on a gasp, pushing her breasts up for his attention. Jesus. What he wouldn't give to pull the top of her strapless yellow dress down and suck his fill. Of course, he *couldn't*, because they were at a fucking barbecue and one of fifty people could walk into the kitchen at any minute.

"Remind me again why we're out of bed on a Sunday?"

Erin rubbed the arch of her bare foot over the curve of his calf, giving him no choice but to rock his hips against her. She slipped her foot even higher in response, teasing the back of his thigh. "The captain just closed on this house and we're christening the backyard with grilled meat and beer."

"Right." *Fuck*, she smelled good. "Not a good enough reason for you to be wearing clothes."

"You either," she breathed, tugging his head down to fuse their lips together. It only took one slide of her damp mouth for him to deepen the contact with a groan. Getting as close as possible to her was always a requirement. As was his habit, he let his hands wander to the hem of her dress, curling his fingers into the soft material. At this point, he would usually draw it up to her waist to give himself access to the sweet flesh beneath, but he was hindered by their surroundings. He rubbed the hem up and down on the outside of her thighs instead, chafing the skin and making her sag against him as he devoured her mouth.

She still favored her combat boots and crop tops, but two weeks ago, his mother had taken her shopping and created a monster. She'd come home with dresses and high heels and painfully sexy underwear he seriously hoped his mother hadn't picked out, trying on all of her purchases for him with an enthusiasm that had stolen his ability to speak. Watching her blossom within a friendship with his mother made him so goddam happy, he hadn't found a way to put it into words just yet. Erin never had to be anything but her beautiful, unique self, and they'd found an unlikely kindred spirit in each other. They'd both encountered difficulties in their past to come out on the other side with their spirits intact.

When Erin started to move against him in that way that signaled the point of no return, he pressed their foreheads together and let her draw oxygen. "You look so innocent in this dress. It's making me crazy." Difficult as it was, he forced himself to draw back the desire she stoked in him. It only got stronger by the day. The minute. "We'll have some fun with that later. Won't we?"

"I might have my middle name changed to *fun.*"

Her excited response did nothing to help his cause. His imagination was already running wild with possibilities for when they got home. Erin had not only embraced his tastes in the bedroom, she'd inspired newer, *better* ones. Just yesterday, he'd come home from the store to find her gone. Before panic could set in, he'd heard a gentle rap on the door. When he pulled it open, Erin stood on their doormat, wringing her hands. *My car broke down across the street. Can I use your phone to call a tow truck, mister?* He was now convinced she'd missed her calling as an actress, because she'd kept up the ruse so long and so convincingly, he'd been ready to move heaven and earth to fuck her when the time came. She'd ended up facedown on the kitchen floor with her ass in the air, still calling him "mister" as he pounded into her like a madman.

Dammit, if he kept thinking about it, they would have to leave. And he kept her to himself too often to drag her away once again.

Suppressing his growing need, he jerked his chin toward the backyard full of cops they'd just escaped from. "How are you doing with all the people?"

"Pretty well, I think." She dragged her fingers lightly down his arm, making his muscles jump beneath her touch. "Anyway, if anyone tries to corner me, I'll just hop the fence."

He smiled, secure in the knowledge that she was joking. "How many steps to the street?"

"I have no idea," she whispered, giving him the same answer she gave him every day now. "All I need to know is if I jump the fence, you'll come with me."

"Damn right." Connor leaned in to kiss her again. How could he help it?

After a slow-burning kiss, she pulled back. "I have to tell you something."

She looked nervous, so he smoothed a thumb between her eyebrows. Didn't she know by now there was nothing she could say that could hurt them? "What is it, sweetheart?"

"You asked me a while ago what I wanted to do with the money. Well, I decided." She wet her lips. "I kept thinking about the schoolteacher…the one you told me about? The one who smiled every day and the children loved her?"

Connor nodded, unable to speak. What was she saying?

"I asked Polly to look into your military file. Find out the name of the village you were in when…the incident happened." She seemed to be searching his eyes for a reaction, but he couldn't give her one yet. He was too stunned. "It was easy from that point on since there's only one school in the village. She… Ashira…still teaches at the school. I sent her half the money and the rest to the school."

So many feelings were at war inside him, he didn't know which to address first. Gratitude, awe, love for this amazing girl. There was another part of him that wished he'd done a better job convincing her to keep some of the money for herself. Convincing her she deserved it, that it might come tainted but if it was hers, it could never remain that way.

"I don't know what she'll do with it," she continued. "Maybe she'll give it to her husband. Maybe she'll leave and find a better life. But if you saw the good in her, then I know it's there."

In the end, all he could do was grasp her face between his hands and attempt to fight the emotion clogging his throat. "Erin, I don't know what to say."

"You gave me a place to feel safe. You made me feel safe. I just wanted to pass that feeling on to someone else." She turned her head and kissed his hand. The hands that were the first to touch her without pain. Thank God. "Connor, you freed me."

The weight of his love for her closed in around him until all he could see was her, the center of his universe. His breath. His sustenance. "No, Erin." He buried his face in her hair and inhaled. "We freed each other."

Austin settled back against the brick wall with his newspaper, pretending to peruse the finance section. He'd gone with the reliable hipster businessman look today, one of his favorites because it only required thick black-rimmed glasses, a fake beard, and a unique suit. The suit in question was camel-colored, with an eagle embroidered on the breast pocket. He'd picked it up years ago at a thrift shop in London, knowing it would come in handy, but also because it appealed to his sense of humor. The mannerisms for this particular character were easy enough to carry out. Look bored, pretend you don't notice everyone eyeballing your silly throwback attire, turn the newspaper page with efficiency. Try to impress on everyone passing by that you are interesting. You are special. But you don't feel like talking.

He tilted his wrist and consulted his watch, once again casting a look across the street toward the dance studio. Five more minutes.

Really, he shouldn't be here. He should have stayed at the damnable barbecue and listened to cops swap potato salad recipes. That's where he *should* be, but instead he was here. Somewhere he'd promised himself he wouldn't go. It only made matters worse each time. Then again, hadn't his entire move to Chicago been about this place? This person? Oh, he'd told himself moving here had been about the job, but he didn't care a whit for the job. Might have quit after the first day, if it weren't for the girl. Polly. Keeper of secrets. Secrets he wanted to know, if only to figure out what was taking place behind her green eyes. Watchful eyes that saw right through him as if he were invisible.

Or so she tried to pretend.

He knew all about pretending, though, so he was supremely qualified to call bullshit.

She'd been the only one who didn't laugh that afternoon

at the barbecue when he'd proven himself a shitty babysitter. One single minute. He hadn't been able to hold the captain's baby a single minute while Ginger, his wife, refreshed her guests' drinks. Not because he didn't know *how* to hold a baby. But because it was too hard. It had conjured memories to the surface like a sorcerer and landed him here. Where he shouldn't be.

Across the street, the dance studio door opened. A smiling woman in an oversize sweatshirt stepped out and propped the exit open with a block of wood. Two tiny girls in ballerina costumes skipped out holding water bottles, their chatter audible all the way where he stood. His gaze remained glued to the open doorway, waiting, the breath frozen in his lungs.

There. A redhead he knew to be three, almost four years old walked out, much slower than the other girls. She looked serious. Too serious. Her head was bent over a cloth doll, her mouth moving as if speaking to the inanimate object. What was she saying? As if he'd asked the question out loud, as if she were close enough to hear it, her chin lifted up and she looked directly at him.

His daughter was looking *right at him.*

Time started to crawl. The newspaper in his hands started to feel like a prop, which meant he was dropping character. *Bored. You don't see her. She's just an extra in your movie.*

The prompts didn't work this time. His palms were sweating so profusely, the newspaper turned insubstantial in his hands. Quickly, he dropped to one knee on the sidewalk and shoved the newspaper into his leather satchel. He needed to sling the bag over his shoulder and disappear into the train station, but he couldn't force his legs to move, knowing she was so close after all this time.

One more look. Just one more.

But when he looked up, she was gone.

Austin nodded jerkily. For the best. It was for the best. Ignoring the looks from passersby, this time centered on his off behavior more than the blasted eagle on his pocket, he shoved his headphones into his ears, turned up Zeppelin to full volume and ran in the opposite direction of where he'd seen her.

Old habits died hard.

ACKNOWLEDGMENTS

To my husband, Patrick, for being the *best* kind of badass man. The kind who isn't cowed by the idea of his wife being the breadwinner, while he does the bulk of raising a child. Our daughter will be *twice* the woman for having spent so much quality time with her father, because *that*, Mackenzie, is how a real, secure man behaves. Thank you, Patrick, for being an amazing man, father, and husband.

To my daughter, Mackenzie. I never would have started writing again if you hadn't shown up. You made me want to be the kind of mother you could be proud of. Thank you.

To my editor Heather Howland, for believing in this series and my characters. For believing in me. And paying such close attention to detail. Not to mention, designing some seriously amazing covers for Crossing the Line. Thank you.

To Liz Pelletier, for believing in the series enough to give me my very first book on bookstore shelves. What a surreal experience. Thank you so much.

To Katie Clapsadl, Meredith Johnson, and Jessica Turner for doing such a great job on the publicity side of things. I'm so appreciative. Thank you.

To Bailey's Babes—we've come a long way! Thank you for sharing every day with me, and for being excited about my books. There are not enough words to thank you ladies.

To the bloggers/reviewers who continually read my books and recommend them to their followers, much of my success is owed to you. Thank you.

READERS ARE RAVING ABOUT THE CROSSING THE LINE SERIES!

RISKING IT ALL

Three years ago, Seraphina Newsom's brother was gunned down by a ruthless mob kingpin. In order to take down the killer, Sera has gone undercover unsanctioned. Alone. Her only protection lies with Bowen Driscol, the reluctant new head of South Brooklyn's crime family, who the NYPD blackmailed into pulling her out. But when the two meet and Bowen feels a deep, damning shiver of desire, he knows there's only one way to keep her safe...to claim her as his own.

HIS RISK TO TAKE
RISKIER BUSINESS

FIND OUT WHERE IT ALL BEGAN WITH TESSA BAILEY'S BESTSELLING LINE OF DUTY SERIES...

PROTECTING WHAT'S HIS

Sassy bartender Ginger Peet just committed the perfect crime. Life-sized Dolly Parton statue in tow, Ginger and her sister flee Nashville. But their new neighbor, straight-laced Chicago homicide cop Derek Tyler, knows something's up—something *big*—and he won't rest until Ginger's safe...and in his bed for good.

OFFICER OFF LIMITS
ASKING FOR TROUBLE
STAKING HIS CLAIM
PROTECTING WHAT'S THEIRS
UNFIXABLE

BROKEN HONOR BY TONYA BURROWS

Ice-cold and unbreakable, Travis Quinn is the HORNET team's hard-ass. Despite the blanks in his memory, Quinn remembers *everything* about Mara Escareno—the curve of her lips, the feel of her body, and how he walked out on her suddenly six weeks ago. Now Mara is pregnant with his baby. But before Quinn can fully process the news, she's kidnapped by his enemies and plunged into the merciless world of human trafficking. Because now Quinn's enemies have discovered his only weakness...Mara.

RULES OF PROTECTION BY ALISON BLISS

Rule breaker Emily Foster just wanted some action on her birthday. Instead she witnessed a mob hit and is whisked into witness protection, with by-the-book Special Agent Jake Ward as her chaperone. They end up deep in the Texas backwoods. The city-girl might be safe from the Mafia, but now she has to contend with a psychotic rooster, a narcoleptic dog, crazy cowboys, and the danger of losing her heart to the one man she can't have. But while Jake's determined to keep her out of the wrong hands, she's determined to get into the right ones. His.

CONVICTED BY DEE TENORIO

Retired Marine and new Sheriff's Deputy Cade Evigan is on a mission to weed out a violent motorcycle crew from a small mountain town. Deep cover DEA Agent Katrina Killian is the last person he needs to fall for—especially when she appears to be one of the criminals he's out to take down. Unable to risk either of their lives with the truth, Katrina has to play both ends against the middle to keep Cade safe. But lies can only last so long and her time has just run out...

PROTECTOR FOR HIRE BY TAWNA FENSKE

After an accident that cost lives and ended his military career, Schwartz Patton vanished into the Montana wilderness. Only his brother, Grant, knows how to reach him, and only if there's an emergency. That emergency comes in the form of a blue-eyed city girl running for her life. Despite not seeing eye to eye on, well, *anything*, sparks fly between them, making it clear his isolated sanctuary will never be the same. Schwartz knows he's screwed. Because even if he can keep Janelle hidden and safe, he's not sure he can do the same for his heart...

ALIVE AT FIVE BY LINDA BOND

When Samantha's mentor dies while skydiving, she suspects he was murdered. Her investigative instincts lead her to irresistibly gorgeous Zack Hunter. An undercover police officer, Zack is investigating his uncle's diving death with the same adventure vacation company. He doesn't want Samantha's help because he's terrified of being responsible for a partner again. Still, Samantha's persistence is quite a turn-on, and he finds it harder and harder to stay away from her. But when the killer turns his attention to Zack, Samantha could be the only one who can save him.

HIGH-HEELED WONDER BY AVERY FLYNN

Sylvie Bissette is the woman behind *The High-Heeled Wonder*, a must-read blog for fashionistas everywhere. Tony Falcon wouldn't know a kitten heel from a tabby cat, but when a murder investigation leads him to Sylvie, he realizes the feisty fashionista may be his best chance at catching the criminals who killed his best friend. But solving that case means going after the people Sylvie cares about, and soon his attraction for her—and the danger she's in— has him wondering if solving the case is worth hurting the woman he can't stop fantasizing about...